To Hell and Back
A
Test of Faith

By
VL Parker

Verna Lynn Parker

Copyright © 2011 – VL Parker

All rights reserved worldwide.

No part of this book may be copied or re-sold.

I would like to thank my children Matthew, Sarah and Jessica for your patience during the creation of this story. I would also like to thank my beautiful and talented sister Gina for believing in me and encouraging me to finish this book.

I am forever grateful for God blessing me with my amazing family, especially my wonderful husband Robert. I thank you my darling husband for your assistance, your love and your support. This book would never be what it is without your insight, and feedback.

I also would like to thank Jessica for her feedback and encouraging me to enhance certain battle scenes. Your advice has enhanced the story.

VL Parker

Part One:
Before We Live, We Die

Prologue:
Something that's Worth Dying For

"Between shadows and death we will reach out for the light." Catherine once told me this in the dark of the night, but I didn't believe her. In the darkness there is no shadow and in death there could be no life, and yet like a moth drawn to the flame I was compelled to follow her.

Our lives were separate as were our paths, still destiny determined they would become entwined. As a plant longs for the sun and the rain, as the desert thirsts, and as we require air to breathe, so too I came to need Catherine. I wanted her to save my soul; to restore my faith in humanity, for she was my last great hope, to resurrect all that had died in me.

I felt some deep force within me forcing me to follow her and yet she was a believer in a god I did not know and a leader of a group I did not understand. Their faith was blind, being led by prophecy and dreams, but I refused to be a pawn of the gods. I would choose my fate and control my own destiny. This is what I had always clung to, but now the world had changed.

I was lost and alone; I was perplexed and confused, as chaos made me victim to circumstance. Catherine would become my cause, she became my dream and I would
  follow her to the ends of the Earth. For her I could live; for her I could die.

As I sit down to write this story I question where I should begin. Perhaps I will tell you just a little about the forces that shaped me, and the circumstances that brought me into Catherine's life.

It was the first year of The Great War, some said it was Armageddon, others World War III. Regardless of what one chose to call it, it was bloody, it was endless, and it had taken on a life of its own. By the time I crept into Catherine's camp I was under its control.

The carnage could trace its roots to the War on Terror, which had been launched by the United States following that terrible September morn in 2001. The attack on Iraq was swift, and then the assault on Afghanistan was legitimate. One war flowed like blood into the next, as decades of warfare shaped our lives.

It was now decades later and Jerusalem was being attacked on all sides. Throughout the previous winter, terror spread across the city, covering it in a blanket of shadows, as rivers of blood flowed through the streets. Israel's enemies, the Palestinians and the surrounding Muslim countries, were besieging her on all sides. They proclaimed that nothing but the complete annihilation of the Jewish people would suffice.

America and Britain endeavored to protect her, but the solution was an enigma. The more we supported Israel in her struggle, the more fervent became hatred of the Jews in the region. Our support only escalated fighting throughout the Middle East. Our War on Terror married into the war to free the Jewish people from Muslim aggression.

We have been in a perpetual state of war ever since, a confrontation against Islamic extremists. We were never resting, nor relenting from eradicating the enemy before they could destroy us. Kill, or be killed, this was why war was waged and this was the atmosphere in which I grew up. It was an age of fear, an age of anger, and an era of broken dreams. Still, in the darkness a small flicker of hope remained and we were determined that our voices would never be extinguished.

I vowed to defend democracy. I would live and die for this ideal. I was always sure of whom the enemy was. There was never any doubt about what was worth fighting for; it was only a matter of which side you're on.

Our allies and our own spies supplied us with ample evidence against terrorist cells and the nations who supported them. We had the technology and the will to destroy them. Then the world began to change as truth was portrayed as lies and our great American nation soon became despised.

The world had long fallen into darkness and chaos as a result of the never-ending bloodshed. It was a world I could no longer understand. The atrocities of war were no longer worth dying for. I was a soldier without a cause, a man without a soul, desperate for some hope, but with a heart that had grown cold.

I had lived for freedom and I was willing to die for democracy, but what was I to do when democracy ceased to exist? I could not give up on this dream. It was in my blood. It was a part of my being. I had to find a way to defend it, to save it from the reign of dictators who swayed the nations of the world.

There was one woman who shared this dream, or at least she shared the same enemy. We were kindred spirits, compelled to fight and die for, if necessary, that which we believed.

Peter Roberts
Captain, USN

Chapter One:
Flirting with Death

It was late into the night when I arrived in Catherine's camp. She was the leader of a renegade group that was hiding out in the mountains of Washington State following the Freedom of Jerusalem Campaign. I arrived at the camp just as Catherine's followers were settling around the campfire. Catherine was speaking when I sat down across from her on the other side of the flames.

"Are you sure you want to hear this tale?" *Catherine inquired to those sitting around the fire with her. They were eager to hear the story even though many had heard it before. She sighed,* "It will take much of the night." *Everyone sat back after pouring themselves another glass of wine, preparing to hear the legend. She poured herself a drink and then she began.*

It was the last day of school in Dublin and I had just returned from my final martial arts class. I was pleased to have done so well in school that year and I was especially proud of receiving my level three black belt.

Master Ming said, "I am pleased you have succeeded in achieving your goals. I enjoyed guiding you and hope you will continue on your journey toward discipline and enlightenment."

Master Ming cautioned his students, "Remember, what you learned here stays here, unless all other alternatives fail, but if you must fight, fight to win." He said this as he punched his right fist into his left hand and declared, "Peace over Power."

We repeated in unison as we punched our hands into our fists, "Peace over Power." Then we genuflected as we all punched the floor bowing before him; we continued with one voice, "Should we fight, we fight to win." We rose and bowed to our sensei. Following that we were dismissed.

I admired the belt around my waist for a moment before changing. I had to hurry back to my room. I said some quick good-byes to some classmates and then I rushed out the door.

I bumped into my sensei as I was running out of the change room, so I took the opportunity to thank him for his guidance as I said, "Master Ming I want to thank you for all you have taught me over the past four years. I hope I will live up to your expectations for me." I knew however, that I was far too impulsive to ever fulfill such an unattainable goal.

I hurriedly bowed to him again and as he bowed back, he commented in his gentle and melodious voice, "Catherine, your physical skills are unsurpassed. You are my best student; however you must overcome your propensity for rash and impulsive behavior."

I giggled and apologized, but I found it difficult at that time in my life to receive a compliment coupled with criticism. I did not know how I should react so I replied, "I will endeavor to overcome my impulsive nature Master Ming, but I wouldn't hold my breath."

I gave him a quick kiss with a foolish smile upon my face. He shook his head as I turned to run, but I noticed a grin upon his face as I turned to wave one more final good-bye. I dashed out the door and rushed to my apartment.

I had to hurry home to walk King, my German shepherd. I lived in a room in an old gray stone house, located beside a church at the edge of the university campus. My father bought it for me to ensure King and I would not be separated. I couldn't survive without my dog. My father and I were not very close. He was always too busy working, however I never lacked for anything financially. He believed it was a man's responsibility to provide for his family and he did that very well.

I do remember being very close to him as a child, but my father was unable to relate to me when I became a young woman. He began to work more and more the older I became, and it was almost like he wanted to avoid me.

I suppose my unabashed expressions of my own opinions, which I was convinced were the only reality and gospel truth, often divided us. The cruelty of life, mainly his preoccupation with the never-ending war and his obsession with economic concerns, tended to divide our family. Still there was nothing I could not afford. Daddy's money was my money. In short I was labeled a, 'spoiled little rich girl.' I was wealthy and opinionated.

I was also introverted and filled with a deep-seated rage that was growing up inside of me, stemming from my resentment of the lack of attention, the lack of protection, and the lack of love that I received from my father. My father and I were not close. Oh well, that stuff does not matter; I'm wandering off topic.

Where was I? Oh yes I was heading home.

When I arrived home King was very excited to see me and was anticipating his walk. "Hello boy. Did you miss me or do you just want your walk?"

King jumped with excitement and I laughed. King hugged and kissed me with a few quick licks and then he brought me his leash. I patted his head and I said, "I see you want to go now. Alright, come on then."

It was late May, but it felt like a hot summer night as we walked along the cliffs above the beach. It was often pleasantly cool by the ocean, but this day it was hotter than usual. I was so warm that I had to sit for a few moments to catch my breath. I had never felt that kind of heat in Ireland, during all of the years I attended university. When I had the opportunity to sit and ponder my future, I was often torn between joy and an overwhelming sense of dreadful apprehension. I didn't know what I wanted to be, or what destiny held in store for me.

King began to bark impatiently. He never did allow me to indulge my pensive nature for very long, so we continued our walk above the beach. I could see the fishing boats coming into shore and hear the sounds of music and laughter floating across the bay. After a long while I sat again and watched the sunset. As the sun vanished so did the warmth of its rays, along with its crimson beauty.

Once the sun disappeared beyond the horizon I walked amidst the shadows of the night until I reached a promontory, where I stood isolated above the vast ocean below. I heard the waves lapping gently against the shore, as I gazed off the edge of a precipice at the darkness below me. I suddenly felt vacant, as if my soul was unexpectedly detached, and a shiver ran up my spine. I resumed my walk down toward the harbor lights in order to escape the chill and darkness of the night.

King now barked again because he wanted to run and play. We continued our decent to the beach below. In our haste down the rocky escarpment, I slipped and scraped my knee. The blood slowly trickled down my leg but I was able to walk, so we resumed our decline after King had licked my wound. I patted his head and I assured him, "I'm fine King, now stop that or you'll give me an infection." I observed that the first star had come out and silently, I made my wish to find love.

The new sliver of the moon shone illuminating a unique alignment of the stars. I could see them shining in a linear formation across the western horizon. Night had fallen and the harbor lights, flickering like candles, beckoned me from the darkness.

I stopped at a quaint little bar along the beach for a whiskey and sat on the patio to enjoy my last evening in town, before returning home to New York the following day. The spirits quickly dulled my pain, and with the removal of this distraction I began to watch the people around me. There were many British and

Canadian sailors drinking in the bar that night, alongside some American Marines.

The bar was a pub with giant fish mounted on the walls and nets hanging in the corners. There were several old pictures of fishermen showing their manliness by holding their largest catches, alongside photos of local heroes lost in the Middle Eastern conflict.

I heard a group of sailors talking about the war. I listened as they talked gallantly, assured that God would support them in their endeavor to destroy the enemy. I heard one sailor dressed in a white wool sweater proclaim, "Sorry mates, but I have to warn you, it's a bitch to be there."

The man who made this comment had worn leathery skin like that of a fisherman. His beard was beginning to gray, showing his age despite his young looking physique. His deep green eyes stood in contrast to his darkened complexion and he spoke with a thick Scottish accent. His tone and the deep furrow of his brow told me that he had his own story to tell. I was sure that the weariness in his eyes meant that he must have been to hell and back.

A young marine with red hair pushed himself toward the older gentleman and said, "How the hell would you know, you old fart?" He was quite obviously drunk.

The older man downed his whiskey and replied as he stood up, "Because boy, I just returned from that God-forsaken place." The gentleman then turned and limped out of the bar with the aid of a cane as he warned, "Prepare your selves for hell boys. This is just the beginning of the third Great War."

The boy shrugged him off saying, "Gramps is just pissed at being a cripple."

Then their commander raised his glass and toasted, ***"Dulce et Decorum Est Pro patria mori."***

Another young marine inquired, "What does that mean Cap?"

I glanced over to see who had asked the question, it was a young boy, barely a man, with wavy dark brown hair. Despite his muscled physique his facial features were still that of a young teenager. I took another sip of my drink after identifying who had spoken and I continued to listen.

The Captain replied, "It is sweet and fitting to die for one's country."

Then the redhead marine that had previously insulted the old man raised his glass and bellowed, "To honor and death."

The whole bar joined in a war cry shouted out, "To honor and death." I refused to join their toast to bloodshed.

My stomach turned at the hypocrisy and futility of war. These young boys believed the myth of the glory of war. I suppose they must if they are to rationalize killing and dying for one's country. Wilfred Owen must have turned in his grave that night, had he known that the irony of his poem was so misconstrued by these young rogues.

The Captain of these men was walking toward me and he noticed my scorn. He stood beside me and asked me to not judge them too harshly, "After all," he said, "If they didn't put an end to the atrocities then who would? These men will eliminate the reign of terror in the world."

"Only God can do that." I replied.

He apologized and conceded, "You might be right, but I still think we have to try, don't you?"

"Perhaps," I agreed.

He inquired, "May I buy you a drink?"

I motioned with my hand for him to sit as he asked, "So what are you drinking?"

"A double shot of whiskey on the rocks." I replied

He smiled with his perfect teeth and perfect lips, and then he ordered one for each of us.

We sat and discussed many topics throughout the evening and he inquired why war unsettled me as he teased, "Are you a pacifist?"

I laughed out loud, "No I would not go that far, but it feels like we have been at war most of my life and sometimes I question why and then I remember 911. I was a little girl, but I recall it as if it was yesterday. That tragic September morn is still vivid in my mind's eye."

I shook my head as the Captain responded, "Me too. I will never forget that day either."

He placed his hand on mine with such gentleness. I smiled as I continued, "I had been deeply troubled by a prophecy that my brother James had emailed me shortly after the catastrophic event. It read,

"Subject: Here is an interesting quote from Nostradamus.

"In the year of the new century and nine months,
From the sky will come a great King of Terror...
The sky will burn at forty-five degrees.
Fire approaches the great new city...
In the city of York there will be a great collapse,
2 twin brothers torn apart by chaos
while the fortress falls the great leader will succumb
the third big war will begin when the big city is burning"

- NOSTRADAMUS

"I never verified that quote, for I was only a child when he emailed it to me at private school. Still, it sent my soul into turmoil whenever I recalled it. I never forgot it. It stayed with me, as did the destruction itself. I still remember my mother holding me in her arms, rocking back and forth, as tears flowed from her grief stricken eyes." I was almost moved to tears as I allowed myself to remember that day.

"I've never heard that quote before, but I have heard of Nostradamus. Didn't he live during the 1600's?" The Captain questioned as he motioned for two more drinks.

"Yes I believe he wrote that prophesy in 1654." I answered

"Where were you on the day the twin towers fell?" He asked as our drinks arrived.

I smiled at the waiter and thanked him and then I continued, "James and I were supposed to be getting ready to go to school, we were both quite young. We were all sitting down for breakfast. My mother turned on the news as she did every morning. My father had been sipping his coffee as the cook served him his eggs and toast. He got up from the table and stared the TV dumbfounded, in shock. My mother slowly walked toward the screen and I did too. She fell to her knees clasping me to her chest, weeping. After a short while when the second plane flew into the tower dad seemed enraged. He stormed from the room and stomped off to his office and shut the door. Mom continued to sit in front of the television as tears streamed down her face. I sat there all day and held her hand. James, my brother, ate as if nothing was wrong and continued to enjoy his day off school; entertaining himself since everyone else seemed obsessed with the attack."

Captain Robert sighed, "Yes, I must confess that day is forever with me as well. It amazes me how some people, like your brother who were wrapped up in their own lives and seemed to be unaffected by that event, it was a turning point for our nation. It shaped our lives."

I nodded in agreement, "I was internally divided that day, as I literally shared my mother's tears and my father's rage. Our lives were changed by 911. The day marked an end to our decadent, carefree life and replaced it with a spirit of fear and a spirit of vengeance and wrath. My parents grew up in an era of security and comfort. I grew up in an age of apprehension, hate and paranoia."

"What is it that your father did for a living? Did he work with anyone in the World Trade Center?" Roberts questioned.

"I don't know if he knew anyone, but it is possible. My father's assets were extensive and our wealth was obscene. He had numerous business interests and relationships with many high profile businessmen. He owned a large high tech weapons manufacturing company that profited greatly from our government's ongoing commitment to wage war on any nation that bred extremist factions of any kind. He also was a majority stakeholder in a large energy company, and many manufacturing companies. He was the majority shareholder in Eco Air that designed energy efficient aircraft. Eco Air opened a few years after 911." I shook my head and laughed to myself.

"What made you laugh?" The Captain asked me.

I replied, "Oh, I was just remembering the dinner parties. Officials were often at our dinner table and I would creep down the stairs, whenever I was home, to listen to their long discussions concerning recent aggressions against the free world. They would talk much about business, but they mostly focused on politics. I gradually learned how closely tied business and politics were. Although few of the business leaders in North America were overtly involved in politics, they were certainly able to influence not only who held power, but how that power was wielded. Many prominent politicians, bankers, as well as industry leaders attended mother's exquisite dinner parties."

I could not help but smile as I continued, "When I was a young child I loved the excitement, the dresses, and the decorations, but what I loved most was hiding and listening to after dinner conversations. I felt like a spy, I would often take notes and make a game of it creating elaborate conspiracies. I would then have to connect all the clues to save the world. It was not long however, before I became a woman and such games had begun to cease."

The Captain smiled, "I'm sure you were the most adorable spy ever. It is sad that such innocence and games are left behind, but I do believe I can still see that childlike fascination in your eyes right now."

I laughed and I believe I did blush a little as I looked down for an instant. I regained my composure and I continued, "I longed for the peace and joy that my mother so often loved to recall. She would tell me about her childhood and how it was in the years before the war. It sounded idyllic, but I sometimes wondered if it were not a mirage, a tainted memory, or fantasy. Our life, because of our wealth, was beautiful and ideal too. In many ways I was shielded from the darker aspects of the world beyond the gates of our estate and beyond the privileged private schools."

The Captain asked, "How long was it before you saw the world through different eyes?"

I was surprised how much we conversed, but I continued to reveal myself to him and I answered, "I was less shielded as time went on. I would watch the news, read news articles on-line and it was not long before I discovered the poverty and the pain all around me. How could anyone help but see the world around them in this age, with information at our fingertips?"

"True." Roberts agreed as he continued to question, "Was it the news coverage that made you anti-war?"

"Perhaps," I sighed, "I was angry and sad, as I thought of where war and hatred had brought us, but my martial arts instructor, Master Ming, also taught us that sometimes our freedom had to be protected. I endeavored to live at peace with everyone, however I was determined to never be a victim, and as a woman I felt this need to defend myself growing with each passing year. I was confused with a longing for peace and anger at all the injustice in our world. Maybe we do have to fight, but sometimes I wonder if violence begets violence. I felt like there were two distinct personalities warring inside of me, one bent on justice and fighting for what was right and another that just wanted peace and security. The news can really warp a child's perspective and I fear it did with mine. I became increasingly anti-war when I saw the atrocities that the soldiers participated in against some of the Iraqi, and Afghani people. I became increasingly critical as I grew older and I realized we only sent our troops to avenge or where we could financially prosper, but if you are a poor country with a desperate need for freedom and equality, no matter how grave the situation then, sorry we can't help you be free.

"I agree, but war is very expensive. The cost is a legitimate consideration." The Captain said sincerely as he noted with some tone of disapproval, "It is sad when some soldiers become inhumane, but the majority of soldiers are risking their lives to better the world, to fight back the darkness, not to become a part of it."

I smiled as I said apologetically, "I'm sorry if I seemed judgmental and harsh earlier when you led your men in a toast. I'm grateful for my freedom, and I am grateful to men like you who protect it, but sometimes I question if the continual fighting does not make the darkness become a part of you. How do you retain your humanity when fighting the inhumane and how do you know if you're fighting a worthy cause?"

He said, "That is a difficult question and a deep conversation that may have to wait for another place in time. I will say this though; I believe it is love and beauty like yours that keeps us human. If I had you at home to return to following the war I am sure I would survive it. I believe there is nothing love cannot heal." He stood up and gave me his hand as he asked, "Now why don't you allow me to alter your opinion of a sailor and share this dance with me?"

I smiled and replied, "Well on that note we can agree, I too believe that there is nothing love can't heal."

He grinned as he led me to the dance floor.

I cannot recall the number of dances we shared, however I remember that the other marines called him Captain Roberts. I recollect getting lost in the music and drinks, and I will never forget what he looked like.

He was about six foot one with gorgeous, hazel eyes and dark brown hair. His smile was the kind that could make a woman swoon and his lips were just the perfect size, summoning you to steal a kiss. His broad shoulders made you feel as if he could hold you forever in his arms.

He embraced me closely as we swayed slowly to the music. I loved the warmth, security and protection his presence provided. He took my breath away and I was becoming entranced by his allure, but I had to maintain the upper hand, so I played the tease.

I felt so sensual and alive when I danced and I took pleasure in knowing the affect my dancing had on the men around me. Our final waltz was tranquil and far more tempered then our previous dances. As we swayed slowly to the music I felt his heartbeat, it was strong and steady. I too was excited and my heartbeat quickened; I apologized abruptly, "I'm sorry, but I have to leave; I have to get up early tomorrow."

He pulled me closer to his body and whispered into my ear, "Surely you will not leave me with nothing before I go off to war, perhaps a kiss?"

As he spoke these words I felt his hot breath flutter past my ear. He brushed my black hair gently out of my eyes. Beads of sweat were running down the hollow of my chest and I allowed him to lift a single drop just below the nape of my neck. He was forward and yet gentle and sweet and I wanted to kiss him, I believe he knew it because he did kiss me. I confess I kissed many boys in my young dating life, but he was different. He was a man and more than that he made me want more. I never experienced that before. He took my breath away.

After our kiss he beseeched me, "May I walk you home? It is well after midnight and it is beautiful night for a stroll, beneath the stars and the moonlight."

I loved his deep and gentle voice. I played with the idea of having him as a lover for just one night, but I quickly dismissed the thought. "I would love to join you however, I am a virgin and I intend to stay that way, at least for tonight." My blunt reply seemed to only intrigue him more. I grinned as he pulled me closer to him and my eyes danced with delight at his confident, but gentle nature.

Some of the more proper of Catherine's followers shuffled with discomfort. They did not approve of Catherine quoting the soldiers' foul language and they hated hearing about her former licentious behavior, but she never allowed them to think she was in any way perfect. Still, they were idealists.

I on the other hand loved her passion, her free spirit, and her beauty. She still had her long black hair, her deep blue eyes that glistened reflecting the fire and a body that drove men crazy, especially me. I could not suppress the smile, which crept across my face as I admired her flawlessness. Catherine put another log on the fire and briefly glanced at me through the flames. I swear I saw her eyes dance with delight as she continued her story.

King barked and gave the marine a threatening growl. I laughed and bent down to give him a hug. After I declined the walk, I thanked Captain Roberts, "Thank you for a wonderful evening, but I must be getting home."

He gallantly helped me to my feet and then he took two steps back, as he bowed and kissed my left hand. Then he replied, "My lady the pleasure, I assure you, was all mine."

"Don't be so sure" I teased.

He smiled and then he continued with an innocent look, "I promise to be a perfect gentleman if you would permit me to walk you home."

I stared at him with equal self-confidence, however I was unable to suppress my grin, "I thank you for your noble gesture, but I already have an escort." I flashed him a smile as I patted my dog's head. With a nod I then proceeded to walk back up the beach with King faithfully at my side, knowing the Captain's face had placed an imprint like a photograph on my heart and his kiss claimed my soul. I was young with a wild heart that needed to be tamed.

Just below the cliffs near my house I bathed my feet in the ocean, as the salt cleansed my skin, the chill of the night air caused me to shiver, and the frigid water caused goose bumps to appear and blemish my once perfect skin.

Catherine got up again to pour herself another drink and she took a deep breath before she continued. I too remembered that night and could only imagine the pain it caused her to remember that part of the evening, so long ago.

I recalled ordering another drink on the patio. I sat watching her walk blissfully unaware, as she strolled back up the beach. I heard however, a group of the men talking about how beautiful she was and crudely commenting about what they wanted to do to her. I won't repeat it. I also noticed they hurriedly paid their tabs as they quietly left the bar, hoping to go unnoticed. They proceeded to follow Catherine up the beach.

Catherine sat down by the fire, and after taking a deep breath laced with liquor, she summoned her courage to continue sharing her story.

"I did not know that some of the sailors had followed me; the wind must have carried their scent away, because King hadn't detected them either. I had just put one of my shoes on when they came and circled me. King growled ferociously as I prepared to fight."

I recognized the nasty redhead from the bar as he remarked, "There was no need for you to get your shoes on lass, and we would prefer you to start with taking them off." I spit at him as they laughed and they proceeded to hem me in.

I remembered Master Ming telling me, "Fear is your greatest enemy, but it can also be your closest friend." I did not understand what he meant at the time, but now that I was terrified I realized I could become paralyzed with fear, or stand and fight with a vengeance. I took a deep breath and I faced my attackers, as adrenaline rushed through my veins.

I noted that I began to tremble in fear, so I forced myself to take another deep breath. King attacked one and I was forced to fight the other three. I kicked the red headed soldier in front of me in the groin with a front snap kick. He collapsed in pain and nausea. Then I turned swiftly and tripped another on my left with a sweeper kick. He fell to the ground with a thud, but the sand was soft and I knew he would get up quickly.

I saw King ripping into the arm of one of my attackers. He yelled in pain and then I heard King yelp. I turned out of concern as I witnessed one of the marine's buddies stabbing King's side with his knife. I sprang in a fury toward him. I was enraged that he stabbed my dog. Murder was in my heart and all my fear diminished, as hatred consumed my soul.

I managed to disarm the one that had injured my dog. I kicked him in the back and he dropped the knife to his side as he flew forward. I lunged for the knife and used it against him, as I slashed his right arm and thigh in quick succession.

The red head sneered, "Now you are going to get it bitch!" I suddenly felt his kick sideswipe me. I had barely managed to lift my arms to block it. Initially I was dazed but I was still gripping the knife tightly. I began lashing out at them in desperation. I fought with a blind rage, as I sliced the arm of the red headed brute.

This only angered the other men and increased their determination to defeat me quickly.

I fought well but with King injured my chances of defeating these men was slim. The marines were too strong and too well trained; still I took pleasure in knowing the knife had sliced two of these beastly men.

A tall blond marine licked the blood flowing from his forearm and then he said with a sinister hiss, "Let me have the slut first. I'm going to teach her a lesson for dancing like a whore. She obviously likes it rough and so do I."

As he uttered these words I saw the blade of his own knife glitter in the moonlight. We lunged at one another and I felt a burning sensation on my rib cage. I was filled with so much adrenaline that I quickly dismissed it.

Then he swore at me, calling me a slut as he kicked me. The kick was so fast that I could not block it, let alone use the knife against him. He kicked me so hard in the ribs that I doubled over in pain. I collapsed; he pinned me to the ground. I was defeated.

He sat on top of me and he held his knife to my face as he said, "You little bitch, you think you can get away with slicing me and my boy without us repaying in kind?"

I replied, "Why don't you go take care of your boy you pig." I spit at him in the face and he backhanded me.

I said, "Does that make you feel like a man, hitting a woman half your size?"

He smiled a wicked grin, "I will cut out your tongue and shut you up, and then I will show you what a man does to women like you."

I was not afraid when I thought he would cut me, but I did fear he would rape me, I would rather die than suffer that. I struggled to free myself, but it was futile and the brutes laughed at my helplessness and then, a gunshot rang out in the night. The men turned around. It was the Captain from the bar.

"Get off her Private!" Captain Roberts ordered, as he kicked him in the ribs. The men moved away from me and faced their commanding officer.

"You sick bastards." he continued as he walked forward. Then the Captain punched one in the nose and elbowed another in the face, and they dared not fight back.

He snarled "I should shoot you worthless pieces of shit right now, but I'm going to need every marine I can get when we ship out for the Middle East. Now get your asses back to the ship."

The men turned with their eyes cast down as they obeyed the order. They helped the cad I stabbed earlier get up and then they slinked away.

The Captain helped me up and asked if I was okay. "I'm fine, but those assholes stabbed my dog." I said as I rushed to King's side. I knelt by him, and he was bleeding heavily. I hoped the wound was not fatal. The officer picked up my dog and followed me to the campus infirmary.

As we walked Captain Roberts said, "For someone who proclaims to abhor violence you sure as hell fight like a soldier."

"Everyone has the right to self-defense, but as you said earlier, 'Someone has to put an end to the atrocities' and I'm so glad you did." I replied.

We continued up the cliffs toward the university grounds as an awkward silence fell between us. I could no longer speak as a lump began to develop in my throat.

When we finally arrived we went to the dormitory located at the edge of the campus. I knocked on the door of a room belonging to a longtime friend of mine, who was named Brother John.

I turned to Roberts as he held King in his arms and I continued to knock on the door, as I explained, "John is a friend of mine who works in the campus infirmary as a volunteer and he has a set of keys. He will unlock the infirmary for us." He must have been sleeping deeply because I knocked for some time.

Brother John and I had developed an intimate friendship over the four years I had attended university in Ireland. We met shortly after I arrived and we spent almost all of our free time together. He was my closest friend and the only person who ever really knew me.

He was studying ancient languages and religious prophecy and I was studying ancient religions and prophecies. The monks were a disappearing order and their own monasteries had closed long ago, so those who chose to give up the world were now forced to live in it. They had to, 'die to the flesh', without the security of seclusion, this was no easy task. We shared some classes together and grew very close. I can't go too deeply into our history for it is too long, but I'll say this, I trusted and I loved him deeply.

"What happened?" Brother John asked as he saw King in the Captain's arms. He hurried us down the dimly lit corridors toward the medical room.

"I'll tell you about it tonight if you will stay with me for a while." I replied.

As I walked into the brightly lit room he noticed the bruises on my face. "Oh my darling Catherine, what happened to you?"

He gently caressed my face and I assured him, "I'm okay, really!"

"My face must have been bruised when I was kicked." I continued and then I noticed my ribs hurt as well. I placed my left hand on them and I felt the gentle stream of a warm liquid upon my skin. I stared down in shock at the blood on my hand. At that moment I did not even remember being cut.

"Catherine my dear, you're bleeding!" noted Brother John with the deepest concern, as he ordered the Captain to tend King, while he led me to the next room.

"Take off your dress!" he ordered.

I protested, "But I, I can't do that."

"Catherine, enough of this nonsense, this is no time for modesty. Besides I've seen you in a night gown and a bathing suit before, a bra is no different." He said firmly. "Here is a small towel to cover your breasts, but I must attend to your wound."

I removed my dress as Brother John got some antiseptic and I covered up, and lay back on the table. He cleaned my wound.

"I'll have to give you some stitches. You are lucky this cut isn't too deep. It slid over your rib cage. " He notified me of this and then he noticed that I began to tremble.

He squeezed my hand gently and asked, "Are you sure you're okay?" I nodded yes, but I could not stop the tears from coming. I hated crying it made me feel weak. I could be strong, but not when he showed me concern and compassion. The tears started flowing. He finished the stitches quickly and then bandaged my wound.

I dressed again and then he came over and held me in his arms. I crumbled and lost my composure. I cried in his arms as he gently stroked my hair. Tears streamed quietly down my face. I took a deep breath and told him, "I needed a few minutes to pull myself together."

John kissed my forehead and he said, "Alright Catherine, but I'll just be next door if you need me." I sobbed a brief reply and he walked out the door.

When I returned to the next room Brother John and the Captain were dressing King's wound and they assured me he would be okay. John notified me, "King's stab wound did not penetrate any organs. He is going to be okay Catherine, but he has lost a lot of blood, you both have. So take it easy, are you light headed?"

"A little," I confessed, "but I'm okay." I said as he took me by the arm. I continued, "John, how can I ever thank you?"

Then Roberts motioned for me to follow him into the hall. I took John's hand and he held mine as I said, "I'll be right back Brother John." I kissed his cheek and he nodded and went to administer another sedative to King, to ensure he would sleep throughout the night.

I followed the Captain down the hallway. "Thank you for saving me." I told him with all sincerity.

He took my hands in his with an odd sense of familiarity. He then carefully touched my face. I cringed, for even the slightest touch caused me to flinch and he inquired, "Honestly Catherine, are you going to be okay?"

I thought, "There is nothing you can do about it anyway, no one can." I didn't want him to worry about me. I refused, to be a victim around him so I replied, "I think I got my arm up just in time to block his kick. There isn't any serious damage.

He said, "I didn't mean your face." I nodded my reply. I felt my throat closing up again as if a giant ball was growing in it.

He apologized, "I hate to leave you like this, but I have to get back. I'm shipping out at dawn and I also want to make sure those bastards didn't go AWOL on me."

Fear took hold of me and I had no voice to speak. I began to tremble again.

Then he looked as if he wanted to kick himself for rising up any fear inside me. He paced a little and then held my hand again and softly assured me, "They couldn't get far if they ran and they all know that. Besides Catherine remember that they don't know where you live and you are leaving tomorrow too."

I took a deep breath and replied, "Of course, of course, I have nothing to worry about I'm just a little shaken."

Roberts responded, "Let me make a call," He continued, "I'll see if they returned to the ship."

He made the call and gave the order to have an M.P. hold them until he arrived. After he hung up he informed me they were being detained. "I can assure you Catherine that these men will be severely punished." I nodded then he lifted my chin. "I really am sorry." He declared gazing deeply into my eyes.

I managed a brief smile and told him, "It was not your fault. I'm just glad you showed up when you did."

He expressed regret again saying, "I really wish I arrived even earlier than I did. I wish I could stay with you now, but I am afraid I must go. I hope you will be all right."

Brother John came out and replied for me, "Catherine will be fine. I will make sure of it." John said this as he placed his protective arm about me.

Then John said, "I just finished giving King a sedative. He will be fine until tomorrow, so let me walk you back to your room." I nodded my reply.

The Captain said good-bye and left after John thanked him for helping me. John blessed the Captain, "May the Lord be with you and bless you for all you have done."

The Captain looked somewhat awkward receiving the blessing but he said, "Thank you"

"Wait," I said and then I walked up to him and kissed him gently on the lips and I said, "Thank you." I knew it was crazy and made no sense after being attacked, but I was compelled to kiss him, fearing it was the last time I'd ever feel like that about any man ever again. It was foolish, and yet I did it anyway.

Then he tipped his hat bowed and walked away. I never saw him again.

Brother John walked across the courtyard with me toward my house. I told him what happened from the time I left the bar, after which he chastened me pleading, "Catherine, I wish you would take my advice more and stop going out alone late at night."

I angrily replied, "I was not alone. King was with me." Then I felt guilty for snapping at him. He didn't deserve my wrath.

I took his hand saying softly, "I am sorry." As we arrived at my room I asked him, "Will you stay with me tonight, at least until I fall asleep. I'm afraid without King."

He agreed, "Of course Catherine. Go get ready for bed."

I went to change into my red satin nightgown and robe. He lay beside me in bed as he held me in his arms and caressed my hair. I lay my head upon his chest as he placed a cold pack on the injured side of my face.

"My darling Catherine you have to promise me you'll stop going out alone at night"

I attempted to sit up as I replied, "I can't live in fear. I won't allow some cowardly scum bags to force me to forfeit my freedom!"

He placed my head back down upon his chest saying in a gentle tone, "Catherine, I'm not asking you not to go anywhere. Just make wiser choices. Stop going to bars by yourself, and places that put you in danger. You fight well, but there will always be a foe with greater strength than your own."

I resented what he said, and yet I knew he was right. I hated feeling weak, but a part of me was afraid and I felt I was partially to blame, so I acquiesced, "You're right, I need to be more careful and I promise I will be." Feeling secure in his arms I quickly drifted off to sleep. Still, I felt him gently kiss my forehead before he left the room.

Morning came all too quickly, as the cold breeze and the sound of the rain falling upon my balcony forced me out of bed. I shut my bedroom window. The weather was so strange lately; one day it was hot and the next it was as if a cold north wind blew in. I went quickly into the shower to escape the cold.

While I was in the shower I was pondering a strange dream I had about Captain Roberts the night before. In the dream the Captain had died and was walking around as if he was alive. I was angry with people around me who did not acknowledge that he was no longer dead. It was the Captain and yet he was not the same man. Then the dream changed. It was as if I was suddenly transported into a different place and time. I was standing with Captain Roberts near a horse track that encircled an open field. I was entered into the horse race. I ordered the Captain to go prepare my steed, but he struggled to saddle a sow for me instead. I was angry and told him that I could not ride such a filthy creature. Then behind me there was a beautiful majestic and spirited black stallion. The trumpets announced the race had already begun. I grabbed some reigns and harnessed the black horse and rode him bareback. He rushed past all the other horses with ease. We ran as swiftly as a rushing wind. We crossed the finish line so quickly that we could not stop and I saw a great cliff before us. I jumped off the horse, while still holding on to the reins. The horse went over the cliff and even though my feet were slipping I would not let go and I refused to be pulled down as the dirt gave way. I slipped further and then I summoned a great strength and pulled the horse safely back upon the land.

Despite my desire to relish the hot water, it was beating against my skin hurting my cut a little, even though a waterproof bandage covered it. I was driven from the warmth of my shower, forced to abandon my thoughts as the cold distracted me from discovering the meaning of my dream.

I then realized the time. I had to hurry if I wanted to attend early morning mass before flying to New York.

I also wanted to say good-bye to Brother John before departing and I had to check on King, so needless to say I was in a rush.

I wore my royal blue velvet dress, and loosely tied it at my breasts. I convinced myself that this was to avoid accentuating my cleavage and it would provide me with warmth, for there was a chill in the air. How I hated the cold. This dress was a heavy warm material with a long flowing skirt and tight waist. A form fitting, blue velvet vest was attached to the skirt and I wore a low cut white blouse with long puffy sleeves beneath.

I had this dress specially made for me based on a statue I had once seen in Ireland of a woman pushing a cart of bread in the market. The outfit accentuated her feminine attributes and I attempted to do the same. This was a case of life imitating art, but unlike the statue whose hair was up in a bun my hair was left down. My long black hair fell to my waist and I brushed it to the side to hide my face. I then hastily decided to tie it partially back with a black velvet band.

I admired myself in the mirror for a moment and was thankful my face was not damaged too severely. I loved how the blue velvet intensified my already dark blue eyes. I grabbed my hooded raincoat and I quickly ran across the courtyard and toward the oratory. I was in some pain; however I did not give myself time to appreciate just how fortunate I was, considering what could have been.

I shivered as a gray fog swirled about me and the cold ocean breeze began to blow in. There is nothing as chilling as a sea fog. It encapsulated my being. I had to draw my cloak more firmly about me. I stumbled as I attempted to hurry my steps, for I could see no more than a few feet in front of me. A disturbing silence hung in the air that day. It made the echo of my heels upon the cobblestone all the more unnerving. The sound of the church bells beckoned me from the lifeless courtyard.

I was flushed and a little late, as mass had already begun. I noted that Brother John could not help but admire my beauty as I removed my hood and handed an usher my cloak. I knew he was looking at my face. I noticed that he allowed himself the brief pleasure of studying the gentle curves of my body beneath my now disheveled dress. I had the courage to allow my eyes to meet his. His eyes were like fire, as the flames from the candles reflected their light.

Then the haunting Gregorian chants sent a chill up my spine. I've always hated Gregorian music ever since I saw the Omen One and Two movies. They were very old movies from my parents' generation. I remember watching them when I was a young child.

I don't know why my parents let me watch those horrific movies, I guess they enjoyed them. I hated them but it didn't stop me from curling up on the couch watching them with my parents. I must have taken some disturbing pleasure in being frightened or, perhaps a distant part of my soul was enticed by the darkness.

The music played during these horror movies made the hairs on the back of my neck tingle as I waited for the impending evil to appear. For many years after I watched these movies, I would be filled with fear whenever I heard that style of music. It is strange how vivid the feelings are that certain childhood memories can evoke in adulthood.

I was an independent young woman, and yet the music still affected me as if I was that scared little girl from long ago. Fear could have easily consumed me had I not noticed that Brother John was staring at me. I felt his eyes burn through me as I blessed myself with holy water. I genuflected before I sat down in my pew.

I gazed into John's brown eyes and remembered how he gently kissed my forehead only a few hours before. It is strange, I was deeply drawn to John, it was not a sexual attraction, but it was a deep longing for a connection and security I only found in him. Yet there was another side of me that took pleasure in his attraction to me. Vanity, pride or arrogance I did not know what it was, but I admit I loved the attention and concern he showed me.

I did not have time for confession today but I knew I would have to confess my sins someday. How often had I sensually tempted John? It was cruel and unfair. I was never really attracted to him, and yet I wanted him to want me. I was however attracted to Captain Roberts. As I sat in church I remembered Captain Roberts' face and his broad shoulders embracing me. I allowed my thoughts to lead down a dangerous path as I bowed my head in prayer in a personal confession to God. He was the man I did desire. He awakened a passion in me that would not be silenced.

After mass I whispered into John's ear, "Follow me." I led him down one of the dimly lit hallways. I wished to say good-bye to him in private and give him a gift of a picture of the two of us together.

I hugged him gently and I kissed his cheek as I said, "I know I will probably never see you again John, but I don't want you to forget me." I handed him the picture of the two of us together as I continued, "Your friendship has meant so much to me over the past four years. You have been a light in my life. I understand why you plan on retreating from this world, but I will miss you terribly and I wish you could remain a part of mine."

John was going to live in the wilderness in the Canadian Rockies. Soon he would remove himself from the modern world and seek the face of God. He took a Celtic cross off his neck, which was made of white gold. It had a single diamond figure of Christ on it and tiny rubies were placed where the nails in his hands and feet had been and a golden crown of thorns on his head. There was a flat circle of tiny diamonds in between the

Celtic chainlike design that encircled the top of the cross. It was so beautiful as it dangled on its gold chain.

John placed the necklace gently about my neck saying, "Catherine, I want you to have this to remember me by, and always remember, Jesus will deliver your soul from death and He is your help and your shield."

I was very touched by this gift. I knew his mother gave it to him as a birthday gift the year he decided to become a monk. Brother John came from a very wealthy family, as did I. He hated how obsessed his family was with the material world and that drew him to seek the spiritual. Still, I knew how deeply he loved his mother and the gift mattered to him. Perhaps this is why he chose to give it to me. It was his way of becoming more detached from the world around him, or maybe he just wanted me to remember him like I wanted him to remember me. Regardless of his motive I felt honored he had given his cross to me.

John touched my face gently and sighed, "I'm going to miss you too, Catherine." He gently kissed my forehead and he turned toward the confessional.

I returned to the side altar to light a candle and I started praying for a safe and swift journey home. I knelt before a large statue of a robust middle aged man. He was very tall, perhaps seven feet, or more. His feet were standing in water and on one shoulder he carried the beautiful Christ child, while in the other hand he held a golden staff carved in such a manner so as to give the impression of wood. His staff had emerald green leaves inlaid along its upper portion, so as to give a subtle impression of a tiny fig tree.

The name of this statue's plaque had been removed, however I knew from my religion classes that this was a statue of Saint Christopher. The local church did not remove this statue, for local fisherman and sailors alike revered it. However the statue's name was removed in the churches' attempt to comply with Vatican orders issued in the twentieth century.

The Vatican de-canonized Saint Christopher in the late twentieth century as they attempted to purge the list of saints. The church questioned Saint Christopher's life and origins, but I loved his story.

Saint Christopher became the patron saint of travelers after he carried the Christ child across a river. Although his story was never recorded in the bible, legend has it that he devoted his life to helping feeble people across a difficult span of water. Then one day as he is carrying people to and fro, a small boy appears before him and asks the large man to carry him across the river. Christopher agrees and carries the lad across, but as they proceeded the child's weight steadily increased and the large man struggled to carry the child across. Each step becomes increasingly difficult as Christopher's strength diminishes and the child becomes so heavy that it is almost impossible for the large man to bear the weight any further. Christopher summons the last of his strength and places the child on the other side, collapsing at the water's edge. After catching his breath the giant of the man inquires, "How is it that such a small child could weigh so much?"

To which the child replied, "Because I hold the weight of the world's sins upon my shoulders."

Mariners, travelers and ferrymen worshiped him for centuries. Despite the fact that his status was downgraded to that of a legend by the church, many Catholics continue viewing him as the patron saint of travelers.

Thus I lit a candle and prayed, "May my journey be swift and may I arrive at my destination safely my lord. Saint Christopher, pray for me. Amen." My prayer was short, but I had spent some time visualizing Saint Christopher's encounter with the Christ child.

The distant sound of a clock chiming and the gentle touch of Brother John, who had returned from the confessional, reminded me it was time to depart. John's hand rested gently on my shoulder as he said,

"Catherine, it is time to go. You go get ready and I will prepare King for your flight. I have to check his dressings and I'll give him another sedative. I will pick you up in twenty minutes."

"You're driving me to the airport?" I was surprised I expected to be going alone.

He smiled and laughed, "Of course I am Catherine; did you really expect me to let you move King on your own? Why must you try to do everything alone?"

I shrugged my shoulders and blushed, "What will I do without you John?"

He beamed as he answered "I don't know Catherine, but I'm sure you will have no shortage of young men jumping to your aid should you request it." I kissed his cheek and he rushed off as did I.

I returned to my room to gather my belongings and change for the flight. I found a beautiful, fragrant bouquet of red carnations, filled with lush, rich green ferns and baby's breath outside my door, with a card signed by Captain Roberts.

It had a sweet and simple message in them that read, "Catherine I chose these carnations for you, for they are flowers that endure, retaining their sweet aroma. My heart aches at the thought of not seeing you again. You have captivated and intrigued me. I hope our paths will one day meet again. Regardless, the sweetness of my memory of you will never fade. Wishing you were mine and I was yours, Peter Roberts"

Catherine gazed into the fire as if lost in thought, reliving another moment in time. She closed her eyes and took a deep long breath and sighed as she continued her story.

I picked up my flowers and I took pleasure in smelling their fragrant aroma. I regretted I could not stay in the moment, but I did have a plane to catch.

I changed into a white lace dress and packed the rest of my things. I had lamented not going to confession before my flight and I felt some apprehension before boarding my plane, but how could I confess that I had extensive sexual fantasies, and confess my thoughts of Captain Roberts during mass as well. At this time in my life I was not quite as transparent as I am today.

Catherine ignored the whispers of the women in the camp. She knew they thought she should not be so candid. "Sacrilege!" One fat woman commented. Catherine grinned and shook her head before continuing with a sigh as she threw another log on the fire.

Brother John took me to the airport and he asked, "Who got you the flowers?"

I smiled and replied "The Captain who saved me last night. That was awfully sweet of him don't you think? "

"I suppose."

"John, you're not jealous are you?" I teased in jest.

"No, I am just a little wary." He replied.

I leaned over and kissed him on the cheek and I laughed, "Oh John, I'm going to miss you watching over me. These past four years have been the happiest of my life. I always felt safe when you were near. You are also my own Jiminy Cricket. What am I going to do without you?"

He grinned and blushed ever so slightly as he replied, "Just try to stay out of trouble. You're only mortal."

"Okay John, "I replied, "I will try to stop playing Russian roulette with my life, but I can't stop living. I have to live before I die you know."

"Well, make sure that Death doesn't call on you before its time. Be more careful!" He ordered.

"I will, I promise." I said with all sincerity

We arrived at the airport and I gave him a big hug good bye. He held me gently and then he said with all sincerity, "God speed, Catherine."

Chapter Two:
Soul Ties

I climbed the stairs and waved my final good bye as I boarded the plane. The captain welcomed me on board, "Welcome Miss Catherine, I hope our flight is not too turbulent for you, we will be traveling through some rough weather. Would you like to delay our departure until, tomorrow?"

I hated to fly and dreaded every trip I had in my father's little jet planes, although these were not so little compared with some of the newer models my father had built for domestic flight, so I inquired, "No I don't want to delay, but can we fly around the storm?"

The Captain answered me warily, "I believe so and we may beat the storm, your father's plane can go quite fast, if we need her to."

"Thank you Capitan" I smiled, "I would be eternally grateful if you could, the faster the better."

Dad owned many businesses and one of them built airplanes for both the military and for commercial use. He serviced the rich with airplanes that used a fraction of the fuel used generations before. He bought the technology for solar powered aircraft and further developed it. He capitalized on people's and government's fears of becoming dependent on foreign oil and diminishing oil supplies, meanwhile he secured oil interests in Alberta and off the Grand Banks decades ago. He was a genius when it came to making money.

Still I feared getting in these machines, especially when flying so low over the ocean. They seemed to be far to light and flimsy for a trans-Atlantic flight. This aircraft was one of dad's newest additions to his solar planes. It was a solar turbine hybrid. Even though I flew to and fro from Europe more times than I can count, I could not calm my nerves. I preferred my feet on the ground. King was not thrilled about flying either. We comforted each other in our fear and buckled ourselves in for the takeoff. I pet King on his head, as he whimpered when the engines started.

I said, "Well boy you should count your blessings. Not all dogs fly in style. If this were not my father's plane you would be placed in a tiny kennel and stored with the luggage in the belly of the plane." King did not seem impressed. The sedative took effect and he began to slip out of consciousness, and yet I knew he appreciated my presence and I was very happy to have him with me.

After a smooth, but stomach wrenching takeoff, I began to think of my four years with John in Ireland. It really began to bother me that I would never see him again. We were so close. No one ever knew me as intimately as John, and despite my many character flaws he loved me for whom I was, while inspiring me to be better.

I sat back and relaxed in my seat. The cabin boy came and asked, "Miss Catherine, would you like the usual, or would you prefer a glass of Merlot?"

I smiled and said, "A Merlot would be lovely Eric, thank you." I took a deep smell of the lovely bouquet and enjoyed my wine as I stared out the window. I lost myself in memories of the past.

I recalled the first day John and I met. I was in a rush, running late again. It was my first day of classes and I wanted to go to chapel before school began. I slept later than I planned. It was a foggy fall morning and I was running across the courtyard toward the chapel. I heard the bells beginning to chime. Fearing I would be late I ran faster, with the clip clop of my heels echoing across the cobblestone courtyard. Suddenly I fell, tripping over my own feet. I scraped my knee on the stone ground. "Oh Shit." I swore out loud when a young man dressed in a in a white wool sweater and blue jeans leaned over and gave me his hand.

He asked, "Are you alright miss?" He helped me get to my feet.

I replied, "I'm fine. Thank you for helping me up."

He smiled and noted, "You have quite a nasty gash in your knee. The cobble stone is quite hard on the skin."

It was bleeding, but I insisted, "Oh it's not that bad. I'll be okay."

He gently smiled and held my elbow and motioned with his other hand as he inquired, "The infirmary is just over there, across the courtyard. Can I take you there? We should really get that looked after."

I grimaced as I looked down at the blood oozing from my knee and then I glanced across the courtyard and replied, "Well I wouldn't want an infection. I probably should get it looked at."

He took me by the arm and guided me across the courtyard and introduced himself, "I'm John, what is your name?"

"I'm Catherine, I smiled as I awkwardly gave him my other hand to shake. "Thank you so much for helping me. It is very kind of you John."

He answered, "It's no problem; I'm glad I was there at the right time to help you, I only wish I could have been there sooner, to prevent the fall. Where were you rushing to?"

"Oh," I sighed, "I was on my way to chapel. I wanted to pray before classes began."

"Well, I guess we will both be missing chapel today." He sighed.

"Oh, I am so sorry to have made you late too." I blushed as I felt the guilt of being a burden.

He let out a gentle laugh, "I was running late as well Catherine; you have given me the perfect excuse for Father Martin. I won't be in trouble since I acted the part of the Good Samaritan." He smiled a big beautiful smile.

I frowned as I inquired, "Trouble? Why would you be in trouble?"

"I'm training to become a monk and I am attending the college to study ancient philosophy, ancient languages, religions and prophecy, but I serve in early morning service as well. Do you know Trinity has an excellent library? They have been steadily gaining access to some of the oldest writings in the world."

I replied, "I didn't know that, but I'm glad to hear it." I further inquired, "John, did I note a little pride in your voice as you mentioned these facts? I mean, I note a very slight Irish accent in your tone, and yet you don't sound like you're from Ireland."

He grinned, "You have a good ear and you are correct on both counts. I'm not from here, I am Canadian, but my mother is Irish and a graduate of Trinity. She is very fond of her homeland. Mom insisted I attend here for at least one degree before becoming a recluse. She is responsible for many of the Religious Studies Department's recent acquisitions. She donated quite a bit of funding to ensure I was exposed to a variety of teachings before I take my final vows."

"She's not Catholic then?" I asked, for I was intrigued that a man would become Catholic and a monk if his family were not devout.

We reached the infirmary where to my surprise he opened the door with his own key. It was not open for another two hours, so we were alone. My eyebrow rose as he quickly informed me, "I volunteer here part time. I open up most mornings until all the staff have arrived then I return to cover the final hours and lock up."

I let him tend my wound, cleaning it and applying a bandage. He continued to speak, "I was raised a devout Catholic, until mom left the church several years ago. She is now a non-denominational Christian. She felt betrayed by the Catholic Church for keeping her in the dark concerning other teachings and even the bible itself. I wanted to attend a Jesuit college, but my mom insisted I come here. She wanted me to receive a more secular education. She feels knowledge is power and that my decision should not be made without an informed mind. I agree and so does the church. Final vows are not to be taken lightly. They are binding."

"Well you do enjoy talking a lot for a monk." I chided.

He laughed, "That is true. I hope I don't ever have to take a vow of silence. That would be difficult indeed. Where are you from?"

I smiled, "Well we seem to have a few things in common; I live in New York, but I was born in Canada too. My mother is Irish Canadian, but my father is American."

"What made you come to Trinity?" John asked

I replied, "I am also taking Religious Studies, specializing in prophecy and ancient religions."

John raised his eyebrow as he queried, "Are you considering a life of service too?"

I laughed as I said, "No, I'm not the kind of women to dedicate myself to such a life. I have trouble waking up for early morning service as it is, let alone at dawn for early morning prayers. Brother John, aren't you supposed to be up before the sunrise, not when the church bells are ringing?"

He grinned sheepishly, "Yes, I'm afraid I'm not much of a morning person." John and I became inseparable after this meeting. It was then I decided to mark our first Christmas together with a gift that reflected our first meeting. Christmas came and he opened my gift, it was an alarm clock that played, "Are you sleeping, are you sleeping Brother John, Brother John. Morning bells are ringing, morning bells are ringing, Ding dang dong." At this point the alarm had a little monk that hit two bells with a miniature hammer. When John opened it he said, "Very funny Catherine."

It was John who showed me to my classes, many of which I shared with him, and he showed me around Dublin as well. I was introduced to Temple Bar as well as the cliffs north of Dublin. They were only a thirty-minute drive and they became my favorite place to explore.

Dublin's proximity to the sea was the most endearing trait of the city. There was an extensive coastline to explore; my dog and I were in heaven. John and I would walk with King for hours along the cliffs of Howth, as well along the beaches below. Sometimes the cliffs would fall abruptly into the sea and you had to watch your footing to ensure that you did not plunge to your death off a precipice. Despite the ominous cliffs, Howth was my favorite area north of Dublin. John, King and I would hike up to Howth Head and enjoy a magnificent view of Dublin and the gorgeous bay. We would often go there and kneel together in prayer and study the scriptures.

The village of Howth was delightful too, with excellent dining. John and I often preferred the village to the inner city of Dublin. I had eaten at many fine restaurants in my lifetime, but the fabulous little restaurants with their rustic fireplaces, stone and wood, made them not only cozy and welcoming, but intimate as well, perfect for deep philosophical discussions. My favorite food was the little fish and chip shops. They were so good; mouthwatering fresh fish with deep fried potato wedges. Mm-mm that was good.

John and I would walk for hours talking and strolling along, discussing our childhoods, our families and our classes. A whole new world opened up before us as we continued in our studies. Together we explored the rest of Ireland during our vacation breaks. We later traveled Europe and we were thankful for our families' wealth. Very few people could enjoy such luxury, without restraint. There was nothing in this world I couldn't have, except John.

I remember when we were in Italy together, it was a hot summer night and we were in separate rooms with a shared courtyard. I had not seen John in the shadows.

We both could not sleep. The moon was clear and full. I was in my red nightgown without the over gown. It was too hot to sleep, but I enjoyed the gentle breeze of the air. I sat by the fountain when I noticed John was watching me.

"John, is that you?" I asked

"Yes Catherine, it's me." He replied

"What are you doing? " I inquired, as he emerged from the darkness.

"I couldn't sleep, so I came out to the garden."

"Me too." I agreed and I questioned him, "Why didn't you say anything when I came out?"

"I was watching you. I'm sorry to say the sins of the flesh are too much to deny. You are so beautiful Catherine. Forgive me if I scared you."

"You didn't scare me John. I was only surprised. How long were you watching me?" I said playfully.

"For a while…" He smiled, "I could watch you all night."

"Thank you." I replied.

He came and sat beside me as I interrogated him further, "John have you ever had sex? "

"No." He blushed and then he responded, "Have you?"

"No." I looked down and bit my lip before I continued, "Have you ever wanted to?"

"Yes, I am a man Catherine." He took a deep breath and sighed "But I must not give into such temptations. Have you ever wanted to?"

"Yes, but I'm afraid. I don't know why. A part of me longs to, but another part of it terrifies me. I always hoped my first lover would be gentle and sweet, like you. Then I wouldn't have to be so apprehensive."

"First lover, did you plan on more than one?" John asked incredulously.

"No, not necessarily, however I never presumed that I would find love and still, I hoped for it."

"I understand." John said supportingly

"Would you ever sleep with a woman, if you had the chance John?"

"I don't think that would be wise. I long to, but after tasting such fruit, how could I ever become celibate after that?" John sighed again and shook his head, "No, no, that would be very difficult indeed."

I looked up at him, "Even if that woman was me?"

He smiled and caressed my cheek as he replied. "Especially if that woman was you Catherine, I already love you that would make things complicated."

"What about a kiss? Have you ever had a kiss?" I inquired.

"No." He blushed again.

"Having no physical relations is unnatural John. We are designed for it. We long for it. We need it." I said this as I moved in closer to him. Then I whispered, "Kiss Me."

John pulled me in close and kissed me gently, then longingly and passionately. I smiled up at him, "For someone who has never been kissed, you kiss very well."

He grinned, "I think that I was helped by an expert." He chided.

I slapped his shoulder, "Hey, be nice. Now how was that?"

It was very nice. I sense that I was very passionate about wanting you, however you don't really desire me, do you Catherine?" He looked at me seriously.

"John I love you, my soul has a security and completeness I've never known with anyone else but you; I even want to seduce you, but I don't physically desire you. I mean you're gorgeous and sweet and any girl would be fortunate to have you, but something is missing." I looked down, as I continued, "Does that make sense?"

He lifted my chin as he said, "I think so; it just means that I'm not the one for you."

"Hmm, perhaps that's true, but would you have me anyways?" I urged and I kissed him again.

"Oh Catherine, you do make celibacy very difficult, but I love you enough to say no. You deserve everlasting love, one man for one woman. Do you love me enough to never seduce me? I have not the strength to say no to you again."

"Alright, I'm sorry John. I do love you enough. I'll behave for your sake. Forgive me" I pleaded.

He kissed my forehead and smiled, "Always, Catherine. There is nothing you could ever do that can't be forgiven." Then he kissed me goodnight and we went to our rooms, to try and sleep.

We were very close to one another, but I wondered if a reason in part for our lack of physical intimacy was not somehow related to the dysfunctional relationship with our fathers. John was not close to his father and I was not close to mine, but we were both close to our mothers growing up.

John's father was an angry, driven man who John recently learned was sexually abused by the priest in their local church for years. He abandoned God because God had abandoned him. His father became dedicated to working hard acquiring wealth and giving money to various organizations that were dedicated to protecting children all over the world from abuse. He was driven, but he was unable to have healthy intimate relationships. John's dad was a bitter and angry man, with good cause. Sadly, John never grew close to his own father. John's mother however showered him with affection and attention. She was determined to protect her son while teaching him how to love. She succeeded in this, but his father became very disturbed and resented John's choice to dedicate his life to serving a church and a god that caused him so much pain and misery. John's father became a workaholic and reclusive in his own way.

As for me, my mother always allowed me to help her plan the dinner parties, have a say in the decorations, and she took me to the spa to enjoy the finer things in life. Of course there was always fine dining and shopping too. Mom and I spent a lot of time together when I was young. So did my father and I, until 911.

After 911 my father grew more distant, busy, and he too became a workaholic, obsessed with wealth and diversification. The more the economy spiraled out of control for others, dad seemed to grow and prosper, even profiting from the housing crisis. He would see a failure in one part of the economy and build up, or purchase significant shares in responsible companies that would succeed. He bought many large and beautiful homes when property values plummeted. He purchased houses that others had paid millions for with few hundred thousand in cash during the era of foreclosures. He also purchased and rented many well-kept starter homes too. It seemed that every business decision dad made turned to gold. He had the Midas touch, but he neglected that which matters the most, family. I often wondered what happened to all those families whose homes he purchased. Were they on the street?

John amazed me; he had nothing but compassion and understanding for his father's pain and loss. It did not touch his faith in God. He had trouble understanding why an all-powerful God could allow such evil to occur, but he trusted justice would be served by God. John believed with all his heart that God would work all things for good. John prayed daily for his father's salvation and healing.

I confess I had little compassion for my dad, but as far as I knew my father did not have such a valid excuse for ignoring his daughter. I had bitterness and resentment and felt as if my father simply loved money and power more than family, more than me.

It bothered me that an all-powerful God did not protect innocent children and women from evil men. It angered me that he made us so weak and dependent, so helpless. I hated and feared abuse my whole life as a woman, this is what had driven me toward developing abilities from childhood, abilities that would make me stronger. I could also thank my father for that. I knew he would never protect me; I had to learn to protect myself.

He taught me in early childhood to depend on no one, to be smart, independent and strong. He gave me the best teachers, and the best militarily summer camps to attend for four weeks every summer. While other children took dance and piano lessons, I learned orienteering and weaponry. Other children went to camps to eat s'mores and sing songs around the fire, while my brother James and I would chart the stars, navigate and practice outdoor survival tactics. I had a strange upbringing; on one level I was pampered by my mother to live a life of a princess in a fairytale and on another level I was sent away to the best schools and camps to be a survivor, preparing for a day when my father would not protect me. He called himself a realist. I don't know what to call him, but I know I felt like I missed out on having a dad.

I became less bitter over time when I realized I was not alone in my experience. I was luckier than many children. I had money, resources and a future with few limitations, but what I really wanted was a dad. I found it difficult to relate to God as Daddy, it was easier to think of Jesus as my King and Savior, rather than of God as my father. I did not know him well then, I was as estranged from God as I was to my earthly father, and yet some deep seed of trust existed. I expected them both to provide for me, to protect me and to watch over me. I also expected them both to answer me when I called, but I didn't know them, I didn't feel loved by them and although I expected their protection, I never felt protected. I felt weak and vulnerable. This was my reality: a conflicting fear for my safety and the feeling I was not loved by God, or by my father, married to the hope that they cared and that they would protect me if I needed them too, from what I didn't know. This was part of my soul's struggle for peace, a part of the deep divide.

John and I both had seen the world for much of our lives from a very narrow prospective. We both loved God and hoped he was more than our narrow teaching about him. We were devout, however we both longed for something more, something beyond ourselves. We longed for a relationship, a purpose, direction and a destiny. We both were avid learners and sought the Divine in different ways, but we did seek.

We were united on so many levels, but John was growing toward discipline, self-control, monasticism. We were soul tied, but physically we were a world apart. I was young, passionate and longing to explore the physical world as well. He was primarily spiritual. In our fourth year we began to spend less time together. We still saw each other, however we were no longer inseparable and I began to seek out other social relationships. He needed to practice being alone and I needed something more tangible.

After this final thought of John the turbulence of the plane took me from my reflection for a while. I began to feel weary and tired, I longed to fall asleep like King, but mild nausea kept me awake, and so I watched the news. A gorgeous, dark-eyed man with pitch, black hair upon his head was on the news. His eyes shone like polished obsidian.

He looked strikingly similar to Captain Roberts, except for those eyes. The man on the news had eyes that penetrated your soul. It was unnerving, but Captain Roberts' eyes were salutary and captivating. I sighed remembering his face. I breathed in the sweet scent of the flowers he had sent me.

The man on the news was talking about the hope for peace in the Middle East; this distracted me from my vision of the Captain and focused my attention to the man on the news again. War had always been experienced in my lifetime. If we were not involved battling a terrorist threat close to home, then our soldiers were involved in one far away. It was an unrelenting darkness that consumed mankind. There was always war, or rumors of an impending war.

My heart felt sorrow for men like my brother James, whose life was taken by the need to fight unending battles that were declared by leaders who would never be forced to fight the wars they waged. James went missing in action three years earlier. We assumed he was dead because the Islamic forces no longer took their enemies as prisoners, except to briefly interrogate and torture them for information.

Courageous men like Captain Roberts, so good, strong, and kind were the ones forced to fight and die in some senseless conflict across the sea. I thought, 'I wish there could be peace and then mankind could laugh, dance and love again.'

I then allowed myself the pleasure of remembering dancing in the bar the night before. I smiled and pleasantly recalled that part of the evening. I remembered his velvet voice that conveyed strength and gentleness simultaneously. John had a similar tone, but his faint Irish-American accent made me smile, whereas Captain Roberts' voice penetrated my soul. It is strange, but when he spoke to me it was as if I had already known him before. He entranced me, my white knight.

The news returned to the war, so I turned off the view screen and I took one last smell of my flowers and then I lay them upon my lap and I fell asleep remembering our kiss on the dance floor. I was hoping not to awaken until our journey came to an end. I drifted off pleasantly remembering dancing in the

Captain's arms. We were swaying to the music and it was as if I transcended time and space. My dream was everything I longed for my reality to be.

I had known John for four years and I spoke intimately with him often; I would miss him, but some deeper part of me would miss and long for Captain Roberts more. Though I had only spent a few hours with him I felt a deep connection to him that I could not rationalize. Spiritually I had connected deeply to John, and yet a part of my soul was tied to Captain Roberts and it always would be.

Chapter Three:
Into the Deep; Trapped Between Light and Darkness

King was barking frantically when I was awakened and the plane was shaking. I was thankful that he was still harnessed into his seat. I was not. The pilot was incapable of effectively dealing with the turbulence that violently jolted the plane; it sent me crashing to the floor. I spilled the last of my wine and stained the cabin floor, and I fought to get myself back to my seat. I lost my footing and fell back to the floor of the plane. The cabin boy reached out for my hand he brought me to my seat and ordered me, "Buckle up! Prepare for a possible crash landing."

I yelled to be heard over the clamor of the screaming engines, "Landing, we are over the Atlantic! There is nowhere to land."

"You know the drill" The cabin boy shouted as he reminded me, "Should we lose cabin pressure be prepared to put your oxygen mask on immediately."

I nodded as the cabin boy returned toward his seat to buckle in as well. The turbulence increased further and I feared the plane would be torn apart. A severe ocean storm had us in its grip. The pilot was talking, but I could not make out the muffled sounds of his voice above the sounds of the engines. I could hear loud cracks of thunder above all the noise. Lighting flashed outside my window followed by a roaring thunder. I saw a bolt of lightning hit the wing of the plane and we were suddenly hurled swiftly toward the sea.

I put my mask on and I noticed that the cabin boy had not made it back to his seat in time. He had blood oozing from his forehead. I felt us hit the water. Somehow we managed to stay on the surface of the water, but I knew we would not last long. I yelled, "Eric, Eric, are you alright?" He made no reply.

The captain came rushing into the cabin and asked, "Miss Catherine are you alright?"

I nodded and said, "Yes Captain, but Eric is not."

He went to Eric's side and ordered me, "Put your life jacket on quickly and prepare for emergency exit."

I struggled to get my life jacket on. The Captain got his jacket on and dressed Eric in one too. He then grabbed an inflatable raft and declared, "I am going to open the cabin door. Then we must jump out and hopefully we will all make it onto the raft but there are no guarantees. It is one hell of a storm out there. We are more likely to survive if we remain calm. Don't Panic!"

The cabin boy had not moved since we hit the water. I managed to get my dog out of the plane with me. We both jumped into the sea. The winds and the waves were fierce. I caught glimpses of the plane whenever the lighting flashed. I was in complete darkness and then amidst blinding flashes of lightning and roaring waves, I could not see the plane or the Captain for long. I was sure the plane was taking on water and that it would be gone before too long. I could only hope the captain and the cabin boy got out in time. The captain saved us, but did he save himself?

I feared this would be the end for me as well. It was almost a certainty. One moment I was pleasantly dreaming about Captain Roberts dancing with me, the next moment I found myself fighting for every breath, a prisoner of the darkness of the sea with only brief flashes of light to see the terror all around me.

I lost all sense of time and prayed God would not allow my dog and I to die. I could see lighting flash across the sky above me. I struggled not to swallow the salt water but I couldn't stop King from choking. The waves were so strong. I was sure he drowned, but I refused to let go of him, until one wave pulled me under the sea.

I lost sight of King. There was only darkness and vague images of lightning flashing above me. I felt myself being plunged deeper into the sea. I bobbed to the surface only to be overcome by another wave and I felt like the sea had swallowed me. It overpowered me. All went black and silent.

I don't recall how much time had passed before I came to my senses and was conscious of the world around me, but I was now floating along the surface of the water. I then heard a muffled sound of a rhythmic chopping in the distance. Then I saw a helicopter flying above me. I was melancholy; still I was relieved to finally be rescued.

I was grateful to feel my body being pulled from the cold waters of the Atlantic. I struggled to speak, but I was unable. I hoped they were taking me home. I swear I could see the shoreline in the distance, I don't know how, for I was unable to move, unable to speak and yet I could see the world around me.

I could not lift my head and my body was numb. Unable to move, or speak I was comforted by the thoughts that I would be home soon and that I was no longer a prisoner of the Deep. I felt very tired, but I was unable to sleep.

When I arrived I heard the pilot say that we were landing in Halifax. I was surprised that my family was not there to greet me. I was loaded onto a gurney and driven to what I presumed was the hospital. I was exhausted and longing for rest. Then all went silent as I felt myself fading and darkness consumed me.

Suddenly I was awake again and I could hear the voices of my parents as they thanked friends and family, "Thank you so much for coming, your support means so much to us."

Mother leaned over and held on to me. She squeezed so tightly I thought she would break my bones and she brushed my hair aside. She kissed me and her tears rolled onto my cold and clammy skin.

I needed a blanket, but I was unable to tell anyone what I wanted. I felt as if I was trapped somewhere between sleep and dreams. I wished I could hug Mom and assure her I would be okay, and then I began to fear I would never be able to walk, or talk again.

Dad held my hand and hugged mom telling her, "Elizabeth, come and sit for a while."

I couldn't see her anymore. I could hear someone who was talking to Mom. I did not recognize who was speaking, but I remember what they said, "Catherine was such a beautiful girl. This is such a tragedy."

How beautiful I was? Was! I panicked, I feared I had been physically mutilated and was unaware of it, and then I remembered the bruise on my face. I wished someone would bring me a mirror and a bloody blanket. Instead I was forced to wait, resigned to my fate. This comatose state was lasting for hours, or days, or weeks, or maybe even months; I could not tell for I lost all sense of time as I seemed to drift in and out of consciousness and yet I found no rest.

They began to move me again. I did not know where they were taking me, but I was thankful to be in the sunshine. I could not feel the warmth of the sun, and yet I saw it shining brightly above me. It nearly blinded me and still I could not absorb its warmth. It was almost as if it were a cruel illusion. The fruitless trees shared my presentiment, as they stood naked all around me.

Suddenly my parents were beside me again and my mother was still crying but silently. She placed a single red rose on my chest, "My beautiful Catherine, I will always love you." Then she kissed me as a procession of mournful people appeared before my helpless sight.

Then I saw Brother John, as he kissed my cheek and placed the picture I gave him on my heart. He bent down and whispered in my ear, "You will always be a part of me." I was confused, as I noticed the shadows growing all around me and the light began to fade into darkness.

I heard a thud and the darkness consumed me. It was as if a heavy lid was closed on top of me. In my mind I struggled to kick and scream, pleading for someone to let me out. I then felt myself being lowered as if deep into the ground. Panic set in; they thought I was dead and they were now burying me alive! I shrieked in terror, begging them to let me out. No one could hear my silent scream.

After some time I felt myself moving upward. The sway gave me the illusion that I was floating. I heard a thump as my coffin was placed on the ground beside my grave. I was elated some one knew it was a mistake. Someone did open the lid. The sun had set and the cold of the night made me want to shiver, still I was happy to see the beauty of the full moon and the stars above me. It was the men who placed me in my coffin earlier at what must have been the funeral home.

"It's a pity," one of the men stated. The other replied, "Yeah," another replied as he lifted the picture of me with Brother John and he said, "I would have loved mounting the bitch." They laughed as they looked at the photograph.

"You're crass bastards!" I thought. Then they set their eyes upon the cross about my neck.

One of the men reached for it but suddenly he pulled his hand back as if he had been burned. "Shit. That hurt." He said.

The other questioned him, "What? What the fuck just happened?"

"Never mind, to hell with it, let's get this bitch out of here" The first man replied.

Together they lifted me out of the coffin, and threw me back into my grave. "No", I yelled inside my mind, "No, I'm alive!" As my body hit the ground I felt a piercing jolt travel up my spine. I was in severe pain. I was sure that more bruises were added to my battered body. I was discarded to the depth of the earth. I realized that I was lost between the light and the darkness.

I heard the men laugh as they threw the red rose and picture of John and me into the grave. Then I screamed as they began to cover my body with dirt, soiling my white dress. I wailed again. My protests went unnoticed, as the weight of the soil smothered any calls for help, which were only emanating from my own mind. I was completely alone for the first time in my life. Time had lost all meaning. I could not tell if it was day or night, nor how much time had passed and my eyes could not shed a tear; I screamed no more. The futility of my wailing was painfully apparent to me. I had flirted with Death and now he laid claim to me, as the earth blocked out all light. I cried silently, while life gave way to death, light to darkness and time gave way to eternity.

Chapter Four:
Hell's Captive

I had drifted into a state of nothingness. My heart and soul were numb like my lifeless body, paralyzed in a semi-conscious state. I was suddenly brought back to consciousness when I started falling. I grasped for roots, but they gave way and I was unable to stop my descent. I fell abruptly with a hard thud, banging my head on a cobblestone floor. My body was bruised and battered; the lace on my dress was ripped and it was no longer a brilliant white. It was now smudged, stained with blood and dirt. My hair was a mess, but at least I was able to move.

A distant voice from deep inside my mind compelled me to get up and walk. I obeyed. I forced myself to rise, despite the excruciating pain. I no longer had my shoes on. I could only see one shoe near where I stood, while the other one was hidden in the darkness. I don't know why I picked my shoe up, but I did. I strained my eyes to see as I inched my way along the ominous corridor, running my hand along a cold stone wall.

The wall was cold and damp, as if it were covered with a hairy moss. I screamed in horror as I felt something crawl across my fingers. I lifted my hand off the wall and precariously moved forward, trembling and filled with trepidation.

My feet were freezing but they refused to go numb. I longed for some relief from the cold but I found none. My only hope lay in forcing myself to walk and seek some form of escape from the torturing, frigid air. I trudged on, drunk with fatigue, but unable to sleep as I stumbled aimlessly in the gloomy tunnels.

I could not see clearly, however I sensed movement all around me as if I was walking amidst a dispiriting gloom. I continued along in the darkness and I would occasionally catch sight of a figure emerging from the shadows and brush silently past me. I would whisper, "Who's there?" No one replied.

A great fear came upon me and I was trembling, as a spirit like creature brushed by my face again. The small hairs at the base of my neck stood up and goose bumps covered my skin. The darkness was so thick that I felt saturated by it. I could not visually detect the form's appearance, but I sensed it stood before my eyes. I was frozen with fear. I dared not move, nor could I find my voice. There was silence all around me.

From the darkness someone whispered in my ear, "I can see you."

"Who's there?" I demanded, but no one answered me, so I continued blindly.

Then the silence was broken again with that same ominous whisper; "I know who you are."

I questioned again with my trembling voice, "Who are you?" No one replied, and suddenly I sensed that the thing that whispered to me was gone. I felt all alone in the darkness.

After some time my eyes adjusted to the lack of light. I could now see countless corridors leading in all directions and I did not know which one to take. I then noticed little cells to each side of me and I was near the center of a circle that spiraled down into a sea of blackness below me. The occasional glow of various rooms glimmered in the darkness. Most were empty, but some had people in them.

I tried to talk to a woman in one of the cells, and I noticed she had blood stained thighs. She sat rocking back and forth. She was holding a small baby in her arms. She took no notice of me; she just kept rocking, singing a lullaby under her breath. Then I observed that she had held out her hand to me. I looked to see what she had offered me. In my arms she placed a skeleton of a perfectly formed human being.

In shock I dropped it and I recoiled from her. The little bones fell, crashing into tiny pieces on the cold stone floor. It sounded somewhat like a broken glass shattering. I backed out of her cell and ran up another corridor hearing her song, 'Hush little baby, don't you cry. Momma's going to sing you a lullaby ...' the song began to fade, like a distant echo as I made my way through the passageways.

I walked a long time through a series of unending corridors, falling at many intervals along the way. I saw a man sitting in another cell; he was wearing a yellow robe, uttering the same phrase over and over again. I did not understand what he was saying. The only word I remember was something that sounded like, "Mitraya."

I pleaded with him, "Please talk to me, I need your help." He did not respond initially and then I managed to shed a single tear, which fell upon his foot and he looked up. I asked him if he could help me.

He said "No."

I asked in frustration, "Why not?"

He answered calmly, "This is all an illusion, from which I could no more help you escape than you could help me."

I told him with indignation, "This is very real to me."

He gently replied, "Just because you think this is real does not mean it is. You can only find peace when you accept reality for what it is."

"See reality for what it is" I cried, "Where do you think we are? This is Hell, or some twisted version of Purgatory." I declared.

He smiled and said, "I don't believe in an afterlife."

"Then what do you call this?" I said sarcastically, "Just because you don't believe in it does not mean it is not real." He didn't respond to me, he just returned to his mindless meditation. I was thinking, 'He's gone mad.'

The monk smiled and said, "This is but an illusion on the journey toward enlightenment."

Feeling lost, as he began to enter his trance by reciting his monotonous mantra, I walked away hopeless and dejected. Before I left his cell he looked up and cautioned me saying, "If you do not wish to lose yourself, accept no drinks, or comfort from the handsome one, for nothing is as it appears, it is how we believe it should be." I did not understand his meaning, but I nodded, appearing to heed his warning.

I continued past countless cells, most of which were still empty. Those rooms, which had people inside were filled with individuals that appeared to be in torment, delusional, or insane. Only the man in the yellow robe seemed undisturbed by his situation.

I finally came across a corridor leading downward and a light was shining in the darkness. I walked toward it and came upon a woman who was sitting in a well-lit room. It was the only bright room I had encountered thus far and it pained my eyes, but I peeked in. I had to squint in the bright light. Still, I was compelled to look despite my distress.

Mirrors surrounded the lady and she looked hideous. She was covered in vile sores on her face and her arms. The woman had ulcers on her skin. They looked tender and red and her tissue was disintegrating on various parts of her body, including her face. Many of her lacerations were inflamed. Some of her skin ulcers appeared as open craters, on the layers of skin that had eroded. She appeared to be in pain as disgusting and foul smelling fluid oozed from her larger abscesses. I feared I would throw-up from both the smell and the sight of her. I stared at her in horror as I noticed her smaller wounds were bleeding. Despite her obvious physical suffering her psychological torment was worse.

She could not help but hate her own reflection as she stared at her blisters in the mirror. She almost caressed her right cheek that had the most severe skin ulcers that appeared as the open craters, revealing both her muscle tissue and cheekbone beneath.

She screamed, cursing her own reflection as she threw herself against the mirrored walls. They would crash into tiny pieces cutting her skin and then almost instantaneously the mirrors would reform, as if time had reversed itself. Then the woman would be forced to see her own gruesome reflection yet again.

She then noticed my reflection in the mirror. My dress was torn and dirty and my hair somewhat disarrayed, but I was still beautiful. She turned and walked over to me. She caressed my face as she said with longing in her voice, "You're so beautiful, so lovely and so divine. You have such lovely skin, perfect skin."

I cringed, repulsed at her touch, I was utterly revolted at her hideousness. I felt guilty for being unable to look at her, and like a coward I turned away to leave, but she pleaded with me, "Please don't go."

I did not turn around as I said, "I'm sorry, but I can't stay. I must leave." I disappeared into the darkness. I could hear her calling out to me as I crept away, "No. Please don't go. You're so beautiful. Pleases come back. Please…"

I didn't attempt to speak to anyone else in the cells after that experience, except for one demented man, who was running through the halls like a mad man. He seized me and yelled, "We are makers of our own hell, but why must we suffer for all eternity? Why? I can't escape him, nor hide, even in death he is with me"

I inquired, "Am I in Hell? Have you ever tried to escape?"

He laughed at me almost hysterically as he replied, "There is no escape!" I would not believe it, so I continued on as he left again running and screaming through the halls totally insane, laughing and crying simultaneously, yelling, "Escape, escape, there is no escape!"

I contemplated why God wouldn't just destroy the evil people, rather than condemn them to a place of eternal suffering. I knew that part of the problem was that God made both angels and men spiritual beings, with an eternal existence. I remember how the Bible said that God has put eternity in our heart, but why didn't that eternity draw us to the light instead of toward the darkness. I felt myself angry at God, descending into despair and confusion.

I crumbled to the ground depleted of all energy and disoriented as I tried to remember the teaching of Hell in the Bible. The word hell in old English usage simply meant to conceal, to hide, or to cover; therefore was hell a concealed, hidden, or covered place? If so what is it hidden from and if something is hidden, or covered, does that mean it could be uncovered?

In Old English the literature records I recalled studying that the word helling referred to the helling of potatoes, or putting potatoes into pits. How does one escape a pit? Is it futile to try?

Helling was also used in Ancient English writings when referring to the helling of a house, or covering, or thatching the dwelling. If we are the dwelling place of God, does his blood not cover us?

Words matter to God; I still believed his word was truth, but I was unable to grasp its meaning. Wisdom and understanding was not to be found in this darkness, still I struggled to remember my teachings, believing they held a key to my escape.

I reflected on my studies of hell and the meaning of this word. Then after I recalled the word hell when properly used could be interpreted as a grave and pit, and this certainly appeared to be where I initially found myself and the deeper I traveled into the darkness the more horrors I discovered. Sheol and Hades are the secret or hidden condition of death. Was I trapped in this hell with no hope of escape? Was I hidden from the living? Was I hidden from God? Did his blood no longer cover me here?

I sat against the stone walls pulling my knees to my chest and hanging my head in confusion. I was delirious with exhaustion; still I could not quiet my mind. I questioned why we were all there, what had we all done to deserve such a horror? If Hell was a place where the dead received punishment for their evil deeds, than what sins had we committed?

I reflected on everyone I had seen, the woman with the baby, the Buddhist monk, and the other woman surrounded by mirrors, which would not allow her to hide from her own horrid reflection. I assumed the first must have had guilt over the death of her child; maybe she committed murder? The third consumed by vanity on earth, or perhaps covetousness, jealousy, or envy; who knew? The monk puzzled me; I felt no darkness in him.

As I sat in reflection I recalled lessons from a religion course that I took in university; Maitreya is a Bodhisattva of compassion. Did he find himself damned for worshiping false gods, or not having enough compassion, or did he fail to keep his vows? I did not know. At least he talked to me with some sense of sanity, as brief as it was. I did not know what he, or what anyone had done to warrant such a sentence. What had I done to deserve a fate such as this?

After a long while sitting deep in thought, I looked up and saw a room to my left. It appeared to be filled with gold. There was a man sitting in the middle of the floor dressed in rags and eating a little bowl of gruel. He was counting a large amount of gold coins. People feasted on tables above him. They were dressed in the finest of clothing. He was hungry, but even his gruel was taken from him and he was forced to count another case of gold coins that were delivered to him. He said aloud, "One million five hundred fifty six, one million five hundred fifty-seven…."

I asked him, "Why are you counting? You should stop and eat; you look like you're starving to death."

I did not enter the room, so the people feasting could not see me. I held to the shadows. The man looked up at me and squinted trying to see who had spoken to him. He said in anger, "Now look what you have done. You interrupted and made me forget where I was. Now I have to start all over again."

Just then a waiter walked by with a succulent meat dish to be delivered to those at the feast. The man smelled it and reached up for some as it passed by him and the server used a gold rod that he had in his hand and hit the ragged man on the back and yelled, "Get back to counting!"

The poor man looked down and started all over again, as another case of coins was delivered to him, "One, two, three, four…"

After watching for a while, I decided to leave and continued down the dark corridor. I descended slowly down a stone staircase and came to more level ground and found that another level of cells encircled me.

I saw a huge, fat man being force-fed. He was morbidly obese; it was disgusting, but he did not want to eat. People would stuff another spoonful of food in his mouth, while another large man would force him to drink. Liquid fell like drool from his mouth. He pleaded, "Please, stop it. I don't want any more. Please it makes me so sick. Stop it, please. I can't take anymore." Just as he finished these words he threw up and they compelled him to eat all over again.

I felt myself getting ill, and I thought I was going to throw up as well, but I didn't. I did not say anything this time. I just kept walking, clinging to the shadows, hoping to go unnoticed.

I heard yelling, swearing and insults as I passed another room. A young beautiful black woman was screaming at a man standing in front of her, "I hate you, you worthless piece of shit. You're a stupid useless idiot. You're nothing but scum." She hit him with the back of her hand followed by a kick to his genitals as she continued berating him, "You scum, who is superior now. I'm going to kill you, you ugly wasp."

The man was white with a shaved head and a tattoo with a red cross on one arm and a swastika on the other. He looked like a skinhead. A large black man forced him to climb a box where a hangman's rope was. I watched in terror as I saw them put the noose around his neck and hang the man. His neck didn't break, so he slowly strangled to death.

I ran down another corridor and knew that I did not want to see any more suffering. This was Hell. There could be no denying it, but what was I doing here. I was so sick and tired. I was stumbling, unsure of how I had the strength to continue. I did not know what else to do. So I kept to the shadows and made my way past a myriad of empty cells.

I passed one cell that was under construction. A fat woman and a skinny man were breaking rocks apart. One was using stone to lay a floor, while the other labored to build a stone wall. They looked exhausted and they did nothing but slave away. I did not bother to ask them what they were doing. I didn't care. I assumed they were forced to work for eternity. They were probably lazy on earth. Apathy was setting in. I didn't care anymore; I just wanted to escape the cold. I shivered as I made my descent. My teeth started to chatter and I forced myself to jog again, hoping to warm up. I did stop shivering, but I was still cold and out of breath. I collapsed against the wall thinking. "I don't belong here. I don't deserve this. Why am I here?"

Just then a large number of rats scurried past me and I jumped up shrieking. I continued stumbling through the corridors, frantically running away. I did not know where I should go. I was just desperate to escape the horror. I ran and came to a precipice, where I almost fell into a pit so deep and dark that I feared it was bottomless. Had I fallen into it, I was certain that I would have never escaped this place of agony.

I regained my balance, and looked below me into an endless sea of darkness; then I saw some firelight flickering in the distance. I heard countless cries of pain and moans of lament, amidst screams of despair and torment reverberate up the cavern. I backed up slowly, inching my way back from the cliff, until I heard a scream directly behind me.

I turned around to witness a most horrific vision before my tortured sight. Before me in a cell stood two figures, one a boy in a long white robe the other a man in a black priest's robe. The man was being raped by a boy; the priest cried in pain. I ran to stop him, but as the boy turned around I saw the face of a beast, and his penis had spikes protruding from it. The priest's anus was bleeding heavily and I moved to help him.

The vile creature said to me in a heinous tone, "Do you not think he gets what he deserves, he did far worse to innocent children."

I shrank back as the creature stepped closer to me and asked. "And what are your sins my dear? Did you lust like this man? Did you act on you deviant desires?" The beast laughed at me, and then he turned and began to beat the priest.

I ran away in fear and disgust clutching the cross on my neck. I ran for so long, I was afraid to stop, but I was also too terrified to go on, so I collapsed feeling wretched, cold, exhausted and demoralized. Nausea overwhelmed me and I had dry heaves as I attempted to throw up, but my stomach was empty. I lay crying and shivering, exhausted, but still unable to sleep.

I began to question God, "What had I done to deserve this? Why have you damned me, why?" I collapsed again and I lay there crying alone on the floor, weeping for my God to save me. A handsome man bent down and gave me his hand.

He was tall with white unblemished skin; his teeth were perfect and brilliantly white as he shone like a midnight star. His hair was black as the night contrasting with his deep blue eyes. Never in my life have I ever seen any being so breathtaking, so alluring. His shoulders were broad and he stood before me in a perfectly tailored black suit. "Follow me" he said, "and you will never be cold or hungry again."

I was amazed, for as his arm was supporting me his warmth emanated throughout my body. Only then did I become aware of how hungry and terribly thirsty I was. I was so consumed with my desire to escape the cold that I must have forgotten my need for nourishment.

I saw him standing before me in the darkness and for some strange reason I was somewhat afraid of him, but in my fear I had to find the courage to take his hand. My heartbeat quickened as I stared into his velvet blue eyes. I shuddered for I suddenly felt as if I was looking into the heart of darkness itself.

I desperately wanted to escape the cold and the pain, so I quickly deluded myself thinking, "The LORD has sent me an angel, to save me." I thanked God above.

The stranger laughed and said "Your god has abandoned you and delivered you to me."

I took my hand from him immediately and protested saying, "My God would never abandon me. He promised in his word that he would never leave me, or forsake me."

He smiled and replied, "Than you must have abandoned him." He continued and said, "Regardless my dear I can assure you, he cannot, nor would he answer your prayers while you remain here. Your feet have come down to Death and your steps have led you to me."

Fear took hold of me and I stood lost and afraid. He reached out his hand again and said, "Now if you wish to escape the cold, come with me."

I had not realized it initially but when I had let go of his hand the cold, which previously caused me so much torment began to return. I could not bear the excruciating cold again, so I took his hand and I allowed him to place his arm around me, the iciness fled and I temporarily dismissed the chill in my soul.

He led me to a room filled with the soft light of candles, and a small fire, which warmed the room. The room was filled with red satin curtains and pillows and a black velvet sofa. A Roman tub of warm water stood alone in the middle of the room. I could see the steam from the warmth of the bath rising up like a gentle mist.

He kissed my cheek and told me, "Disrobe and prepare yourself my lovely for an evening that will change your life forever." Then he left me with six beautiful women to help me prepare. I was apprehensive, but I did not resist. It was as if my mind were no longer my own. I was entranced.

They removed my dress, which was now a dull gray. No sign of white remained. I lifted the cross off my neck and placed it on my dress. I allowed the women to guide me to the bath.

The warmth of the water felt luscious against my skin and the six bathed me. My skin burned with pleasure as they caressed my body with scented soap. I was entering a hypnotic state of ecstasy.

I was taken out of the tub; I was massaged with scented oil all over my body. The pleasure was intense. The six dressed me in a seductive red satin dress, which wrapped around my body. Two of the females kissed my shoulders, another my neck, and then he came back for me.

I took his arm and he guided me out of the boudoir, down the hallway and into a bar with a dance hall. It felt so good to be warm again. Candles and small fires throughout the hall lighted the bar. People were laughing and dancing, while some were drinking. My body relished in the heat.

He requested, "Give me the pleasure of this dance." I quickly lost myself in the music and shared one seductive dance after another with him. On the sixth dance he swayed to the music from behind me. He slid his hand up my thigh and up toward my breast. I did not move his hand as I felt myself lost in a trance like state.

As the dance ended a waiter passed by with drinks. He grabbed the goblet and wrapping his arm around me he held it to my lips and offered it to me. I was parched and was about to drink, when I heard a voice whisper in my soul, "No."

I looked around and noticed the people all around me were not just dancing and drinking; many were engaged in sexual activity in the darkness. I witnessed sin in the shadows. I saw figures of men having sex with men and women with women, as their silhouettes were cast upon the walls all around me. I turned to see a woman lap dancing for a man to my left. She was beginning to remove her deep purple clothing. Then he kissed my neck and told me, "Drink my queen, drink."

His voice was hypnotic, but I heard a voice echo again in my soul declare firmly. "NO!"

I threw the goblet to the floor, and watched as the crimson liquid flowed like blood before my feet. I ran towards the door in disgust, listening to a distant voice in my soul, which compelled me to leave. It commanded; "GO!" and I obeyed.

I collapsed to my knees just outside the hall, crying with shame. I looked back appalled to think that I was about become a participant in the orgy behind me. I saw the six women who had bathed me dressed in seductive red dresses. One of them was having sex with another man in the shadows, as the other women danced around the couple with one another. I noticed that they licked each other with a serpent tongue. For a moment I felt deeply ashamed and I was consumed with self-loathing, as well as disdain for the others in the hall.

My tempter followed me in hot pursuit and he grabbed my arm and warned, "If you leave me, there will be only suffering and no pleasure."

"I prefer the suffering, rather than losing myself to you and your serpent women." I replied disparagingly. I turned my back on the haunting flames and continued walking back toward the room that I had changed in earlier.

He followed me and told me not to be such a fool. He asked, "Why would you rather suffer than stay with me?"

I told him because my God had answered my prayers. I said, "I foolishly believed earlier that God sent me you, to deliver me from my misery, but I was wrong. Now I know he still cares and he will guide me out of this vile pit of debauchery. He says in his word, that he has delivered my soul from the lowest hell."

The Devil sneered, "You are here. I am the ruler in this world. Where is your faithful god now?" Then the devil continued with a snicker, "Why do you presume to think a praise written by David in a psalm thousands of years ago is a promise to you? You have arrogance to claim this as a promise. Who are you, that you would have such pride, that quality alone proves you are meant to be here." Then he laughed at his own words.

I did not answer. I disrobed and threw the red satin dress into the fire that was burning near the center of room where I had bathed earlier. I put my chain with the crucifix about my neck. I was about to put my white dress on, but as I reached for it he grabbed my arm.

His voice was filled with contempt. "How can you trust in a god who condemned you and made you suffer? I was your only relief and still you follow him.

Why would you want a god who denies passion and pleasure and offers you only pain?"

I answered fearlessly, "You were right earlier; I abandoned Him. I allowed my passions and my lust to rule me. I gave into my desires and temptations of the flesh, without considering the consequence. I was angry and distant from him because I resented my lot in life. I resented my weakness and I did not trust his strength enough. I lived in bitterness rather than gratitude. The question is not what did I do to deserve this; it's what didn't I do? I did not trust him. My God did not condemn me; my heart did. I cannot serve my flesh and expect my spirit to live. I cannot claim salvation when my heart holds on to that which is anything but love. I will not follow you ever again and he will not leave my soul in this evil place."

"You admit your sin and yet you refuse to allow me to give you pleasure. Why?" he asked this as he held both of my arms and I stood naked before him.

I replied, "Because I love my God; he is my creator, my father, my savior, and his Spirit is within me."

The Devil laughed as he replied, "If His Spirit was within you, then wouldn't you be in Heaven?"

I declared, "My Lord conquered death and died to take away my sin. He will save me!"

"Then have him save you from this." He said this as he threw me into the fire. I screamed in pain and rolled onto the floor, as the cross branded me. I looked at the rest of my skin and it was bubbled and blistered. I don't know how I could see them, but I noticed microorganisms and bacteria swimming in the vesicles on my skin. I was covered with these vile sores.

He smiled and said; "You see those organisms, they are the filth which embodies you. Your god is too pure and you are contemptible to him. He will never accept you as you are, but I will. I do not judge you for being passionate and free spirited, I welcome you and that is why you followed me before. Follow me now."

"Never!" I said this as I clutched the cross that had seared my flesh.

He took hold of it and laughed mockingly, "Do you really believe this has the power to save you?" He said half laughing as he continued, "It is a foolish trinket."

I pondered this for a moment and then I responded, "No, it does not have power by itself, but you hate it because it is a symbol that reminds you that Christ's Father gave him power over you, power over life and death. It also reminds me that he suffered and died to make me clean. I will never give myself to you; I will suffer an eternity first."

"As you wish." he retorted. "You may join the other fools who insist on tormenting themselves, or you may follow me. The choice my dear is yours, but know this, I will not protect you from the cold, nor from the hideous organisms, which now live on your once beautiful body, unless you give yourself completely to me. Only then can you find relief and joy. I am the only one who has power here! I had victory the day the angels followed me." He said with pride.

A single tear rolled down my cheek and I choked out the words with barely a whisper, "No, he had victory on the cross." My tear rolled down my cheek and fell upon my hand. I looked down to see the organisms disappear. I grabbed my dress and put it back on. It seems funny, but suddenly I smiled, happy to know that at least I would no longer feel the chill in my soul and a small flicker of hope grew into a flame. I stood up determined to never lose myself to the Devil again.

All went black as he waved his hand and obliterated all fire, all sources of light and warmth. I was alone in the darkness and tormented by the cold yet again. All of the sudden he kicked me in the left side of my ribs and I was thrown against a wall with an unearthly force. My arms and feet were suddenly chained to a wall. I knew I was now in my own cell. I was hanging on the cold stone wall.

My head was aching from hitting the wall when I was flung into the chains and it began to throb. My headache was intensified by the shrieks of terror that rang out through the darkness. After hanging there for some time my wrists and ankles were rubbed raw, for I had tried to escape. I failed. It only increased my agony by making my wrists and ankles bleed.

The enemies of the Almighty God could be heard laughing in the distance with heinous delight. It was probably the demons torturing the lost souls, or were they laughing at my plight, or at my blind faith in my God that I could not see?   Another single tear of pain and defeat ran down my cheek as I prayed, 'My God, I believe your word is true, it is written that if I make my bed in Hell, you are there. Where are you now God? It is written in the Psalms that you would not leave my soul in Hell. Deliver me. You redeemed many souls from the grave, so why don't you reclaim mine? You delivered Jonah when he prayed to you Lord, out of the fish's belly. Jonah cried out in his affliction to you Lord and you heard him. I cry out to you God, hear my voice and rescue me as you liberated others.' My dry throat hurt as I howled, "Father, save me!" Alas I was Hell's captive. Heaven made no reply.

I then heard the serpent's voice, "Now child," and gradually I could see his face. I saw him standing in the darkness as he inquired, "Really my dear, do you prefer this to me? Am I really that repulsive to you?"

I looked down at him and said, "You know I will never willingly give myself to you again, so you have to chain me up and hold me prisoner."

He smiled and replied, "You are a prisoner my dear, but I assure you I am not the one who holds you here." With that he left again.

I hung my head, exhausted, cold and confused. "Everybody talks in bloody riddles!" I thought to myself. I had no conception of time and though I longed for sleep, I could not. If it wasn't the screams of torture echoing their haunting cries through the corridors, then it was my own pain, and the unrelenting cold that kept me awake. I was Hell's captive, but I still believed Jesus could set me free. Just when I thought I would lose my mind, I was broken in heart and spirit and unable to set myself free. I cried one last plea, "Jesus, save me."

He stood before me in a long white robe. His robe shone like a light in the darkness. It had a hood that was pulled forward on his head, so that I could not see his face. He commanded me to follow him.

I cried, "I can't. I'm chained to this wall. I don't have the strength." He walked over and made my left hand free from the shackle. I tried to get the other wrist free and though I succeeded I screamed in agony as I pulled my other wrist free myself; while he broke the chains about my ankles with a touch of his finger. I was unbound. I would have come crashing to the ground as the chains gave way, but he caught me. Finally, I was liberated.

He led me down twisting corridors, of darkness. I felt compelled to follow him, drawn by some distant hope hidden deep within my soul. I was still shivering, bruised and bloody; however I made myself follow him closely. The closer I came to him the warmer I felt and so I hurried my pace to absorb some of his warmth. There was healing in his presence, and I could feel my body beginning to mend.

I could hear cries mixed with screams of affliction in the darkness, but I had grown weary and deaf to the incessant howling. We passed the bar I had been to earlier and Satan was enraged as he took sadistic pleasure in tormenting his subjects. Some were being tormented with fire others by whipping and beating them. I assumed they were being punished for failing to recruit me. We passed by quietly and continued down the corridor.

I recognized the monk as we turned a corner. He was still sitting in his cell reciting his mantra. I insisted, "Please Lord, can we stop. He deserves freedom too." As I said those words I felt my stomach tighten. I became nauseous, for I realized that I didn't deserve freedom. I was no more worthy of be saved from this hell than anyone I had seen earlier.

I fell to my knees crying in pain, weeping at my own unworthiness to escape. Crying like I never had before for all those souls whose voices were echoing through the darkness. The pain of their hearts flooded over me; I became awakened to their suffering, loneliness and despair.

Jesus beckoned to me patiently, "Come, follow me." He saw tears flow from my eyes, which were no longer dry. He looked at me with compassion, as I looked towards the monk with pleading. The Lord reached out his hand and wiped away my tears with a gentle caress. He grinned down at me and then he walked toward the monk.

The monk looked up at us. I begged him, "Please, come with us." Before I was only concerned with ending my own pain and suffering, but now I was desperate for the monk to be led to freedom too.

The monk said, "There is nowhere to go." He then got up and stared into the eyes of Jesus whom I was following; the monk was staring at him quite perplexed. I knew he believed that this was all an illusion, but he must have wanted to escape it regardless because after staring into the Lord's eyes for a moment he followed us.

As we walked I asked the Lord, "Why are you here?" He smiled and simply replied, "I am here in response to a prayer."

I did not have the boldness to question why he did not come for me earlier. I was rendered to silence and I knew not why. I was speechless. Words lost all relevance as I followed both men. They however spoke easily. The monk was talking with the Lord saying, "I have spent a lifetime and what seemed like an eternity meditating and seeking enlightenment. I have developed perfect mind control, in that I feared nothing, nor was I shocked by anything."

The Lord replied, "Apathy and resignation is not self-control."

I pondered their words as I walked behind them. The monk had appeared to have been unaffected by the severe cold, which had tortured me earlier and he demonstrated no sign of physical discomfort. Nothing seemed to anger him, or move him emotionally. He acted as if he were devoid of emotion. As far as I could see he dismissed much of the horrors I had witnessed as a reflection of truth rather than reality itself.

The monk noted, "On this journey I have sought to become one with the universe. I would experience this oneness after hours and sometimes after days of meditation, while in the monastery. Here I found myself dependent on that feeling of oneness, thus I never ceased meditating, hoping that I may enter into nirvana. I could not sustain it though; it was far too fleeting. Like the distant wind it would come upon me, but I never knew from whence it came, nor could I predict when it would come again."

Jesus smiled, but he said nothing he just walked on beside the monk silently. The monk spoke a little more and when he did speak I found myself confused by his refusal to see the situation for what it truly was. He spoke in such a manner that reflected his firm beliefs that this was all an illusion, his perspective often escaped me. Still I liked him; his peaceful demeanor soothed my soul. He was a much-needed company and a sharp contrast to my emotional and impulsive nature. Furthermore, his face had a pleasant familiarity.

When we arrived at the place I had entered Hell, the Lord informed me that I would have to climb out. The monk gently grabbed my arm saying, "This won't be easy for you." He cautioned me again saying, "The enemy knows your worst fear and will use that against you, you must remember it is all an illusion."

The Lord replied, "You must walk by faith not by sight. Follow Me."

I must admit, I did not know what he meant, but I protested saying, "I can't climb. My wrist is broken and I feel like my shoulder was ripped from its socket." The Lord touched me and immediately I was free of pain, so I began to climb ahead of them. I tried to clear my mind, but as I ascended my worst fears came alive. The tree roots I had grasped to pull myself out transformed to snakes. I released them and fell. I came crashing to the bottom, but they both caught me before I hit the ground with full impact.

The monk helped me up and said, "You can climb up or stay. The choice is yours." Snakes were my greatest fear. I hated them, but I hated Hell more. I then closed my eyes and refused to open them. I recited my own mantra in my mind as I climbed, "Those that the Lord sets free are free indeed." These words were from the scriptures; I also remembered Jesus said in the New Testament, "What you believe will be." I felt for the roots one at a time. I struggled through the tight tunnel, slipping only occasionally and scraping my skin. My eyes stung a little as sweat, blood and dirt leaked into the corners of my eyes. My ascent was slow, the climb was steep and I struggled back into the world above, using every muscle of my body. I emerged from the darkness below. I did not look back and I forced myself to climb out.

The soil softened, it was wet and slippery and I dug myself out of the ground. I gasped for air and laughed as I reached open ground. I sat upon the grass laughing foolishly. My eyes were blinded by the sunlight and I was unable to focus, but I relished the light and I rolled back and forth as I laughed out loud, then abruptly I remembered the monk and the Lord were coming after me.

The monk walked out of the ground easily, as if ascending a staircase with the Lord walking up beside him. I did not understand why I struggled and they escaped with ease, but I did not even attempt to comprehend it; I was just happy to be free.

Euphoria consumed my very soul as I realized I was free. My grief was ended. No more sorrow, no more pain, no more listening to the cries of helpless people echoing in my mind. I had escaped the fiend's evil lair and I would never be Hell's captive again.

The sun was shining as I turned in circles with my face toward the sky. Rain began to fall on me gently washing the soil from my skin. I cried tears of joy. The grass had a fresh scent of life-giving breath, which only comes after the rain. I heard an eagle's cry, as a rainbow appeared in the distance.

Catherine got up and stretched as she noted some of her soldiers had fallen asleep. She grinned and stoked the fire as she continued the telling. No one questioned her, nor interrupted her; they simply delighted in the listening. Some never tired of hearing her visions, while others could not fight off the calling of night.

Chapter Five:
Heaven's Gate to a Father's Love

"I fell to my knees, as I was overcome with weeping." *Catherine continued with a slight smile upon her lips. I swear I saw tears slowly falling down her cheek, glistening in the firelight, as she continued telling her tale.*

The Lord smiled at me. His teeth looked brilliantly white against his dark complexion, which shone like fine polished gold. He smiled and gave me his hand and gently helped me up. I watched in awe as the Lord walked off into the distance speaking with the monk at his side. I don't know why I did not follow. I just stood there staring, unable to move.

Then another man of immense beauty appeared, standing before me. His eyes were like that of a tiger's and his skin was similar to the color of polished ebony. He told me with a voice that sounded like the rushing wind "I am pleased to see you have escaped the darkness."

He continued, "I would appreciate it if you would come with me."

I was only slightly apprehensive so I answered, "Why, where are we going?"

He gently replied, "To Heaven's Gate."

"Who are you?" I inquired.

He smiled and said, "I am a servant of the Most High; my name is Gabriel." He gave me his hand and continued, "Please come with me."

I took his hand as I nodded in agreement.

We turned away from the grave and we began to walk toward the black iron gates that exited the graveyard, when suddenly a wind came like a swift ocean storm and the soil from my former grave swirled about my knees and beneath my dress. I swallowed my feelings of guilt and attempted to hold my dress down.

The awesome being beside me held my hand and as my dress lowered the wind subsided. My shame began to slowly dissipate and peace spread over me like a warm, gentle breeze. Then the devil dressed in black came up from below as if rising from the grave.

His skin was pasty white like the under belly of a beluga whale. His eyes now looked as if they were that of a blind man unaccustomed to the light. He repulsed me in every respect and I was angry for ever allowing myself to be attracted to him.

"I want her back; she was condemned to below." He said this statement in a demanding and furious voice.

I felt apprehension consume me for an instant, but I was too disgusted in both him and my former actions to fear him for very long. I told him with defiance in my voice; "I will never go back!"

"Fool." He laughed at me and declared, "You have no say in your damnation; your actions speak for themselves." He continued with vengeance in his voice. "Your actions condemned you and escape is impossible."

I looked to the man beside me for help. Gabriel gently squeezed my hand like a big brother and then this awesome figure spoke and said; "Monarch of Hell, you know the limitations of your power. Are you really going to fight for her? Who is she to you? The LORD loves her and he has chosen to set her free."

The Devil laughed and said, "That is precisely why she will be mine. Besides she is the second to leave." Then he stopped speaking as a sinister grin crept across his mouth. His grin turned into a wicked smile with the realization that he was no longer restrained, as he laughed out loud he said, "Time for the dance to begin."

I was horrified to think I had loosed his powers and gave this creature corporeal form, but the man who was with me began to guide me told me to walk away. Just then the Devil shouted, "Give her to me! I will make her my bride."

Satan grabbed my arm and I turned and gave him a swift kick in the gut. "Like hell you will!" I declared as my kick sent him smashing his back into a gravestone that crumbled behind him.

He got up and slowly brushed the dust off his suit and then he walked toward me and said with a smile, "My queen you surprise me, beauty is not your only gift, but like your God I demand fear and obedience. He attempted to strike me down with a backhand for kicking him.

My magnificent protector grasped his arm and declared, "She is already spoken for." He fought in my defense.

Satan somehow managed to twist my defender's arm. He then kneed him in the back. My protector keeled over and the fiend kicked him in the face with a round house kick. The Prince of Darkness paced about him, like a prowling lion that takes pleasure in tormenting its prey. Still this did not keep Gabriel from striving to protect me.

My noble defender forced himself to rise up and he stood between the Devil and me. He kicked the Evil One with a snap kick and attempted to punch the villain several times and yet the fiend managed to block him at every turn. The savage Lucifer was winning the battle.

I suddenly realized that although Gabriel was a servant of the Most High, he could not defeat Satan. He was a good fighter, but the snake was better. Lucifer was swift and struck hard with cruel accuracy. The Devil laughed out loud at defeating an angel of the LORD.

He began to move toward me as he said, "Come my bride" I was repulsed and I went to punch him and the Devil smiled taking pleasure in my resistance as he grabbed my arm with ease. I lifted my knee swiftly to his groin as my hand grabbed his wrist. He was faster than me. He blocked my kick with ease and grasped both of my wrists, forcing me to my knees. Simultaneously I was praying God would send help and save me and I struggled to my feet. Just then an angel swooped down from the heavens above. Satan threw me to the ground as if I were as light as a small child.

This celestial being's size was intimidating, his muscled physique was awesome and his smile playful. A fierce fight ensued behind me. The two fought, kicking each other as if they could become suspended in time and space and then moving a moment later with lighting fast speed.

I ran toward the angel of God who had fallen earlier in the battle to see if he was all right. He assured me he would be fine. As the Devil and the other angelic host fought the wind picked up and dirt blew around us from the ground while the sun emerged yet again from behind small dark clouds, which had lingered above the graveyard. Nature reflected the struggle between light and darkness in the battle for my soul. The two beings continued to fight and the first messenger of God suggested we leave. Although I wanted to stay, for I was in awe of the battle that was before me, I listened to the angel that guided me away from the graveyard.

Later the second angel caught up with us and jovially asked, "Are you two okay?"

"Yes." We both replied to his question. I assumed that the being now towering beside me was the great archangel Michael and he seemed elated from the fight and his nature was now easy. My suspicions were quickly confirmed.

The angel beside me said, "I take it you won Michael."

Michael laughed and I detected a small grin upon his lips, as he replied, "No, The Lord rebuked him, but I enjoyed my part in it." He moved with a confidence and authority of one who leads many.

Michael lifted me into his arms as we flew toward the heavens; I asked, "What about the monk and the Lord?" I was somewhat unnerved and my sentences were disjointed. I attempted to compose my thoughts as I asked; "Will I see the both of them again?"

The warrior of God smiled and the first angel replied, "That is not for us to see. We do not know of the monk."

I stared up into Michael's eyes, which were blue like sapphires and his skin was like a dark tarnished gold. His hair was blond with golden highlights that fell about his shoulders. I asked, "Why was he unable to defeat Satan and you managed to so easily?"

Michael declared, "Gabriel has heart, but he is blessed with brains and I am blessed with brawn. We are who God has designed us to be."

I smiled and nodded. I expected I should feel an extreme reverence for these angelic beings but to my surprise, although I admired their strength and beauty, I felt none.

We flew at lightning speed toward the sun. I feared I would be burned alive. I was still imprisoned by my limited understanding and expectations. When we reached the sun Michael placed me down at the base of a diamond staircase that led into the light. A rainbow of color surrounded me, as the sun shone through the staircase like a prism.

Gabriel took my hand and said, "You must choose to walk through alone. You cannot pass through Heaven's Gate without faith and unless you first cross through the fire of redemption.

I feared the pain, but I felt the need to be clean, so I walked slowly, as I ascended the staircase and allowed the fire to burn my soul. The heat that I had longed for so desperately before now caused me immense pain as the cross around my neck seared more deeply into my flesh. I became one with the cross.

When I arrived at the other side, I crossed Heaven's Gate and the Lord was waiting for me. He was dressed in a long white robe and he stood before me and held out his hand. He was the most beautiful man I had ever seen. White light radiated from his being. His hair was brown and it looked as if it were highlighted by the sun. Jesus had eyes that were green like an emerald sea. His hair tumbled to his shoulders like a lion's mane.

He hugged me and wiped away my tears. My own dress was white again. "Jesus?" was all that I said.

He nodded and said, "You know that I am."

Then I asked a barrage of questions. "Why did I have to suffer in Hell and why did I have to walk through fire if you died for my sins?" I continued rapid fire before waiting for his reply, "Why did I have to fight my way out of Hell, when the monk left so easily?"

He was gentle and replied, "I did not condemn you, nor did my Father; I came to save the world not judge it, but the time of judgment will come. You were filled with guilt for your actions and judged yourself to be unworthy to stand before your God. My Father made you and he knows, as do I. We are aware of the temptations and passions of humanity. I came to set you free from your guilt and to reconcile you to my Father, who is purity and love. Alas, humans are stubborn and have allowed Satan to mislead you, to accept this separation and commit one sin upon another because you feel you were unworthy of the Father's forgiveness. You believed in me, but you did not receive me.

What desires are in the heart are good, however man allows these desires for good to become tools for evil. You allow them to rule you instead of you governing them. My grace and mercy saved you. You refused to submit to Satan and you refused to allow him to condemn you; this is why you were able to leave the hell you were in and come into the light.

Our Father heard your prayers from the darkness for we know and see all. You were unable to hear me in your guilt and sin and your inability to hear the voice of God was because you were not of God. As you began to turn to me in faith, then you began to hear the Spirit of truth speaking to you. All you had to do was listen and I would guide you home. Sadly, few humans choose to repent and have faith in me and walk in the Spirit.

The sun purifying you originates from your guilt as well. You know the Father is all that is good and you could not allow yourself to enter his presence knowing you almost gave yourself to Satan. You needed to be cleansed, but had you truly believed my blood was shed for you and had the power to reconcile you to the Father, then none of these things would have come to pass. My Father made you; you are his and he knew you well. All has happened, as it should. "

I was so confused. I had a million questions running through my head as I inquired, "Why was it so hard for me to leave Hell when it was so easy for the monk?"

He placed his hands on my shoulders and smiled, "Because my child, you did not listen to me. I said, 'Follow me.' You chose your own path and climbed out on your own."

"Relax and enjoy what is now." He commanded, as he said this he opened the doors to his throne room and an intense heat ran through my body, but it did not burn. I collapsed to my knees and a soulful weeping consumed me as the fire continued to burn through me, then wave after wave like a waterfall washed over me.

I wept for my own unworthiness to be in his presence. I had cried for my sins and the wasted years I had dwindled on Earth. I wept for the dammed, I shed tears for the countless souls who did not know the Lord and I wailed for the pain and rejection he had suffered for my salvation. I knelt before him lamenting, as all of human history flashed before my mind's eye.

I saw the joy and intimate fellowship Adam and Eve had shared with the Lord prior to the fall. I witnessed great moments of joy lost amidst the great evil that had swept across the span of time. I saw history sweep before my eyes. Then I yielded my spirit as I knelt before my king.

The only words that poured from my lips again and again were "Thank you. Thank you." Waves of gratitude washed over me.

Heaven was filled with life, white light, peace and beauty. I could hear the most beautiful angelic voices singing songs of love and glory. Some angels were quite busy serving the Lord, by receiving orders from the throne, while others whispered petitions in his ear. The throne room was a myriad of activity. Other angles were singing, 'Holy, Holy, Holy Lord…' like a choir in the background. There were other beings like myself, who seemed at peace, others were petitioning the Father and the Son for I know not what.

Men were walking hand in hand embraced in brotherly love. Some women were hugging one another, as children ran and played with animals nearby. A couple walked holding hands as a child ran up to be embraced by them. The Spirit of love and life interconnected all fathers and sons, daughters and sisters, animals and humans together. I felt the breath of life surround me at every turn and a sense of wholeness I had never felt before. All that was flesh had died and all that was spirit was one with God. Jesus sat at his Father's side, and a beautiful woman with long golden hair sat on the other as I entered his court, filled with thanksgiving and awe.

I was presented before the Father; my dress was as white as snow. I was now holy through Christ Jesus and a cloak of silver was placed about my shoulders by two angelic hosts. I was cloaked with his righteousness. He was life. He was light, peace, knowledge, love and power. He was spirit. He was everything. I fell to my knees once again and his brilliance was brighter than the sun itself. His illustriousness was so powerful, as his light blinded my eyes. I could barely even make out the outline of his face.

"Come, my child" His voice was powerful like the rushing wind. I climbed upon his knee like a child does when she is but two or three. He laughed as we looked across the floor at the pattern of little golden footprints that led to his giant throne. We laughed and I had finally felt the love of the father I had longed for. I was filled with peace and joy. He held me in his arms and in an instant he communicated his every thought in his plan for me. A moment later his glory left me. I found myself floating in the ocean of life. I had died, but in death I found life. I had entered through Heaven's Gate and rested in my father's love.

Part Two:
Discovering Destiny

Chapter Six:
Waking from the Dream

I was in the ocean gasping for breath, as salt water began to fill my lungs. I lost all consciousness until I felt my body thrown upon a rocky shore. Great waves came rushing in, each one more forceful then the next. The sheer pain of my body made me aware of the need to pull myself farther upon the shore. I managed to back up against a cliff. I clung to the rocks determined to find security inland. The night was dark, and the clouds were low. The ocean's waves appeared to reach up to meet the sky. Lightning flashed across the heavens. My back ached as I prepared myself for the raging storm, which would surely last the night.

I found myself thinking of the continued escalation of global climate change that was causing severe ocean storms, with huge waves that had devastated coastal communities for decades now. Each year seemed to break all records for sheer power and destructive capabilities than in times before. Our hearts had grown cold in our hopelessness to the seasonal cycles of human suffering. Now I was in its grasp; I had to find some way to survive the torrents and not fall victim to death yet again.

I was exhausted, but somehow I managed to fall asleep, curled up in the crevice of some rock. Suddenly barking awakened me as the warm gentle rays of the sun penetrated my clammy skin bringing me back to life. I briefly saw a black Labrador retriever before me, but my mind refused to be summoned to consciousness for more than an instant. At least I was warm.

I opened my eyes. My body was too sore to move and my head felt battered and incapable of any form of motion. I felt the warmth of a fire and the smell of rosemary and mint filled the room where I slept in a warm bed. Days or weeks passed as I heard the crackling of the fire and the most peaceful melodious voice singing with the gentle strokes of a piano in the distance.

It was a man's voice, and he sang songs of love and songs of mourning. He sang songs of fragile hope, of lovers who had yet to meet. He also sang about eternity. Though I couldn't summon my eyes to open as I drifted in and out of delirium, I remember that I longed to see his face, for his words soothed my soul.

I heard that same gentle voice commanding me as I opened my eyes and attempted to rise, "Please don't move." His voice was like velvet to my ears. He placed his hand on my arm and said, "Lie back down and don't try to get up. You are very injured, but you are safe. I am going to summon a doctor. Please stay in bed, I won't be long." With that he rushed out the door and I heard his footsteps run down the stairs.

The doctor entered my room and was a beautiful brunette, with long wavy hair and soft brown eyes. She smiled and said, "Hello I am Dr. Ash. You are going to need a few more days of rest, but you are out of danger, if you take care not to rush things." She gently redressed some bandages and then I faded back to sleep.

A few days passed and he tended me. He read poetry by my bedside and at times the Book of Psalms. Sometimes I could hear him playing the piano again across the hall as he sang quietly every night. His voice softly rang out like the sound of an angel carried upon a distant wind. One day he entered the room with a breakfast tray and was pleased to see I was sitting upright.

He was bald-headed and his eyes were the color hazel. His teeth were perfect, as white as pearl against his beautiful dark brown skin and his jaw was strong.

He had broad shoulders with which he carried his body with utmost confidence and grace.

He said, "I'm happy to see you up, but don't push yourself; you have been through quite an ordeal. Are you able to speak?"

I was unsure, and yet I nodded as I said, "Yes." I was surprised to hear how weak my voice was, but I was pleased that now someone else could hear it.

"My name is Edward, Edward Stephens. Do you remember your name?" I was surprised that I didn't. He smiled and said, "That's all right, but we should give you a name, is there any name you prefer?"

"No, I don't believe so."

"Well, until you remember, or we find out who you are, can I call you Catherine?" I did not know why he chose that name, but I felt like it suited me even though I didn't know who I was. It was strange, but the name was familiar nonetheless.

"I would like that Edward." I replied, as I attempted to clear my throat. My voice was audible, but just barely, it was still weak. I didn't know why, but my voice box hurt, like I had screamed so long that I nearly lost it.

I gradually regained my strength, but not my memory. Feeling well enough to walk one day, I asked if I could go outside. He smiled and took my hand as he said, "Let me show you my garden." He had flowers too numerous to count, but some I still remember as if I were there today. The blooms were red, orange and white; the violets were blue and purple; his tulips were silver white and pale pink. His flowers when seen through the trees amidst the lilacs and cherry blossoms all reminded me of the sunrise across the ocean. The colors were like a rainbow and from the balcony of my room I could see fields of daffodils blowing gently through the distant trees.

We often sat on my balcony and he would read to me. One day he read,

"Incline your gentle ear to me
And let your lips answer my call
As I summon thee to love,
To steal a lover's kiss

For what lasts forever but love?
Let passion's truth be told.
Surely love transcends time and space
And true love is eternal

Before I saw your extraordinary beauty
My eyes could well have been blind
But you have shone so intensely
Faithful devotion was revealed

No longer does shadow lengthen my days
Time has lost all meaning
Our love will not fade

For our love is now immortal
True love will endure
Though I lost my love, my life
She waits for me beyond the grave"

I commented "That is so lovely who wrote it?"

Edward replied, "I did for someone I love"
I surmised, "Well she is a very fortunate woman to be loved so well, she must love you too."
"She did." He replied.
His poem placed an ache in my soul, but I didn't know why.
He smiled gently and reached for my hand as he said, "She passed away years ago."
"I'm sorry to hear that. You must miss her terribly." I said as a tear fell down my cheek.

He gently wiped my tear away and said, "Yes, I do Catherine, very much."

At night I would often sit on a balcony and I would gaze at the stars above. I would search my mind for memories. My soul felt like it was still asleep, without my memories I could not be at peace. There was a void inside of me, I somehow felt separated from all humanity. I was not close to anyone, even though I had been under Edward's care for many months, I did not know him well either. I felt very lonely. He cared for me for so long that he felt responsible for me, and he treated me like a father does his own child. This comforted me deeply as time passed, but I had to remember.

I did love to share my time with him, but he knew my mind needed to remember who I was and what my God's plan for me was. One night we prayed that God's Spirit would guide me and let me know his plan.

That night we sat drinking wine by the firelight where I found out he was once a pastor of a large church. He retired from ministering to others when his wife died. He said he was filled with too much pain and resentment after the loss to be of help to anyone.

He spent these past few years soul-searching, praying, fasting and mourning.

He held my hand and I asked him, "Why did you want to call me Catherine?"

He knelt before me and gazed deeply into my eyes, I felt him touch my soul as he replied, "I called you Catherine because I once heard that it means 'God's gift'. You are a gift from the heavens above. My wife and I could never have a child, but if we had a girl, we would have named her Catherine. I believe the Lord sent you to me to save me from myself. My heart was never able to reach out to help anyone since my wife died six years ago, until I met you. You were so helpless when you washed upon my shore, and I knew

God sent you to me to care for you. I would remember my purpose too."

"You have been a great help to me, but how do you know God sent me to you?" I inquired.

Then he replied, "I know. I see the truth in your eyes, the gentleness of your heart and the light of God emanating from deep within your soul. So although I don't know if you will ever remember who you used to be, I know he has a plan for you, and there is a reason he brought you here. I also know you are most definitely his own."

"How can you know that?" I said trying desperately to grasp some sense of how he could be so certain, when I did not know who I was.

He smiled and caressed my cheek and gently touched the cross that was seared into my flesh as he replied, "Because of this and I know because I feel it in my spirit. You have made me think of someone other than myself. My pain vanished when I saw your pain. I was compelled to help you and I'm compelled to protect you."

Tears fell from my eyes and rolled slowly down my face, as I touched the cross on my neck; I often wondered why it would not come off. I must have been burned in a fire. Like so many other things I did not know, it was a mystery to me.

Suddenly he stood up and apologized, "I am so sorry. I did not mean to make you cry, Catherine. " He walked across the room and got me a box of tissues. He then went and rested his arm on the mantle of the fireplace and then he turned, looking deep into the windows of my soul as he inquired, "Are you tormented, struggling to remember who you were, or are you anguished because you are afraid of who you are?"

I walked to him and held his hand again, "I don't know Edward. I feel happy and safe with you, but I feel something is tugging at my mind. I feel my spirit struggling to remember who I am, especially in the night, as I look at the stars above me. I need to know who I am and yet I'm afraid and I don't know why?"

"I will help you find out who you were Catherine, and I know who you will become tomorrow will change. Change is inevitable. It is a part of our growth and walking in our destiny. No matter what you discover, I want you to know that I will always be here for you. Our life is like a novel, the past may have affected you deeply, but it is finished. We need to embrace the next chapter of our lives as a new story begins."

I did not understand why I was afraid, but at that moment I felt warmth travel through his hand and somehow touch my soul. He leaned over to kiss my forehead, like a father kisses his child. I felt safe in that moment. I smiled and I was comforted by a brief sense of déjà vu.

It was now late in the summer and I knew a change in the seasons of our lives was coming. A strange apprehension filled my mind whenever I would go to sleep. I felt like a part of me belonged to another, someone whose face I could no longer see.

I also felt as if there was a storm raging deep within my soul, and then I began to remember. I was a prisoner in my dreams. Edward did not know what to make of the nightmares, which would wake me in the night. The scene of Hell tortured me in my dreams and I would wake up screaming and Edward would rush into my room and comfort me back to sleep. He believed it was a spiritual battle, but he did not know its depths.

Edward called Doctor Ash back to reassess me. I told her my dreams and the feelings they evoked. "I'm frightened; these hellish nightmares torment me night after night. I fear falling asleep and when I do I feel like someone, or something is in the room watching me, waiting."

"What does that person feel like? Why are they watching you?" She inquired.

"It is not as much as a person, but more like a presence, it feels sinister, and it feels evil." I replied

She raised her eyebrow; I could see she thought I was crazy. There was no point in trying to explain it to her. I sensed that the doctor believed it was just a painful part of the process of remembering who I was. I did not know who I was, but I didn't want to know anymore.

Then one night as I was asleep I found myself entering into a state of ecstasy, when Satan appeared before me. He kissed my neck and I saw the fiend. I kicked him across the room, but it was Edward who screamed in pain. My tormentor was gone.

Edward came in the room to check on me because he sensed something was wrong. I rushed to Edward and cried as I apologized. I felt as if I was a tortured soul plagued by the failure of my own inability to remember who I was. Then I heard the Devil laugh at me and say, "Ha, ha you thought you fooled me, eh." I didn't know what those words meant, but I recognized the voice. I told Edward what I had seen and heard. I was sure he would not believe me. To my surprise he did not have a look of shock, or disbelief upon his face, just concern.

Edward confirmed my suspicions of what Doctor Ash believed, "A part of me thinks that Doctor Ash may be right Catherine; your mind may be playing tricks on you. You may be hallucinating. You may be confusing reality with your dream state and memories."

"Edward, how can you call yourself a preacher and not believe me when I tell you, it is the Devil who is attacking me." I continued with annoyance, "I know that snake and I know I'm not crazy or imagining anything. I don't fully understand this, but I know it is real. I saw him when I kicked you."

Edward sighed as he declared, "Catherine, you know I believe in the Devil. I have witnessed his work and felt his presence. Possession is very real, but he has never appeared in corporeal form before. He is limited and restricted to influence on our plane of existence. You can't literally see him. You were dreaming. He does attack us in our dreams, but it is an illusion, not real."

I sighed, Edward was more sympathetic than Doctor Ash and he was more open to my experiences, which were only amplified with each passing day, but a part of him shared the doctor's opinion.

I was walking toward the kitchen one day when I felt a shiver run up my spine. I suddenly felt cold and the hairs on the back of my neck stood up as I heard a whisper in my left ear utter, "You can't fool me, I see you. I know who you are."

I turned, but saw nothing as I boldly questioned, "Who are you? What do you want?" It gave no reply, but I knew it was Satan. I recognized his voice from a different time and place. I felt that cold before, but I didn't know when. Every time these incidents happened I told Edward everything. He grew more and more concerned for me.

Days later I was in the study, when Satan made a big mistake. I had just been deep in prayer and the Devil had come and stood before me. He stroked my hair and smiled his wicked grin and asked, "Hello my dear, do you remember who I am?"

I emerged from prayer remembering everything about my past experiences, and with confidence and I faced my tormentor. I got up from my knees, and with a swift motion I swatted away his hand as I declared, "I do remember you. Now go away; I am no longer afraid of you."

The Devil laughed with a hint of intrigue in his tone as he commented, "You should fear me my dear."

He continued mockingly, "I preferred you kneeling before me."

"I was kneeling before God, you snake; not before you." I replied in disgust.

"Well," Satan looked about and said irreverently, "…my bride I don't see him around, so I have come for you."

I stood my ground; "I only feared what I did not see, and that which I did not understand. Now I remember you. I see you for what you are, a pathetic creature consumed with jealousy and envying a power and love he cannot possess."

Edward was passing in the hall and was about to inquire what was wrong, but instead he stood by the door. Edward was staring at us in disbelief and he listened as we talked. He was shocked when I addressed the man as Satan.

Just then Edward burst into the room, "Catherine, what's wrong?"

Satan swirled around and with a smile and side kicked Edward, who was thrown clear across the room with that unearthly force that I now remembered all too vividly.

As Edward crashed against the wall the Devil laughed, "You stupid mortal who do you think you are dealing with? You should fear me; you both should fear me, for I have power that your limited nature could never fathom." Satan adjusted his suit and shook his head back and forth as he said with a tone of arrogance, "I don't know what this world has come to. I suppose the time has come to reveal my glory and power to all of mankind."

When he said that I kicked him with a heavenly force and he flew into the bookcases behind him. To my surprise he grinned and chuckled with delight as he said teasingly, "My queen, your beauty is now married with a force I thought you had forgotten."

He said this as he walked across the room and reached to caress my face. I went to hit him, but he grabbed my wrist with ease. Grabbing my other arm he forced me to my knees saying, "You have forgotten my power."

"You only have power over those who give it to you. You are still weak and helpless before God! It is him alone whom you fear." I shouted and then I prayed, "My Lord, deliver us and protect us."

As I said this Michael, the warrior of God, appeared and said, "Are you going to leave now or give me the pleasure of kicking your skinny behind yet again."

"Michael," Satan grinned "I am afraid you are getting too proud. You know that was my down fall." Satan laughed and then politely excused himself with a bow, "I really do have a very busy schedule, so I must decline this dance. Watch your back Michael. As for you my lovely, I will be back for you." Satan said this as he kissed my hand. Before I could pull it away he disappeared in a puff of smoke.

I ran to Edward's side and Michael helped me lift him up. He carried Edward to the sofa and gently placed him down. Once Edward regained consciousness I gently explained to him everything he needed to know. Michael sat himself on Edward's desk and told me to be watchful, as Edward looked on speechless and dismayed.

I asked him, "Michael, Satan is called the Master of Illusion; is that because he is like a magician and able to perform magic tricks, or is his power real?"

He sighed, "Catherine," Michael cautioned me, "I want you to know that although he is a master of illusion, in your realm his power is real. You must be careful! He can appear to manipulate time and space, but that is only from a human perspective. The laws of physics and the universe still apply to the heavenly hosts, but on a scale you could not fathom. He has been mastering the art of illusion for millennia." He sighed as he shrugged his shoulders, "This is complicated, but the pain he inflicts is very real and he can hurt you. God will reveal the truth through the Spirit inside you, but I can tell you this; he can do nothing without God's permission, unless humans surrender to him and let him into their lives. Don't let him in, resist him. Stand guard, for you do not know when the serpent will strike, or how. I have to go. Watch yourself, but don't be afraid." With that Michael walked out on to the balcony and swiftly flew toward the Heavens.

Edward and I spent the whole night sitting up talking, as I told him everything about my accident and death, and then we prayed that I would regain my entire memory. We fell asleep, only to be woken at eight o'clock by the doorbell ringing. "Oh I forgot the doctor is coming for a checkup. Do you want to see her?"

I told him, "I don't need to, but you should get her to examine you. You were kicked very hard." I opened the front door and led her into the study. The doctor wanted him to go get x-rays, but Edward refused. She loosely wrapped up his ribs believing three were cracked, if not broken. She wanted to know what happened and looked accusingly at me.

He held my hand and assured the doctor, "Everything is fine."

Doctor Ash replied, "Edward you could have suffered spinal cord trauma, if so, this is a medical emergency requiring immediate treatment."

"I'm not going anywhere!" Edward was adamant as he continued, "You can prescribe something for me to reduce the swelling, but I will not go to the hospital."

The doctor appeared frustrated as she replied, "Fine, I will prescribe a corticosteroid, to protect from swelling and perhaps some possible long-term effects. The time between the injury and proper treatment is critical Edward. When were you injured?"

Edward winced as he replied; I was injured a few hours ago. I have been here on the sofa ever since."

The doctor threw a glare in my direction as she said, "Proper care will be a factor that will dramatically affect the eventual outcome. You could be paralyzed."

"If I were paralyzed the pain would not be this apparent. Give me the prescription." Edward reasoned.

"Here is some dexamethasone, I will go get some more and I will return tomorrow. " She replied with a hint of frustration in her tone. Then Doctor Ash continued, "It should reduce the swelling and hopefully prevent further damage to the spinal cord. If spinal cord compression is the case and it is caused by a mass such as a hematoma, or bony fragment, then we can have it removed at the hospital before your nerves are completely destroyed."

"Doctor..." Edward said firmly.

The doctor acquiesced, "Alright, alright, I will leave, but you should go to the hospital."

Edward did not give her any explanation as to the details of how he suffered the injury. He was non-compliant and the doctor had little influence upon him. Without his permission for further treatment she took her leave of us. She was annoyed and perhaps worried, but she respected Edward's request to be left alone, except to drop off the rest of the prescription and re-examine him later.

The next day Doctor Ash returned with Edwards's prescription and instructed us both concerning proper care and drug administration before departing. I felt a great relief as she walked out the door; Edward could finally understand my struggle. I was liberated, as if awakened from a dream, which haunts you in your waking hours, and yet can never be entirely remembered. I was rediscovering my destiny.

Chapter Seven:
Waging War

The next day I rose early and brought Edward his breakfast and tea. As I poured the tea and handed him his breakfast tray I asked, "How are you feeling?"

Edward responded, "Well thank God I'm not suffering any pain, the disturbing thing is, I feel nothing from the waist down." I felt guilty, I should have protected him.

He warmly took my hand and said reassuring me, "My darling Catherine, don't blame yourself. My life is in God's hands, every single part of it. He will work all things for good for me. I am his and I know I am still called to serve him. Don't worry child."

I smiled at him and sat down across from him with my coffee after I had poured it for myself. I announced, "I've fully recovered my memory with respect to my destiny and much of my past."

Edward beamed, "Praise God, I knew you would."

I grinned and then after a sip off coffee I confessed. "I'm a little unclear as to what has happened in the war on terror. Can you update me? I have not kept up with any current events."

"What do you remember?" Edward inquired.

"Well Israel was surrounded and being threatened on all sides, as usual. The Palestinians, Iran and Syria were all still dedicated to a complete annihilation of the Jewish people. I'm sure that has not changed. Egypt managed to somehow stay out of it, but the region in Jordan was heating up." I recalled.

Edward sighed, "I'm afraid that is still the same, not much has changed. The war in the Middle East had escalated and the US government had declared a state of emergency. The United States was forced to wage war against Pakistan in the battle against yet another terrorist faction from the Middle East, the Warriors of Dar al-Harb"

"Who are they I've never heard of them before?" I inquired.

Edward took along sip of tea with sadness in his tone he told me, "Their leader is Abdullah Ameer, a Pakistani. His country of origin has been both protecting him and the other leaders of this terrorist group who lived within their borders, while laundering money for them from donations sent from abroad through various rescue organizations and relief efforts.

Conscription in the United States has been mandated. The armed forces were needed on a multitude of fronts, to liberate Israel from the enemies surrounding her, to protect North America at home from terrorist attack, and from the constant threat from North Korea."

"Will this war ever end?" I sighed.

"Not until even more lives are lost. The war is escalating even further. Our government was monitoring Chinese aggression in the Middle East for decades, but recently it has been growing daily. China is bold and few can predict what move she will make next, but her power is growing. The great powers are all preparing for war on various fronts. "Edward replied

He shook his head as he continued, "Russia became our enemy following their backing of Iran's recent attack on Iraq as they attempted to further secure their control of the rich oil resources of the Middle East. Although we left Iraq way back under the Obama Administration, it looks like we may have to go back. Iraq is not one of our allies, but we can't allow Russia and Iran to gain control of the oil and China desires the rich mineral wealth beneath Afghanistan as well. America's success in Afghanistan allowed them to pay for a large portion of their debt to China by mining iron, copper, cobalt, gold and critical industrial metals like lithium. America mined much of Afghanistan after it was stabilized, and two decades later America pulled out when the reciprocity agreement expired. Afghanistan's sovereignty was short lived. China herself is ready to step in and continue the mining."

"Greed..." I shook my head and declared, "They're escalating the war for financial gain. That makes me ill." I finished my coffee and rose to pour myself another cup.

Greed is Russia's primary motivation, but it is married to their dream to regain the ancient glory of Mother Russia. They have been in bed with Iran and China for decades. North Korea is also a part of their designs for world power." Edward stated as a matter of fact.

I looked confused and I inquired, "In bed, what do you mean by that?"

Edward motioned for some more tea as he explained, "China and Russia have been enabling both North Korea and Iran to develop nuclear weapons for decades. The CIA discovered their covert operations a long time ago, as well as a small part of their conspiracy. However it has only been recently that they have announced that they are fully prepared for nuclear war."

"Oh dear Lord, do you think they would actually launch a nuclear attack?" I said dismayed as I handed him his tea.

"Yes" He sighed again, "I'm afraid they have been plotting to do it for some time."

"But don't they realize they would destroy everyone, including themselves?"

"Perhaps some of them do. However I believe they're planning an assault on Israel, Europe and America simultaneously."

"I remembered that Canada and the United States feared China's growing power and North Korea was threatening to exercise its nuclear abilities. China was the only nation to effectively deter Korea from launching an all-out nuclear attack. I had not even suspected, let alone believed that they were merely staying their hand for an even more devastating attack in the future. Don't the Iranians have any concern about killing other Muslims as well in their attack?" I asked in shock.

"No." Edward stated firmly, with a slight edge in his tone, "Abdullah Ameer believes God is on their side. He tells both his followers and the world openly that the Jews should be fought against in every field. He is convinced, and so are his followers, that his actions in attacking Israel will prepare the way for the coming of the Hidden Imam. This is his apocalyptic world view, and his followers firmly embrace this belief."

"They cannot attack their own people, the Koran forbids it." I continued in exasperation, "It is written, 'You shall not shed your own peoples' blood.' This is a sin of aggression against their own people.

Edward took a sip of tea and continued, "Radicals will always rationalize their sins and madness. Ameer and the Iranian leadership are very close to one another; they have a long standing relationship. They have no qualms about launching a nuclear attack. They are ready to use their atomic weapons against Israel and her allies. They're not worried about killing their Muslim brothers and sisters because they devoutly believe that infidels go to Hell and Muslim believers will go to heaven. They believe that killing the nonbelievers will earn their place in Paradise with seventy-two virgins; what difference does it make if you kill yourself as a suicide bomber, or by launching a nuclear attack against the infidel?"

I gasped, "That is insane." I paced the floor exasperated as I said, "They have no idea what Hell is like and that is where they're going if they murder all those people. How can they behave that way and even consider themselves Muslim and children of God? We are People of the Book! Don't they realize we are all made in the image of God? How can they even contemplate committing mass murder and expect to live? It is utter madness." I was very upset. "How could so many believe such lies?"

Edward replied, "China agrees with you. Some Chinese officials believe that religion is a virus that is destroying mankind and should be exterminated. They believe that a world without religion would protect us from the wars of religious extremism. They are not supporting America or the other Christian nations because terrorists on both sides are responsible for the countless deaths of innocent civilians. It is a world gone mad."

"How can they blame Christianity? We are not a faith of hate; we are founded on love, non-judgment and peace. Those religious extremists are not representative of what it means to be Christian, just as Islamic terrorists are not a reflection of true Muslims."

Edward continued with his gentle tone, "I know Catherine; Muslims are not the first people in history to kill in God's name and declare wars assured, 'God is on our side', and then proceed to slaughter millions in the name of religion. Remember the crusades, the Spanish Inquisition, the Conquistadores, giving smallpox to the Native people in North America intentionally and hunting them for land, gold, or religious fervor. Our own histories reek with such madness."

"I know our history Edward, and the violent past of our own country. It sickens and angers me, but what century are we living in?" I could not fathom how mankind could be so cruel, so deluded.

Edward smiled and said, "You are very passionate Catherine, but be careful, passion and spiritual fervor is a double edged sword. There are two sides to every coin. It is difficult to understand, but don't judge them, even though the terrorists are foolish pawns of the Devil. Just as Iran and Pakistan are foolish pawns of China and Russia, ultimately our lives and the lives of everyone on this Earth are in God's hands. History is not in the hands of a madman, even one as influential as Ameer."

I knew Edward was right, but I could not help but complain, "Still fighting for so many decades on so many fronts, and for what? We stop one madman and another rises to take his place. First it was Al Quada and now the Warriors of Dar al-Harb. When will it end? If that is not enough to worry about, there are the rumors that some leaders in China want to put an end to all people of faith. It is sickening."

Edward was wise and could easily see both sides of the issue. I knew he was saddened for the many Americans who lost their lives in the wars, as well as many who lost their financial security, but what else could be done? We had to fight and we had to win.

The wars on so many fronts were steadily weakening the once great American nation. The United States was becoming a war-crippled country. If it were not for the remainder of the debt America still owed to China, our nation would have remained strong.

Ironically as we were forced to escalate our commitment to war; it was well understood that America could still emerge victorious. If world war resulted and if America and the allies continued their vigilance, then to the victor would go the spoils. The other nations, especially the oil rich ones in the Middle East responsible for the chaos would pay the bill in full. North Korea and Iran were the wild cards. If a nuclear attack was launched against the U.S., Israel and Europe in an all-out nuclear war, then nobody would be victorious.

The only thing holding everyone's extremism at bay was the fear of complete human annihilation. The long-term effect of nuclear fallout could not be ignored. The world was anxious, aware that it only took one madman to change the entire course of human history.

China was the most powerful nation in the world. She alone could influence the nations by force. She had the strongest army and her political involvement was an enigma, a quagmire of rumors and intrigue. Who knew where she stood in all this, but either way she would capitalize on the continued war against Islamic extremism.

The war had crippled both the Christian and Islamic economies, and China was left positioning herself to gain world dominance. What if China did decide to put an end to nations of faith altogether? Would she really support nuclear attacks against America? I didn't know, nor did I understand the political nuances. It was very complicated, but I feared that Iran, or Korea would act on their threats to launch a nuclear war.

I could not get this out of my mind. I knew God was sovereign, but I also knew this was a world founded upon the law of sowing and reaping, choice and consequences, action and equal and opposite reaction. It was this reality that I feared.

Later on that day following our discussion, conscription papers came for Edward to report for duty. Edward had called the doctor and was forced to go to the hospital for an evaluation. Dr. Ash was very pleased that she had this opportunity to properly diagnose him. I was relieved that he was temporarily pardoned from conscription due to broken ribs as well as his spinal injury. It was also discovered that he had a fracture of two of the bony outgrowths that protruded from the spinal cord. They were small hairline cracks. Edward also had a bulging disk. The army naturally insisted that Edward go through further examination by army doctors. They confirmed that he was unable to serve at this time, due to what they labeled, 'Temporary Paralysis".

I nursed Edward as he had nursed me many months before and we became even closer. Edward and I grew to know each other well and our spiritual union increased in strength and power. I had remembered my near death experience and my past with vivid clarity for some time now, but I was not ready to call my father. Edward respected this and he let the Spirit guide him in every decision.

As the months passed, he gave the excess of his possessions to the needy. Shortly after he did so the government announced the need to seize all assets for the war effort. Edward smiled and was happy that his money would not become blood money. He was torn because he did not want to support the killing of another human being, but he knew that our enemies were not rational and that the war must continue.

Ameer had already stated that, "Only the annihilation of Israel and her allies can lead to the establishment of the era of Muslim dominance and freedom. The Infidel must die." We often heard his threats on the news.

I was listening to the BBC one night as the radio broadcaster announced, "In world news tonight, war continues to escalate and famine sweeps through Africa and Asia. The Nile and the Tigress rivers are both drying up. Last week a group of refugees was sighted crossing the Nile on foot. A remnant of African Jews has returned to the food rich country of Israel. In other news, China invades Afghanistan. These stories and more will be discussed over the next hour with our select panel of experts."

I got up and turned off the radio. I wasn't in the mood to contemplate war anymore. I was glad Israel took the Jewish refugees in from Africa. Many felt that resisting terrorist aggression was preferable to starvation. Israel had plenty of food but the Nile no longer flooded and food was scarce throughout the region. Her enemies were starving and Israel was hated even more for her abundance.

These days the whole world appeared to be in chaos. Canada and the United States suffered flash floods, and disease spread throughout North America. Europe was on edge, waiting to see if Iran was planning to launch a nuclear attack against them. Israel was surrounded on all sides, as terror and war raged incessantly through the Middle East. Meanwhile hoaxes from religious zealots ran rampant. Statues were purported to be crying or bleeding, and sacred images were sighted in soap, on dry wall and on trees, and still the war raged on. The news was filled with stories and quotes from crazy religious fanatics everywhere.

One day we ran out of supplies and I was forced to go into the city to see what I could purchase. Edward insisted on coming, so I wheeled him to the jeep and helped him to get in. Inflation was out of control, so I thought I should bring things that I could trade instead of money. At first I looked for gold and silver and then the Spirit from within spoke to me and whispered into my spiritual ear, "Bring only water and a knapsack filled with clothing." Edward had three fresh water springs running through the property, so I filled some jugs and went to the city.

I drove the jeep and I was able to fill the entire tank with fuel in return for only one bottle of water. I learned the city's main water supply was tainted from excessive flooding and water was sold only in bottles at a horrendous price.

Many who could not afford the water died of thirst, others turned to stealing and murder simply for a clean glass of water to drink. Chaos lurked behind every corner, but still I walked confidently through the dark alleyways where I could hear groans and the cries of little children.

After getting enough supplies I found myself in a dark, dingy part of the city, and I saw a family sharing a loaf of stale bread over a trash can. I gave the children some food, and their feeble mother my jacket. Most needed was fresh water and I told them to come to my jeep for there was one jug of water left and I would share with them. We went back to the vehicle where Edward was waiting for my return, and I began to pour some water for them to drink.

We were near a store, which had been selling water, and when people could see that I was giving away water for this family to drink without charge, others came and begged for water also. The crowd grew and people began to push to the front of the line fearing that the water would run out. A panic was about to break out when I raised my hand and all became silent.

"There is enough for all of you to drink. Please don't push." I yelled.

A frail and desperate looking woman cried out from the crowd, "Do you have more than one jug?"

"No!' I replied.

Edward smiled and said, "There is only one jug, but with Jesus nothing is impossible." The crowd was a mixture of those filled with a desperate hope and those who mocked us. I searched the eyes of desperation and fear, but little faith was found, still an ember of hope remained in some of the children's eyes.

A tall lean man with an unshaven face bellowed, "What are you going to do? Are you going to make water appear out of thin air? Who do you think you are Moses? I don't see a stick, or a rock for you to strike here, preacher." Some in the throng of people laughed at the jeer, but most simply hung their heads feeling disheartened.

Edward bowed his head and gave thanks for the water and prayed that the Lord would provide. He did. My jug did not empty as every mouth was quenched.

The man who heckled us earlier yelled out again "If your god is so powerful why is he paralyzed? Shouldn't God reward his faithful servants?" Everyone looked at his wheelchair in the back of the jeep.

Edward replied, "The Lord allowed my injury to occur because it was not my time to die. Why should a Christian willingly accept blessings from God, but not tribulation? Our Savior was called to suffer, why not I. My reward shall be claimed when I reach heaven." Edward spoke and then he was filled with the Spirit as he preached to the glory of Jesus Christ and taught about the miracles of the Gospels and how the time to repent was at hand.

Two shopkeepers had come to listen as the crowd grew. Edward told the story of Jesus healing a certain blind man and of the glory people gave to God. He quoted many scriptures and finished with a sermon of the woman who met Jesus at the well. One of the shopkeepers was moved to tears and gave away all of his water supply to those in need. The other went to call the police.

The crowd was peaceful as they listened to God's word. As Edward spoke, one bitter man who had mocked us twice yelled out a third time. "Enough preaching Moses, if your God is real, then get up and walk."

Edward held my hand and whispered "If I walk I will be sent to war."

I squeezed his hand back as I replied, "It is your choice to submit to God's will," I paused and looked around at the crowd and continued, "but look at how many will be saved. You no longer have to protect me. I will be all right. I know who I am."

Edward smiled and said aloud, "I do not pray to test you my Lord for I know your awesome power, I ask for those here who believe that they may see your glory and for those who do not believe that they may witness your power. God, heal my body; in Jesus' name I pray." The sky had been gray, however as Edward said these words the clouds parted and a bright light shone down upon him and he was healed immediately.

Catherine looked around at her followers, some of whom were asleep and snoring. Others were engrossed by their first hearing of this tale. Catherine got up and stretched. She added another log to the fire and poured herself some wine as she smiled and recalled, "Some fallen Christians collapsed in tears of repentance, while others broke out in song, singing Amazing Grace."

"You all know that old song I speak of." *Catherine said, as some of the soldiers who had dozed off earlier awoke. They were forced from their dreams as the whole camp began singing this song,* "Amazing Grace, how sweet the sound...."

Catherine laughed, as an old fat Irish woman said, "Alright, enough singing, let her finish the story already."

Catherine gave her a gentle smile and sat down with her wine and continued the telling, "Edward got up and placed his hands upon the heckler's shoulder and he said, 'God has healed me so that you may see and believe.', and the man was incredulous."

The man backed away in horror saying, "No. No, I don't believe it. It, it is all a hoax." He stuttered as he drew further away. He continued struggling for a rational explanation to what he had just witnessed and he concluded, "You were never paralyzed."

"Open your heart to Jesus." Edward said, but that man just turned and ran away.

Then the shopkeeper who called the police came before us as he fell to his knees crying out loud, "Truly, Allah has sent you. Please forgive me. I beg you to run away before the police arrive. I called them; I am sorry, please go!"

"Peace be with you brother." replied Edward as we all heard the sirens swiftly approaching. Edward continued, "The police are coming and I forgive you. Do not fear, because Christ is with me and He will come again." The storekeeper returned to his shop and priced his water at a reasonable rate.

Then Edward gave me my knapsack filled with food and water and told me, "Catherine my darling, you must immerse yourself in the Spirit, so that you may do God's will."

I hugged him and I promised, "I will. Don't worry about me. You be careful Edward."

He quoted scripture from Ephesians 6, "…be strong in the Lord and in His power and might, and put on the whole armor of God, that you may withstand the wiles of the Devil." He then reached into the jeep and gave me a second backpack filled with survival gear.

As he put the pack on me he kissed my forehead and said, "Take this and head toward the mountains. God will shelter you and show you the way. Now go before they arrive and arrest you too, for disturbing the peace."

I told him, "I will never forget you Edward. Thank you for all that you have done for me."

"No, rather thank you Catherine for saving me from myself. I'll email your account with updates. If the city is safe, come into town for supplies. We can keep in touch. Use the library computers, they're free" He pushed me away as he said these last words to me. I walked away as the police arrived to arrest Edward and disperse the crowds.

Then someone yelled, pointing at me, "Arrest her too! She is with him." I ran and leaped over the hood of a car. One officer grabbed my arm, but I elbowed him in the face. I disarmed him, and then I ran. He lay there holding his nose, which was bleeding profusely. In their attempt to pursue me, one police car crashed into another in its attempt to avoid hitting me. With lightning speed I leaped out of the way. The intersection was blocked and I was lost in the crowd.

I continued to walk on when I passed a rundown church, where a priest was saying mass, but no one was there. No one was listening. He was dressed in a long flowing robe embroidered with gold thread. He was old and weary, but faithful to his duty. I was about to pass by when I recognized Satan standing inside. He was attempting to taunt the old priest, but the clergyman was ignoring him, or he could not hear.

I walked to a pew at the front of the church, and genuflected before rising to take my seat. The villain smiled and looked at me. "I love when you kneel before me my bride. Shall we get married here, or shall we simply fornicate?" He laughed and spoke as he came to sit beside me while placing his arm around my shoulder, "Look at that old fool; I have been tormenting him for years. No one is even attending this hovel and still he insists on performing that pointless ritual every day. There is not a soul in sight to listen to his rhetoric. He is a relic of the past."

"I'm listening and so is the Lord." I replied.

The Devil grew angry and marched toward the priest. He leaned over the priest's shoulder and sneered, "Rituals, rituals, these are useless rituals, and useless relics."

I took pleasure in his anger, and I taunted him, a grave mistake. I smiled and said, "If they are pointless rituals and useless relics, then why do they bother you so much?" With this statement he became enraged and threw a long heavy candlestick toward me like a spear.

It would have impaled me, if not for Michael, who appeared at my side. He caught the elongated rod just before it reached me.

Michael walked toward Satan spinning the candlestick like a martial arts master with a Jo staff in a blur of motion. The priest continued his recitations oblivious to, or ignoring the war around him.

I suddenly recalled hearing that Lucifer once led the choirs of heaven. He was God's most beautiful, gifted and perfect creation among the angelic hosts. I believed Michael could handle the fiend, but an idea formed within me, so I acted on impulse. I went out into the street and saw a young hooker on a corner advertising her wares and I asked, "Would you like to come to mass with me?"

"Who are you talking to, me? Do you know what I am?" She replied.

I smiled and I responded, "Yes, you are a sinner like me. We are all sinners, but God still loves us."

"Hmm..." She mused and then continued, "You are the woman from the square giving out water with the preacher, aren't you?"

"Yes. " I answered her and then I placed my hand on her shoulder as I maintained, "I was also the one who gave the woman my jacket and her children some food. That is where you first saw me."

She took a step back and said with a look of distrust married with curiosity, "How did you know I saw you? Your back was to me?"

"I see many things." I pleaded, "Please come with me to service."

She shook her head as she noted, "I don't know. I don't know God, and I don't believe he ever loved me. I'm sure he still doesn't"

I wiped a tear from her cheek as I stated, "He does love you Clarissa; God has always loved you."

"How do you know my name? How can you say he loves me? You have no idea what I have been through." She said as more tears flowed down her cheeks.

"Clarissa," I said in a soothing voice, "I hear the voice of God, he counsels me, and he is the one who led me to you. He is the one who told me your name. He is the one who wants to save you, to heal you, from your past, and from your pain."

"What do you know of my past?" She snapped.

"I know your father and your uncle raped and molested you from childhood. I know the depth of your pain, your heartache, your history. I physically feel it in my stomach and my throat. It fills me with rage and lament." I shared her tears, as I sensed her pain.

"Well, where was God then? Why didn't he stop them? Why didn't he protect me? Where was he then?" She raged.

"He was with you under the deck, he was with you in the closet, and he was with you in the forest." I assured her.

"He was with me when I was hiding? He was with me when I cried and prayed they wouldn't find me?" She sighed and cried some more.

"Yes, Clarissa, he was with you and he was with you when social services came and rescued you from your home. Don't blame God for the evil that men do. God is good and God is love. Your father and your uncle were not, and I can assure you they are suffering in torment for the evil they committed against you and your brother."

Clarissa looked down at her clothing she felt ashamed because of her attire. I looked in my backpack and gave her my long raincoat lined with a thin layer of sheepskin, which was rolled up, inside my bag.

"The Lord welcomes you just the way you are. As long as your heart still beats it's not too late. Please come." I pleaded once more.

I said this as some teens and children, who had followed me at a distance ever since I handed out water to drink, gathered round. I bid them, "Please, all of you come to mass with me." They came into the church two at a time, and walked down the aisle together, and then we knelt in prayer.

The priest had just finished his ritual when he looked up and he saw the church was filled before him, with ears ready to hear the truth. He prayed silently and we sat and listened to the gospel. He talked of revelations and the promises made by our Lord to those who will listen to his voice. I could see the hope from the Holy Spirit flicker in his eyes and as he preached from the pulpit and I saw that his face had become transformed. The weariness of his countenance faded like the fog, which melts away with the coming of the sun.

The battle behind the priest continued and both Michael and Satan fought bitterly. It was only then that I realized no one else could see them. Only I seemed able to witness this war. The priest was unaware of it as he removed his robe and sat on the steps of the altar. We went up held hands and prayed the, 'Our Father' and then we all broke out in song. Satan covered his ears and vanished in a cloud of darkness. We all sang, 'Amazing Grace,' just as we did in the street earlier in the day. Following this we sang an old Catholic hymn that asked Yahweh to show us his way, to teach us his path and keep us in the ways of his truth. We sang to our savior together with one voice. The Holy Spirit filled us and all that were there repented, turned over their life to Jesus and began to walk with the Spirit.

That same fat Irish woman in Catherine's camp interjected, interrupting Catherine with condemnation in her voice saying, "Surely Satan can't enter a church?" *The woman huffed.*

Catherine touched her hand and replied, "The Antichrist is now poised to take over the world. He sits in Rome this very moment and soon he will take his seat in the Temple. He has entered churches since they were formed; he is in your temple right now."

She gasped and took her hand from Catherine. "Impossible" *she said,* "Impossible" *Catherine bowed her head in silence for a moment and then continued her tale.*

As I left I saw Jesus smiling from the side of the altar. His smile filled me with warmth and comfort. Immediately I was filled with a sense of peace and complete security. That peace I had longed for was found in his smile. I heard him speak to me through thought, "Catherine, leave them, they are all in my hands. Now you must go." I obeyed my Lord. I quietly got up to leave and I left the new flock with the Lord and his priest.

As I walked through the city streets alone towards the edge of the city, I saw my own brother sitting on a street corner smoking with a half empty bottle of whiskey in his hand. One of his legs was missing. He must have lost it in the war.

I was only slightly surprised to see him, because a small part of my heart always felt he was still alive. The Lord had not revealed to me that I would find my brother here, but here he was. I was so happy that he was alive, but I was sad at what the war had cost him. I knelt beside him as I called his name, "James! My poor James."

He looked up angrily swore and cursed, "Who in the fuck are you? I don't need your pity. Haven't you ever seen a man with one leg before? How the Hell do you know my name?"

I said, "James stop using such foul language! It's me Catherine, your sister."

"You liar... My sister died two years ago. She died in a plane crash. Get lost bitch!" He replied with venom in his voice.

"I'm not lying; it is me and I'm sorrowful not because of your leg, but because of the pain of your heart. My soul weeps for you James"

He threw my arm off him and retorted. "You're psychotic wench, now get lost. My sister is dead. Now get lost before I shoot you." He pulled out a gun and aimed it at my head.

I touched his shoulder gently with one hand and pushed away the gun with the other as I cautioned him saying, "James you can't kill me, I have already died once. I have gone where you don't want to go. Put that bottle down and follow me, so that you may be saved as the Lord has saved me."

He laughed at me as he recognized me from earlier in the day; "You are that crazy Christian giving water away in the streets. You are a fool. You talk of Jesus, but I have been to war and I live in these streets. There is no God and if there is I could never submit to one who allows his children to suffer."

I stood up; "Do I look like I'm suffering? I did when I was separated from God, but he saved me and he can save you too, if you repent." I continued gently, "Jesus loves you James, once long ago you believed in Him. Do you recall when you were fourteen you were fascinated by the book of Revelation. We would read it under the willow tree by the river, even when it rained… remember, please remember."

He looked at me puzzled and he began to cry, "Is it really you Cathy?"

I gave him my bible from my backpack and I said. "I don't have my original bible James, but take this. It is cleaner anyways. I haven't sealed this one with my own blood."

"Cathy it is you, it really is you. I thought you were crazy when you cut your own finger with my knife and put your bloody finger print inside." He said as his eyes glistened with tears, yet to be released.

I laughed out loud as I said, "As I recall you were too afraid to slice your own skin."

"I was not afraid; I just was not crazy like you, Sis."

I laughed and I gave him my hand as I helped him up. He hugged me for a long time, not wanting to let go. I then warned him with a solemn tone, "James, it is me. The time of revelations is at hand, repent and come with me."

James leaned over where he sat and picked up his artificial leg and strapped it on. He walked with me at my side and although it was difficult for him, he left the whisky bottle behind. I knew my brother could not walk for long so we circled back toward the jeep where it was left earlier that day. Thank God it was still there. I put our stuff in the back and we made our way across the country toward Colorado.

James asked me, "So why are we headed toward Colorado."

"The Lord told me to go there. We will be heading deep into the rocky mountains." I replied.

James was concerned and sarcastically stated the obvious, "Cathy, I don't know if you realized, but I'm missing a leg. How am I going to be able to tromp through the mountains without my leg?"

"Of course I realize how difficult it will be for you brother, but it can't be helped. The Lord has sent me there and I must go. The time of revelations is at hand, you must come with me."

"That is easier said than done, Cathy." My brother replied with concern in his voice. He said no more about the matter as we journeyed westward.

Edward had been arrested and I had heard on the radio a few weeks later that the preacher who had been giving out water had been sent to the war. The story was reported like the countless hoaxes that had been told for the past several months with a flair for sensationalism, but I did not turn away as the reporter announced, "Today news from the frontlines in Iran, the Preacher known as Edward Stephens may soon have to face a court-martial as he refuses to shoot anyone. Army officials tried to accommodate the pacifist since he is a learned man, they offered to make him a strategist, however Pastor Edward still refused. Officials' patience for the pacifist is diminishing." I turned off the radio and smiled to myself, admiring his resolve.

That night while I was parked along the side of the road and I was deep in prayer, I had a vision. Soldiers were beating Edward, they attempted to humiliate him and still he refused to be used as a tool of hatred. Finally after much suffering and noncompliance, he was ordered to serve as an Army chaplain.

Sarcastically his commanding officer, Captain Roberts said, "Fine you stubborn fool, you can give the soldiers their last rights while bandaging their wounds, and if your God is so powerful maybe he'll let you save a few. Go preacher. Do whatever you can in this God forsaken place." It was here that my vision ended. I prayed for Edward's protection, but I could not sleep so I started the jeep and drove through the rest of the night as James slept deeply.

I turned the radio on hoping for some good music, but the news at the top of the hour was on. The radio broadcasts were dominated by updates of the war in the Middle East. Soldiers suffered greatly during the war. The fiercest fighting occurred outside Baghdad and throughout Lebanon. James awoke and rubbed his eyes. He turned off the radio.

I said nothing for a while. Then James uttered, "The news does not tell you half of what is happening over there. Chemical weapons are used and when towns are taken back by the insurgents, the male civilians are tortured by their own kind for supporting the infidel. They're shot after the rebels are done seeking information, and the women are raped repeatedly, and the children treated like dogs. How can you do that to your own people? Hate is rising on both sides and hopelessness has long replaced any sense of purpose in the war. I don't even know why we are fighting anymore. It is chaos and madness over there. All the schools we built a decade ago have been destroyed. They hate us even more now than they did at the beginning of the war. A whole new generation of hate and extremism has been given birth due to the ongoing atrocities. They blame us for the war. Its madness, Cathy, nothing makes sense anymore."

I did not know how to reply, so I just continued to drive silently through the night. Alone in my thoughts I remembered how Edward often shed tears when we used to listen to the news back home. I was enraged by this inhumanity. I was sure Edward was crying even now as he walked in the Spirit. He prayed often for these lost souls.

We stopped one morning at a roadside diner, and I saw Edward on television. He was preaching to the soldiers about how he witnessed the transformation of his unit and of the town he was stationed in, which was not disclosed. The news was happy to report that the insurgents had stopped raping the women and torturing the men. The women could now comfort their children. People were rediscovering their humanity.

The army was incensed as the soldiers laid down their weapons at Edward's request and they refused to fight as he spoke from the middle of a dust-ridden street in the center of town. On that day the enemy began to shoot at Edward from their hiding places and Edward's men shot back in fear. Edward walked out into the crossfire. He raised his hand and the guns fell silent as the soldiers witnessed the poison from their chemical weapons begin to swirl about Edward and descend into the earth below his feet.

He preached as both sides listened to God's words. Though the enemy spoke a different language they were amazed at how they could understand Edward in their own tongues. The commanders on both sides ordered their men to fight, but they refused. Three thousand were saved that day on the battlefield. They witnessed the clouds part above Edward's head and in an instant he was taken up to heaven, as the poisonous gas swirled about him. Thousands who witnessed this on TV were also saved that day, but still many refused to believe.

A film crew recorded all that had happened as Edward disappeared in the yellow smoke. One soldier fired his weapon in fear after Edward disappeared. An alarm of shouting rang out breaking the calm, "GAS! GAS!" Soldiers fumbled for their masks as the cameras captured the continuing horror. They recorded men who were not quick enough choking and frothing at the mouth until blood burst forth from their lungs.

The war raged on, and still many soldiers laid down their weapons and refused to fight long after Edward left us. They were imprisoned and beaten, but they refused to submit to the darkness of man. The news reported mass amounts of soldiers on both sides announce that they were no longer willing to fight.

At home people had a small ray of hope in their eyes as peace talks began in the Middle East. The United Nations met around the clock in their struggle to end the atrocities of war, and many feared the imminent threat of nuclear war and the possible devastation which would result from the ongoing chemical warfare.

The days had passed and the President of the United States boasted of the assurance of peace on the horizon, but the United Nations had discovered the United States was beginning to profit from the perpetuation of the war. China and Russia were both accused of this crime as well, for manufacturing and selling chemical weapons. All three nations were kicked off the Security Council and the UN was dissolved and their seats replaced by three new eastern countries in return for agreeing to end the war. The UN was reformed and named The Alliance Republic of Nations or ARON for short. A new constitution was agreed upon and a new security council was formed.

The one man responsible for seeking out and unveiling the treachery of the great powers was applauded by the whole world and he was instrumental in bringing about peace in the Middle East. For the first time in my memory peace was everywhere on Earth. The man responsible for the peace negotiations sat by Israel's Prime Minister as he signed the seven-year cease-fire agreement. This man who established the peace could trace his lineage back to Cypselus, an ancient king of Corinth. Many admired him as a man of greatness. Augustus' mother was of German, decent but his father was a Greek. Augustus was born in and grew up in Italy and he was fluent in several languages.

The world economies began their painful recovery as industries were forced to diversify, and the war economy transitioned into providing goods and services again. It appeared to be the end of war and swift reforms were instituted to get the economy moving again. The United States was like that of many other nations that had a massive war debt to repay, but they still had direct access to oil, water and lumber resources from Canada. They experienced difficulty, but they were able to begin their road to financial recovery more easily than most other countries.

The once weak and desperate Russia had been increasing her wealth for some time now. Russia was enjoying the rebuilding of their society funded by even more oil deals struck between their former allies who were very grateful for their support.

Despite the loss of their seat among the seven permanent members in the Security Council, the United States remained one of ten most powerful nations in the world however their power was increasingly limited as the months followed. Currency had been officially eliminated since far too many countries were printing paper money that had no real value, and the new United World Federation was formed.

The great demagogue and diplomat, who brought about the peace and was instrumental in promoting economic recovery around the world, entranced all the nations. He became known as the Peacemaker.

He managed to convince the World Bank to wave all interest payments from nations around the world, and it was agreed that the most desperate countries would have all of their national debt written off by the World Bank. This was on the condition that all nations united their currencies and all private banking institutions were eliminated. Thus the countries of the world had one currency and run-away inflation was ended, as the World Bank then served each nation's banking needs. It was not long before the need for all currency itself became meaningless. This was completed by the end of the first half of the first year in New World Order.

Many people bartered when water became scarce, but now there was a new system of world citizenship and economic equality. To ensure equality was possible, each citizen had to be counted and cataloged. Thus every person was ordered to have a microchip implanted on the back of their hand or on their forehead. This chip functioned much like a bar code, thus allowing your ID number to be scanned whenever purchases were made. This enabled the World Federation to not only monitor acquisitions, but also to properly allocate the world's precious resources. The whole process was projected to take an estimated ten years. This announcement was made in the second half of the first year of the New World Order.

The wealthy and most technologically advanced nations were among the first ordered to implement the devices. Many citizens were not informed the chip was also used to locate the exact position of any citizen with an implant. An extensive satellite tracking system would enable the government to track its citizens around the globe with the aid of an advanced network of computer systems located in Geneva, Washington DC, Moscow and Beijing. It was argued that this could protect the world from the evils of terrorism and war. Leading citizens agreed out of fear.

There was an immediate uproar from Christian and Jewish extremists. Religious zealots were labeled paranoid freaks. Although the longing for peace and financial security was shared by all, the religious sects, led by centuries of prophetic writings, could not ignore the signs. They were afraid, but they had to respond to their faith.

One day I was in town bartering for hunting supplies. I was trading my jeep for some much needed long-term survival equipment. As I made my way through the city streets, I stumbled upon a couple that was quarreling. The man argued, "It's no different than you having your precious social security number babe. Come on, the government needs to know who its citizens are. Besides how can people be equal without ensuring everyone has access to food, water and clothing?"

She sighed as tears fell down her face, "I guess that's true, but I remember hearing warnings when I was a little girl about the Mark of the Beast. The warnings of the mark are in the Bible, Sayid"

She could not proceed as the tears continued to flow, so her husband hugged her and said, "Oh sweetheart, now are you trying to tell me Allah is against brotherly love and equality? That's what this chip protects, now come get it with me."

She refused to go and I touched her arm as I said, "She's right, beware the Peacemaker and the Mark of the Beast. Flee to the mountains and remain faithful. The end is at hand and few in the cities will have the strength to withstand the tribulation."

He informed me. "I too believe in Allah, our merciful Lord. I do not fear man or Death, but I do not believe these troubled times are the end; and even if it were so, why run? Can the mountains hide you from whatever the Lord allows? Can a person avoid the Last Day?"

I replied, "No one can run from the Last Day, and I no longer fear Death, for I know my destiny and where I will spend eternity." Then I quoted the Koran, *"Indeed the faithful...those who have faith in Allah and the Last Day and act righteously-they will have no fear, nor will they grieve.* That includes people of the book, who worship the one God does it not?"

He raised an eyebrow and replied with a furrow of his brow, "Yes, it does."

"Hmmm… well your wife and I worship the one God" With that said I walked away.

I heard her pleading with him, "Sayid please, please come with me!"

He told her, "You're crazy, I am not about to live like a bloody caveman."

She ran up to me pleading for advice so I replied, "There is no marriage in heaven, but your choice today may determine where you will be for eternity. Have you accepted Jesus as your savior?"

She nodded yes and I said, "Then the only question is: do you choose to stay and become a martyr, or flee and await the return of the King? The choice is yours."

Her husband looked at us like we were mad, but she turned to him and pleaded again, "If I'm right you can have a chance at eternal life; if I'm wrong you need only live in the bush for a few years. I love you, but I have to go."

He looked concerned as he said; "Mary, You can't survive in the bush alone."

"Then come with me; teach me! You can come back to the city, if you must." She challenged him.

I later discovered that Sayid was a wildlife photographer and an ex-Navy Seal. If anyone could teach her to survive he could. *Just then Sayid added more logs to the fire and interjected*, "Thank God I did. I don't know how you would have survived without me. Praises be to Allah."

Another soldier touched his arm, "I didn't know that was you Sayid"

Sayid laughed, "Yes, I was a skeptic to say the least."

Mary touched her husband's shoulder, "A skeptic, you thought we were crazy, but no one is happier than me that you decided to come."

*Then Sayid kissed his wife, "*I always thought you were crazy love, still someone had to help you survive this war. I guess it was Allah's will that I fall in love with you.*" Then he apologized to Catherine for interrupting, and bid her to continue.*

"Yes, since my encounter with the Devil many months before, the night Edward broke his ribs, my memory had completely returned and I knew my destiny. I woke up daily with a clear purpose, a clear vision and the enemy waged war against me, but I would stand and fight. I was no longer afraid. I walked in God's sacred assurance and strength."

*As Catherine continued I could not help hear the fat woman who spoke earlier utter in whispers to another woman beside her, "*I despise Sayid. How could that other woman have married him? Canadians were always too tolerant, to trusting and naive. How could Catherine have a Muslim in her troop, let alone functioning as her right hand? They are a duplicitous and deceitful lot. I don't trust him."

*The other blond woman beside her replied in very hushed tones, "*I don't trust him either, but I trust Catherine. She knows what she is doing.*" Catherine's eyes penetrated through the flames across from me. It was not me whom she was looking at, and the strength of her look silenced the women.*

I had fought The Muslim extremists for too long, and it made me wary. I was angry to hear he was her right hand. I don't know why. I didn't know him, but I could not dismiss a Navy Seal. I was glad to know Catherine had someone protecting her, loyal to her. I would watch him closely though, because I trusted no one. I was aware of a jealousy and a possessiveness that surprised me. Deep within me I battled an envy that he was by her side and not me, nevertheless I was glad to have him guard her all the same. I would not allow such foolish emotions to influence my judgment. It was not necessarily his religion that upset me; it was his proximity to Catherine. Seeds of jealousy were planted and in my heart, and I waged war against it.

Chapter Eight:
A New World Order Breeds Resistance

The nations began to unite under the guidance of the diplomat that brought about peace in the Middle East. As his influence grew so did his popularity among the masses, everyone praised, Raficial Cypselus Augustus. His first success was securing universal peace for a period of seven years. All nations agreed that they would neither attack each other nor produce an excess of weapons.

Prior to the end of the war the US had been found responsible for beginning an arms race as they developed an extensive defense system across North America's coastline, known as the Defense Perimeter. This resulted in the creation of thousands of missile launching installations, and other nations ramped up their military industrial base to match the perceived threat. The Peacemaker negotiated an end to that arms race.

The new dictator's power was still limited. He attempted to force the US to remove the missiles from these instillations, but America refused. They knew they needed those bases to defend them against Russia, China and Korea, or anyone else who decided to launch a nuclear attack.

The United States had been removed from the Security Council when the UN dissolved, along with China and Russia for their involvement in promoting world war, and it was not long before Canada and Britain were found guilty for being in collusion with the US. Heavy natural resource fines and technological penalizations were placed upon these countries.

These wealthy nations would supply much of the natural resources to ensure economic equality was enjoyed by every country in the World Federation. The wealthy nations were obligated under the peace agreement to provide for the less fortunate societies. Commodities were exchanged between countries according to need rather than bought and sold.

China did not submit to the Peace Maker immediately, however their cooperation was acquired when they suffered enormous food shortages. China faced hail destroying their crops, and disease struck large sections of their agriculture, followed by a plague killing much of their livestock. Suddenly the guarantee of the sharing of food from North America, Russia and Europe proved very appealing.

The government operated with utmost efficiency and corruption was quickly quashed. Any factions working in any way that threatened the peace were dealt with severely, as their economic privileges were suspended and all nations were treated impartially and granted equal access to the world's resources.

The World Federation also used ARON to serve as an international policing force. Initially peace keeping proved a simple task, but as it increased its military power so did resistance and the necessity for peace making grew. The United States, Russia and China found that they had no voice in the New World Order, so their opposition grew even stronger.

Prime Minister Augustus chose six world leaders to serve as council leaders under him, and six hundred politicians served under them as legislators. Every member was hand-picked for his or her upstanding character, influence and abilities. The nations treated each other with the utmost honor and respect.

The six leaders were all representatives of countries surrounding the Mediterranean Sea. It was believed that these men were essential to maintain the peace in the Middle East. Prime Minister Augustus resided in Italy and the ministers under him represented Greece, Turkey, Syria, Jordan, Egypt and Libya and the world hailed them as the, 'Seven Kings of Peace.' Later during the second half of the first year, he also appointed members from Spain, France and England to sit on the council, but their voices were weak.

For three and a half years the world appeared to embrace peace, and the former United Nations had finally achieved all of the goals issued many decades ago in its year 2000 convention. Every society in the world had equal opportunity, health, economic security and access to home computers. The Internet was instrumental in promoting and maintaining the peace.

Then a mandate was issued that every world citizen would be micro-chipped in either their hand or forehead for security and greater efficiency. The chip enabled immediate trade and commerce, as well as satellite tracking.

Most Christians refused to submit to the government's demands, as did many Jews. Jewish extremists engaged in mass demonstrations alongside the Christians, objecting to the government's directives. Violence erupted and both groups were labeled as intolerant and radical and eventually as traitors and terrorists.

Catherine paused and then asked us, "Did I already tell you this? Probably, the wine must be getting to me. Still I'll continue".

She did continue the telling and no one seemed to mind. "The traitors were hunted down and many hid in the mountains, but most were found. Some had managed to stay free and became known as the Resistance."

"Is that what we are called? It is not a very original name is it?" *Sayid declared,* "Oh, sorry Catherine, go on please." *Catherine got another glass of wine and then continued.*

France grew to resent the emerging dictatorship within the government, as ARON seized increasingly larger amounts of food and wine from their region and favoring what was allocated to the countries who served on the Security Council. Three and a half years after it was established, Prime Minister Charles Bourbon of France led a public resistance against the increasing control and loss of autonomy. Russia, China, Canada, Britain, the United States and Japan all joined in condemning the actions of the new government, however China and Russia were trusted about as much as ARON.

The microchip process was going slower than anticipated and once France refused to submit to the process another world war became inevitable once again. The Peacemaker began to become frustrated as outright defiance grew. Zealots were arrested for treason everywhere, and Bourbon was forced to flee into exile with a few loyal soldiers at his side.

Just as the persecutions began to mount the Rapture occurred. The world could not deny prophecy any more. Christians walking in the Spirit disappeared from factories, offices, beds, fields, kitchen tables, cafes, hospitals and cars. Wherever a Christian who walked in the Spirit was, they had disappeared in, 'the twinkling of an eye.' Sad to say few Christians were ready when the rapture occurred, so most of us were left behind.

Fallen Christians ran away into the forests in fear of ARON and their ever expanding security force. Many people, who were terrified by what they witnessed when loved ones disappeared, ran from the cities, fearfully seeking their God.

"Today there are countless pockets of resistance units like ours who are forced to choose between martyrdom or fleeing to the wilderness." *Catherine stood up and went to place her cup by the rows of empty wine bottles.*

Catherine's camp lay deep in the coverage of the mountains and I could not fathom from where they got their supplies. They slept in caves and socialized under a special, massive, camouflaged canopy, which prevented satellites from detecting their presence through thermal technology and infrared tracking devices. So the government could not see them, and in this isolated vast mountainous region they appeared to lack for nothing.

Many women in the camp found it hard to accept that Catherine could claim to serve God on one hand and kill humans on the other. Even Mary, Sayid's wife was heard saying, "Catherine, I know why we chose to hide from the new world government, but why do we kill, fight and die? Can't we just hide until Jesus comes again?"

She just replied to the women of the camp as she shot a grin my way, "Someone has to put an end to the atrocities. Besides the more people I can stop from getting the Mark of the Beast, the better. Surely a soul is worth dying for. Think what would have happened to Sayid if you didn't try to stop him."

Mary smiled and nodded. Then Catherine ordered everyone to bed. "Alright soldiers only a few hours to daylight, so put out the fires and get to sleep." *With that everyone, except the watchmen who were just waking up, took to the caves and went to bed.*

The Night Squad was a specially trained force, which Catherine and Sayid prepared to fight ARON. They attacked by night and used the darkness as their shield. In a few days it would be a moonless night, a perfect opportunity for their attack. Catherine stayed up with Sayid talking strategy and finalizing the plans. To prevent unnecessary killing she had chosen Eric, one of her intelligence officers to design a specialized gun, which would only fire if the government microchip was detected in the targeting scope of the rifle.

Catherine never permitted anyone to kill someone who did not have the Mark of the Beast. Nevertheless she did not neglect to knock them out if she suspected them of endangering her cause.

Catherine was a paradox whom few could understand and even fewer dared to question despite her candid nature. I however felt like I always knew her since our eyes first met all those years ago in Ireland. I remembered her, strength and beauty, her passion and her smile. How could I forget? Tonight I would walk up to her and hopefully revive the connection we once briefly shared.

"Hello Catherine" *I said* "Shouldn't you get some sleep too?" *Oh, she was beautiful. She looked up to see who it was speaking to her. Her blue eyes captured my soul once again, as they had so long ago.*

An exceptionally large African American man stepped in front of me, blocking my way to Catherine. He looked as if he was about to crush me like a bug.

I was very pleased and relieved that she smiled as she declared, "Well I don't believe my eyes! It's alright Jacob." *She said*, "You can let him through." *Catherine said this as she patted her large protector on the back.*

I laughed nervously, "After everything you've seen Catherine, I hardly think I am that remarkable a sight." *Then I carefully made my way around the giant of the man and smiled awkwardly up at him as I passed by. He did not return the grin; he just stared down at me as I walked by.*

"I guess you're right Captain Roberts; I thought it was you I saw in the firelight." *She said with a slight laugh in her voice.*

She grabbed an Irish whiskey and poured me a glass, and insisted I sit with her to share a drink, which I eagerly accepted. "Now you must tell me, how you found me here in these mountains so far from home?"

I took it and sat beside her as I replied, "It's a long story do you have the time?" *She nodded yes as she drowned her drink, so I began my tale.*

"I was stationed in the Middle East as part of a ground troop after our ship sunk in the Mediterranean Sea, en route to the Middle East. We lost most of the crew and men were needed desperately to fight on land. We discovered furthermore, that the enemy developed a weapon that rendered air assaults and attacks from sea impossible. They were able to take control of our computer guidance system, causing both our ships and planes to crash and run off course. We severely underestimated their technological capabilities.

It was Hell on Earth. After a couple years of senseless fighting, a middle-aged man was placed under my command. He took me by surprise when he reported with a bible in his hand. I ordered him to fight, but he wouldn't, then I ordered him to join the strategic command, he refused. Finally my commanding officer ordered me to have him beaten, to make an example of him. After three torturous days he still refused to participate in the war, so I told him to report to the medical field office. He did."

"I know; I saw that happen in a vision." *Catherine replied.*

I touched her hand and apologized; "I am so sorry Catherine; I was such a coward. I should have never followed those orders to beat him. I'm sorry." *I repeated those earnest words and hung my head in shame.*

Catherine looked at me with such gentleness as she sighed, "You did what you thought you had to. Edward also wrote to me about your courage Captain, I know you are no coward."

"How did you get his emails when you are so secluded?" I asked, and she replied. "Eric, my technical expert gets me my email. He was at the library with his partner, Jason when I first arrived in Boulder, Colorado. Eric saw me trying to use the library computer system to get my email. The government is still not able to fully control the Internet, thank God. It is the last venue of free flowing information. Accessing a computer and the Internet itself is the challenge, but Eric saw me and had pity on me. I'm afraid I was experiencing technical difficulties. Anyways please continue."

"Well Catherine I am sorry; I was a coward." *I declared with regret.*

Catherine touched my arm, "Trust me Captain Roberts he is in a far better place. Anything you did, God allowed." *She put me at ease as I knew in that instant she had forgiven me and my years of guilt were released in that moment. Still I blamed myself for allowing him to walk onto that city street with some blind faith that his god would save him from the gas.*

"Now Captain"

"Call me Peter." *I interjected.*

She smiled, repeating my *name out loud,* "Peter."

"I was pleased at least you never forgot me." *I remarked flirtatiously.*

She smiled and insisted I tell her how I found her, so I did. "Edward perplexed me. I had heard some of my men praise him and hold him with the highest regard; meanwhile my commanders called him a zealot and insane. I went to his tent one night when he was holding a prayer session and I waited outside for him. After the other men left, I entered. I went to warn him of my commander's increasing displeasure with his disruptive behavior. They felt a little religion was good for the men, it enabled them to face death more boldly, however too much of a pacifistic faith destroys a unit. Blind faith proves deadly on a battlefield. He did not heed my warning."

Catherine smiled, "Of course he didn't."

I continued, "He had his bible open with the most angelic picture I had ever seen. He noticed me admiring your photo."

Edward commented, "Beautiful isn't she."

"Yes, she is the most breath taking woman I have ever seen." I replied. *Catherine blushed a little as I noted;* "He informed me that you were a close personal friend, whom he prayed for every day. From that day on I shared many hours with Edward. I had to get to know him as a way of knowing you. He spent much of the time warning me and reading to me from the book of Revelation, Daniel and other prophetic scriptures. I'm not what you call saved Catherine, but we appeared to share the same enemy. I often swore that I was fighting the Devil himself, but whereas I led an army of vengeance, Edward led an army of love. He was also worried about you. I never knew they caught his death on TV. I'm sorry you had to see that."

Catherine looked at me puzzled and then said, "I'm glad the world saw it. We are better for it.

I found her reply somewhat strange, but I shrugged it off and continued. "I'm glad I found you. It was difficult, but countless Americans and Canadians are continuing to network in secret organizations such as yours to regain our freedom and democracy. Who would have thought those bastards would have such a delayed success decades after September eleventh. They wage war through terror and when we fight back we look like the aggressor and now all of the nations we were at war with are prominent members of the Dictator's government. How is that for iron**y?**" *Catherine thought everything occurred according to some divine plan. I couldn't accept that, but I was glad we were now fighting on the same side.*

I told Catherine how desperately I wanted to believe in this Prince of Peace, "I was honestly hoping the Peacemaker had the answers to the problems which had plagued the world for generations now. That's why I initially considered joining the International Peace Keeping Force; I was ready for peace. Then when he turned on America and her allies, I gave up hope. I could no longer support a government that was limiting democracy." *I paced to and fro like a caged lion as my anger grew.*

"I went to war to protect democracy and freedom." *I continued*, "When the United States was accused of perpetuating the war in the Middle East, well I had enough" *I stopped to take a deep breath and calm myself, while downing my whiskey.*

Catherine interjected as she poured us another drink, "So how is it I came to meet you in Ireland all those years ago? What were American troops doing docking there?"

"Well" *I sighed,* "Our troops had a stopover before joining up with the British Navy. We were simply awaiting final orders for our mission."

I stood up and walked over to take a seat beside her, "Enough about me Catherine, now tell me how you are doing?" *I lay my hand on hers as I continued.* "Edward was very worried about you. It must have been so hard for you to watch his demise on TV. Is that when you became militant?"

She stood up and turned her back to me, as she replied, "No. I became militant shortly after Edward left us. When the enforcement of microchips became mandatory and our feeble Canadian and American governments refused to resist. I had to do something. When the power of the American government became nullified, I knew we had to fight or die."

I sensed a slight sadness in her voice, which I presumed was guilt, so I attempted to comfort her. Placing my hands on her shoulders I said, "God does not require martyrdom of us all you know. Besides there is some hope; our former president is acting in an underground arm of the American government. He has contact between French, British, Russian, Chinese and Japanese cells. He is looking for a Canadian contingent to operate with the Russians in a network of systems to organize a full scale opposition movement."

She turned and smiled at me with those beautiful white teeth and she had a skeptical twinkle in her eye, and she asked me how I knew all of this. "I have been sent here by the President Davidson to enlist your cooperation." *I responded to her inquisitive look. I did not know if she was interested, but she had a coy smile cross her lips as if she knew something I didn't.*

She then replied, "I have to sleep on it, but I assure you Peter, I will seriously consider it." *Then I was pleasantly surprised as she kissed me gently good night and said,* "I have some more work to do, but you may sleep here in my cave tonight." *I bowed in gratitude.*

The following evening Catherine was leading the soldiers through an intense work out as I emerged from the caves. She stopped and walked over to get some water as she said; "Well comrades, I would like to introduce you to an old friend and perhaps a new ally."

"Captain Peter Roberts, These are the men and women who serve in the Night Squad. Comrades welcome Captain Roberts." *I shook a few of her soldiers' hands, as I informed all of them that they could call me Peter.*

"Well," *Catherine questioned*, "Are you going to join us, or are you just visiting?" *Then she got a mischievous glimmer in her eyes as she taunted*, "That is if you're physically able to keep up?"

I shot a smile back at her as I answered her; "Are you challenging me to a physical test, Catherine?"

She looked confidently into my eyes as she said, "Yes I am, Peter." *Then she came closer and put her arm around me as she explained,* "It is customary for all new recruits to go up against the most physically fit member of the squad, in order to test their physical capabilities."

I relished in her challenge and delighted at the opportunity to demonstrate my physical prowess before her. "I accept, so who is it that I am to compete against?"

I heard the soldiers laugh and I feared I would be forced to fight her giant who was standing faithfully at her side. I never cowered before any man, but this time I was suddenly tempted to withdraw from the challenge as I stared up at him. He was truly fearsome. Everyone laughed again as I looked at him with trepidation. To my surprise Catherine replied, "Me."

I looked at her with disbelief and she taunted me again saying, "Now Peter, you're not afraid to be beaten by a women, are you?"

I assured her, "I'm not opposed to competing against a woman, but I must admit, I am surprised." *I signaled to her that we could proceed, and a series of traditional military obstacle courses, of which I was familiar, were laid out before us. I admit that it had been many years since I actually ran in any such courses, but I exercised frequently and did not hesitate in accepting the contest.*

Catherine was exceptionally agile and swift, much like a cat. She was strong and she moved with ease and skill. I was somewhat ashamed she beat me so convincingly, but the men laughed out loud and one young man said, "Don't worry sir; she has beaten all of us."

I could not believe it, but Catherine smiled as she questioned, "Peter are you up to one more challenge?" *I nodded my reply, still catching my breath as she led me to a series of three rings.*

"Peter, in these rings we engage in hand to hand combat," *She said this as she walked into the middle of the circle. She continued to explain,* "The further you are forced out from the center ring the fewer points you receive and the goal is to immobilize your opponent, or remove them from the ring."

She asked me if I was ready, I protested, "Catherine I've seen you fight. I know you may have improved over the years, but I'm much taller and stronger than you are. Furthermore, I have spent my life in combat. I don't want to hurt you; this could prove to be..." *I hesitated briefly searching for the right words and I continued,* "to be dangerous for you."

The men laughed again as Catherine assured me, "I assure you Captain it is I who does not wish to hurt you. Never underestimate your opponent Peter. *"She assumed her stance, and we began circling each other as we engaged in hand to hand combat.*

At first I was fearful of hurting her, but after she kicked me a few times and after a succession of blocks I began to fight more vigorously. She was quick and each kick and punch seemed to come from a complete body transfer of energy, and yet I sensed she was holding back. I ceased to be on the defensive. I was intrigued by her abilities. Her blocks were unusually strong and I was unable to defeat her. She was much faster than I was. I could not comprehend her strength and speed. The fight lasted many minutes, and I was successful in avoiding defeat. My years of combat experience did work to my advantage and I am sure I still held back a little, not wanting to hurt her.

She must have known and said, "Now Peter I expect you to give me your best effort."

"Fine, I will." *I replied, but I hesitated and suddenly she dropped low to the ground as I was in the process of kicking toward her and she succeeded in sweeping my leg from under me. I fell with a thud to the ground as my head hit equally hard. She stood above me and ordered the medic,* "Sky, take care of the Captain's head. Make sure he does not have a concussion."

"Yes Catherine." *The young Native American medic replied as he helped me up and led me to Catherine's quarters.*

Although Catherine showed no mercy toward me in front of the soldiers, she did have me sent to rest in her bed. She brought some ice to reduce the swelling and told Sky, "You can leave now. Come check on him in a few hours."

"I will." *he replied.* "I'll return when the moon is high." *With that he left us.*

She gently touched my head as she moved my hair aside to look at the bump forming at the base of my skull and she apologized for causing me pain. I held her hand as she sat next to me and I said, "No, I'm the one who owes you an apology. I should have known better than to underestimate you, Catherine. Edward warned me you had one hell of a kick."

She frowned for a moment and then dismissed what I said as she continued, "Well Peter I just wanted you to know, next to Sayid you were the best competition I've had in many years."

I thanked her; "I am happy to have provided you pleasure."

She smiled at me coyly and said, "Behave yourself, Peter." *Then she asked me if there was anything she could do to make me more comfortable.*

So I took the opportunity to boldly plead, "Let me hold you in my arms, stay and lay with me for a while. I promise to be a gentleman."

She informed me, "Now Peter I don't think I should, that could prove to be… too dangerous." *She bent to kiss my head and said,* "Now I have some work to do. You be good and get some rest. I will be back later."

I smiled mischievously as I assured her, "I'm always good, Catherine."

She laughed gently and replied, "Somehow I doubt that my dear Captain." *I sighed and agreed as Sayid came and called for Catherine.*

Catherine did come back later and we lay together and talked. I told her about my childhood and my family's military background, and she told me of her opulent upbringing.

I went first, "I was raised in a military household with a long military tradition. I was sent to Marine Military School, after which I dedicated my life to service. My entire life has been devoted to the preparation for warfare. I cannot see any other path than the one I have chosen, or that was chosen for me."

"That must be refreshing." *Catherine interjected,* "I have always been searching, until now. If you saw me as a child you would never believe I am who I am today. I was wealthy, carefree, and enjoying all of daddy's riches as a little girl in my protected, parochial world. My dad spoiled me and he was pretty much perfect in my eyes, but he was always working. I grew closer to my mother over the years, and the older I became the farther apart my dad and I became.

When we got a little older he sent my brother and I away for continual military training and outdoor survival. We too were prepared for war from early childhood. It was quite a paradox, I was prepared for war by dad and I had a longing for peace instilled in me through mom."

She laughed quietly shaking her head, "I was a radical environmentalist when I was young too. I viewed my father's oil companies in the tar sands as equivalent to raping the land. It caused a division to develop between us and yet I enjoyed the privileges our oil based wealth provided. I was a judgmental and opinionated young woman."

Catherine sighed as she continued reflecting, "I remember one time I set up a picket line along the driveway with signs protesting daddy's oil company, on a night when his investors were coming to the house for dinner. Dad insisted I tear those signs down before his guests arrived. I refused and he threatened to spank me. He placed me over his knee and whacked me three times; I was nine at the time. Usually I would howl, and then I realized the spanking didn't hurt. It never really hurt anything but my pride. I felt empowered, so I stood up looked him straight in the eye and said, 'There daddy, I hope that made you feel better.' With that he sent me promptly to my room."

I chuckled, "Did you comply?" *I asked with a raised eyebrow suspecting I already knew her reply.*

Catherine grinned, "Initially I obeyed, stomping up to my room. However when the guests arrived I was determined to be heard, so I dressed in my best clothes, I went down for supper and I introduced myself to all of my father's guests. One man inquired as to my interests over dinner and I informed him, "I am an extreme environmentalist, and I'm especially displeased with the raping of the land for economic gain." Needless to say my dad was not pleased, but the president of the company asked if I would grant him the opportunity take me on a field trip to view the fields and the processes from start to finish and reserve my judgment. I looked to daddy and he agreed that it could prove to be very educational. So the next day I flew to northern Alberta and I went to tour the tar sands.

I laughed out loud, which hurt my own head a little. I held my head as I inquired, "Well, what was the outcome?"

She replied, "I discovered that my father did sell ethical oil and that they had managed to not only make the process more environmentally friendly, they also replanted and cultivated the forests to be even healthier than before the process began. I came to realize that either a man like my dad could get rich providing America with oil or our enemies would, so I reserved judgment."

"Was your father pleased?" *I asked her.*

"Well, he was pleased enough to give me a peace offering. He lifted me up onto a very high table and gave me some cookies that were by the coffee station. They were delicious." *She smiled and then she continued,* "Dad said, 'So am I off the hook Catherine? Can you see that Daddy is a good guy after all?' I pondered my reply before I said, 'Well, I'm not sure, but I think another cookie could convince me.' So Dad and I made amends."

I laughed out loud, and she smiled as she commented, "Dad laughed too, but I got another cookie."

"Of course you did. Did this really mend your relationship with your father?" *I inquired.*

She sighed, "A little, but it was fleeting. He always wished I was a son, I remember him saying, 'Catherine, I am so proud of you.' then he moaned, 'If only you were my son.' We grew farther apart after that and I developed a passion and fervor for various movements over the years."

I held her hand and asked her, "Did your father's words permanently divide you. It must have hurt to hear such an awful thing."

"No." *She replied,* "It was a turning point, but the biggest turning point in our relationship happened years later when I was dating a young man and he hit me. The boy's father was a close personal friend and business associate of my father. My brother James and I were on a double date. James liked the boy's sister. We got in a political discussion and my opinions apparently offended this boy, who felt women should remain silent. When I said, 'Are you threatened by a woman with an opinion, or by a woman with a brain?' He slapped me in the face."

"What did James do?" *I inquired.*

"Absolutely nothing, James sat on the hood of his car and watched what was unfolding before him."

I was shocked by her reply. She continued, "I told the loser never to talk to me, or look at me ever again. I warned him, 'I better never even see you around me or my family ever again.' He did not fear me, but he was worried about James."

The boy laughed uneasily, 'What… are you going to sic you big brother after me?' James had already joined the military by this point, but he had not been deployed yet.

James laughed, 'You don't need to worry about me, my sister is ferocious, and she can kick my ass.'

I replied, 'I don't need my brother to protect me. I'm real handy with a baseball bat.' With that we left.

I laughed out loud again as I said, "You were ferocious even then, huh."

"I suppose." *Catherine sighed,* "Still, he did not heed my warning; I was so angry. I was enraged. When we got home dad asked what happened and James told him everything. The next morning that six foot four boy in a man's body showed up on my doorstep and dad let him in. I was utterly livid, even psychotic. I pushed my own father against the wall and yelled at him to throw the bum out. When he didn't, I did.

My dad walked outside and said, 'Boy you better not show your face around here again. There is no telling what she will do to you and none of us could stop her."

"Did, he ever come back." *I asked*

"No." *She continued*, "I think he thought I really was psychotic and he was a coward. Dad thought I was a little crazy too. When he came back in I was so angry that I yelled at him asking, 'Why didn't you throw him out? Why didn't you beat him, or threaten him? What kind of father allows the man who hit his daughter in his house?' Dad gave me no reply."

"It is shocking. I would have ensured that boy thought twice before ever harming another woman again. Any man who hits a defenseless woman is a coward and a snake." *I said and then I qualified my statement saying,* "Not that you are defenseless. That is very apparent."

"I was pretty vulnerable at that time in my life." *She informed me*," I had some military and weapons training and plenty of survival training, but I had no hand to hand combat skills. I was defenseless. That is why I asked my father to put me in martial arts. I realized I could not readily protect myself from a grown man, if he chose to hurt me. I found that repulsive. Dad refused, he said, 'I cannot in good conscience enroll you in martial arts. With your temper, you're likely to abuse your husband. I could not put any man in such a situation.'

I was so angry, I would not take no for an answer. I replied, 'You would rather have me beaten by a weasel like that pathetic excuse for a human being that you allowed into our house, or even worse, raped? You obviously won't protect me. You taught me that I must be ready to protect myself.' He would not budge so I got a job and paid for my own classes, until Mom badgered him into paying for the rest of them."

"I'm sorry you had no protection and no support from your father. A father should protect and defend his own children, especially his daughter." *I stated empathetically.*

"Yes he should." *She agreed and then she reasoned,* "Still, had I not been forced to learn to protect myself, I would not be who I am today. It all worked out for good in the end."

"Perhaps," *I smiled and I noted,* "and you are amazing and remarkable."

"Captain Roberts, you do flatter me." *She chided.*

"I only speak the truth." *I replied as she kissed my cheek.*

I took the opportunity to hold her cheek and kiss her on the lips. I was pleased that she did not pull away. She kissed me gently and softly and then she got up and sighed, "Oh, my dear captain you are such a sweet temptation."

I replied, "I remember how passionate you were when we first met. I loved that about you. I never thought you would give this marine a chance. I am glad to know that spark still flickers inside you."

She smiled and said, "Yes, well I better leave you to sleep and get back to work before that spark becomes a flame."

She left me to sleep, but I couldn't as I tossed and turned restlessly. I tried to relax, but I could not get her out of my mind. She dominated my every thought; my fondness for her over the years had never diminished, but now that I was near her she was becoming my obsession. I succumbed to exhaustion with a smile upon my face as I remembered her saying, "Oh my dear Captain, you are such a sweet temptation." *With that I drifted away, not to be awakened until sometime later when Sky brought me back from the land of dreams.* "Captain, Captain, wake up sir."

I looked at him with unwelcoming eyes as he said, "You had me worried for a moment, sir. You were somewhere very far away; you were in a very deep slumber."

I smiled, "Yes, I was somewhere wonderful." *He raised a questioning eyebrow, but I did not tell him I was dancing with Catherine in my dreams.* "Where is Catherine?" I inquired.

"You will see her soon. She has left with Jacob, to pray." *He answered my query and then he continued,* "Now tell me how you're feeling? Any headaches or vision problems I should know about?

"No" *I replied,* "I feel fine."

He gave me his hand and said, "Good, now let's get you up and walking around to see if you experience any dizziness."

I walked around the cave, and he inquired, "Well, any symptoms?"

"Nope, I am fit as a fiddle." *I assured him.*

"Good, Catherine must have prayed for your swift healing."

I did not believe in such things, still I could not help but smile as I replied, "Yes she probably did."

"Well Captain," *he grinned and then said,* "I have breakfast ready for you if you would like to come with me."

"Please call me Peter."

"Hello Peter, I am Sky, Sky Little Wolf."

"Nice to meet you Sky; what are we having for breakfast?" I patted my stomach and said, "I'm starving."

"Another good sign, Sky replied. We are having moose meat sausages and eggs, with fire roasted bannock. Delicious."

"Ah sounds great, a Native dish?" *I assumed.*

"No, it is a Canadian one. Bannock was actually developed after the white man arrived in the land, but it is a delicious invention." *He informed me.*

"I can't wait." *I smiled and I was very pleasantly surprised to discover we had apple juice to drink as well.*

Catherine returned and she brought me to her quarters for a frank discussion. "Peter, I must ask you something directly."

"Go ahead, ask me anything Catherine." *I was expecting her to ask me more about the president, but to my surprise she didn't.*

Instead she looked directly to my eyes and said, "Do you realize that as a Christian and as a leader that I cannot sleep with you?"

She was being very serious, but I could not help but jest, "You slept with me the other night."

"Peter I am being serious." *She was resolute, and yet she could not hide the smile in her eyes and then she added,* "Besides you slept while I worked."

'Oh that is true." *I grinned.*

"Well do you realize this fact?" *She questioned me with a commanding tone.*

"Yes I do. So how am I supposed to behave, my dear Catherine, when you obviously are attracted to me too?"

"Just behave yourself Peter. Think of it as an exercise in self-control and discipline."

"I can do that my dear Catherine, but you should know I have never forgotten you, even during the darkest days of the war I had memories of my brief night of drinking and dancing with you. I know my duty and I will always be a soldier first and a man second. I will always honor your wishes, Catherine. I could never bear to violate your trust."

I knew from all that Edward shared with me and from our brief discussions that trust did not come easily to Catherine. I would never willingly betray her. I was only slightly melancholy that her religious beliefs divided us; at least we had shared principles and a common purpose. Comforted by my words of assurance, we talked late into the night until sunrise surprised us and then she fell into a deep sleep in my arms. I was dreaming of what could be and pondering our destiny, while she lay sleeping easily, for she already knew her future. We were preparing and hoping for a new world, a new beginning, but first we had to resist the existing order.

Chapter Nine:
Suspicions in the Darkness

I awoke the next night and Catherine was already gone. I got up and I decided to walk toward the entrance when I heard voices just outside the cave. It was Sayid and Catherine.

Sayid sounded agitated, "Catherine, how well do you know this Captain Roberts? How do you know he can be trusted and how did he find us?"

"Don't worry Sayid" *Catherine assured him saying,* "He was Edward's former commanding officer and he once saved my life. We can trust him, I know it!" *Sayid was not convinced and I saw her put a hand on his shoulder as she continued,* "Remember Sayid, some of the resistance fighters did not think I could trust you because you're Muslim. They thought I should not trust Eric because he is gay and as for me, well I know a few who question my leadership."

Sayid protested as he interjected, "Catherine all of us would lay down our lives for you. You know I find it strange Catherine that you Christians follow a faith based upon the foundation of grace, which you all claim to receive, and yet so few of your fellow Christians are willing, or they are unable to show that grace to others."

Catherine smiled at Sayid and said, "Truly God has made you wise beyond your years Sayid, it is my earnest prayer that more Christians will come to see that which you have observed. Don't judge them too harshly, living like Christ is no easy task and those few who succeed only do so by the strength and guidance of the Holy Spirit. It is difficult to let people grow in Christ when one is deluded into thinking that they know how this should be achieved."

"Still, you have my loyalty and trust Catherine. I would die to protect you!"

"I know you would Sayid" *She replied as she sighed*, "However, many people feel one cannot be a Christian, a woman and a freedom fighter. They can't trust the pieces, which don't fit together in their own parochial view of the world. I wish they knew how big God is, full of mercy and grace. God is love and so few truly know this love."

Then Catherine noted, "However, I too am disturbed that Captain Roberts found us so easily. I'll ask him exactly how he did it. I'll try to remain objective, but do you remember when your heart was lost to your wife?"

"Yes" *He smiled remembering*. "It was almost instantly."

She put both hands on his shoulders, "Despite yourself, she stole your heart"

Sayid grinned, "Completely."

Catherine smiled as she declared, "Well he has always had mine. Since I first met him he has had that hold, but don't worry, I will guard it none the less. I hold to the scriptures, 'Trust no man, but trust in the LORD your God.' Trust has never come easy to me; I promise I will keep my guard up."

Sayid replied, "I think that would be prudent and I will be watching him."

"As will I." *Jacob stated in his deep powerful voice.*

"Thank you both." *Catherine replied*, "I am confident all will be well."

"Catherine you are insightful and Allah has given you the strength of his arm as well, I just hope you don't make Samson's mistake. *Sayid warned. He continued*, "May Allah continue to smile upon you."

"Thank you Sayid" *Catherine replied as she returned a blessing*, "May God reveal himself to you and all of his truths." *Sayid trusted her, but I knew he didn't have any faith in me. I did not trust him either. I could see his expression change and the distrust appear in his eyes as he acknowledged my presence in the shadows before he marched off.*

"Have I caused any dissension in the ranks Catherine?" *I asked as I emerged from the darkness. The large African American was standing on guard just outside the cave. He remained silent, but I felt his intimidating presence to my right.*

"No!" *She replied with a grin, but I noted a slight furrow of her brow for she realized I must have been listening the entire time. She informed me,* "He is only protective of me and suspicious by nature. He makes a great first officer though."

"So," *I replied,* "If you're Samson, does that make me Delilah?" *She laughed as she took me by the hand and I acknowledged the giant's presence with a nod. He did not return it as Catherine led me to breakfast, with her bodyguard walking closely behind us.*

After our breakfast of eggs and moose-meat sausages she took me to another cave and showed me the suits we would wear for a raid she had been planning with Sayid. "These are the suits you must all wear tonight. " *She informed me* "They're camouflage, specially designed to maintain an external temperature of zero degrees, while your internal body temperature remains normal."

I noted, "These suits are an old model. I haven't used these for over a decade."

Sayid walked in to join us and he informed me. "They will only throw off the heat seeking eyes of the skies if they remained undamaged." *He said this as he firmly placed one against my chest and he warned me,* "So move carefully." *I nodded in agreement and I did not miss his double meaning.*

It was an odd lifestyle I had to get used to, having breakfast after sunset and lunch by moonlight. I used to hate nighttime attacks, but now I was older and much more experienced. I have come to see the darkness as my friend and shadows as a place for solitude.

The night for our raid had come. The darkness enveloped us and only the wolves, coyotes and creatures of the night were on the prowl. Like us they found solace in the black of night, as they too stalked their prey.

Catherine led us to a small computer chip factory at the base of the mountains in Boulder City. We left after breakfast and it took much of the night to come down from the mountains. Just before sunrise she signaled the orders to bed down. We removed our night vision goggles after we dispersed to find adequate cover before the sun rose.

It was only then that I noted neither Catherine, nor Jacob, her giant bodyguard, wore night vision goggles. I swear their eyes appeared to glow. This puzzled me, but I dismissed it for it lasted but an instant. I assumed I was seeing things due to my fatigue.

Catherine found a crevice in the rock. She sat up with her legs tucked into her as she prepared for sleep. Jacob stood on guard above her. He did not sleep. He did not wear a suit like us and he did not require night vision goggles. I did not know why, but it bothered me. I presumed he was so large that there was not a suit that fit him. I could not ask Catherine why he didn't wear the goggles for she did not allow talking on mountain missions, so I took my position beside her and I too prepared to fall asleep.

I could see the whites of Sayid's eyes glaring at me through the darkness. I could not see his face, but I knew it was him. I closed my eyes and slept. It is amazing what conditions a body can sleep in when it is exhausted.

***

We all awoke to the sound of a chopper in the distance. Sayid signaled everyone to stay still as the chopper flew back and forth around the area. We had enough shrubs and rock around us to camouflage our position, and the chopper was unlikely to spot us from the distance it was surveying. I would have to wait until Catherine and I were alone before I could ask her any questions about Jacob; I suspected that the search satellites must have seen his heat signature while they were surveying the area.

We were not permitted to move until sunset. The night was black again as we made our way toward the plant. Catherine said the plant was producing microchips for implanting them in our hands or foreheads. I thought she was nuts for attempting the destruction of the factory, but I was compelled to follow her.

She would not allow me however to enter the perimeter. She said, "I cannot allow you to follow me any further. I only allow believers to fight by my side." *She put her hand on my shoulder as she said,* "There is not much worse than dying for something you don't believe in." *This surprised me for I knew Sayid, although faithful to Catherine was not a believer.*

"Why did you bring me along if I am not going to fight at your side Catherine? I am the best and most highly trained in this squad next to Sayid." *I paced in anger like a lion and then I challenged her,* "Sayid is not a believer either. What is the real reason you won't allow me to fight?"

She pulled me aside and revealed her weakness as her eyes welled up with tears she said to me in hushed tones, "I can't have you fight and die knowing I will never see you again. I can't bear that. It could far too easily destroy me, knowing my decision sent you to your death."

I placed my hands on her shoulders and gazed down upon her beautiful face, I smiled and said,

Catherine I'm a soldier, a fighter, a warrior like you. You cannot, nor should you protect me. As a leader you cannot deny my uses, which could very well lead to the protection of your men. I do not want to die, I want to live a long life, but should I die, I would have it be in an honorable battle." She looked down and I raised her chin and said, "Honestly, if I were any other man would you keep me from this mission?"

"No, no I would not, but you are wrong Peter, I can and I will protect you. Stay by my side."

I smiled, "There is no place else I'd rather be."

Then she ordered, "Alright, everyone move out. You all know what we must do.

At the trainee challenge the other night I noticed Catherine herself and all of her soldiers, with the exception of Sayid and her giant, were branded on their left arm with a Celtic cross. The cross had a banner on it. The banner itself read, 'Jehovanissi' I would ask her later what that meant, nonetheless everyone knew what the cross represented. On their right arm was a Latin phrase, In Luminetuo Videmes Lumen. I only knew a little Latin, but I knew what the motto meant.

We all headed for the warehouse. All of the guards that we had encountered around the perimeter fence had chips detected in them. Catherine had them eliminated swiftly and without remorse. When their chip was detected a green light would blink on our gunsight. The soldier closest to the guard would sneak up behind and slit their throat before they were even aware of our presence. We only fired our weapons when necessary.

We silently approached the side of the gate to the enclosure. Eric had some sort of handheld hacking device. He managed to disarm the alarms with little effort. We made our way undetected through open yard.

Our suits were so well camouflaged that you would have to be expecting us to even see a glimpse of us. *We waited in the shadows by an entrance to the plant. Sayid said,* "Eric what is taking you so long? Are you slipping man? "

"Give me a break Sayid, this code is a series of eighteen characters. Who has an eighteen digit code?"

I noticed a sentry draw near. Sayid noticed him too and we both hid ourselves in the entryway. I silently motioned to Sayid who surprised the guard and broke his neck swiftly and I helped him drag his body toward Eric. I held the guard's hand up near the panel that Eric was working on. The door slowly opened before us. Eric sighed and shook his head. I shrugged my shoulders and patted him on the back as I stalked past him. The factory was shut down for the night and we could detect no one else inside.

Eric and Catherine followed in behind me and Sayid laughed quietly while he whispered, "Don't worry Eric; the rest should be easy enough, come along boy." *Eric followed in behind Jacob. We set many explosive charges with timers on the equipment as well as on the boxes ready for shipping.*

Catherine motioned for Eric and I to follow her to one of the offices. "Eric, can you hack into this computer?"

He tilted his head with a smirk and did not even reply as he made his way to the desk, to determine which operating system it used. He said, "I have to go to the server room first; do we have time?"

She replied, "The timers are preset, I can't change that. You have sixteen minutes." *Eric ran to a room that was surrounded by glass and full of computers.*

He waved to us to come over, when we got there he said, "I'm in, what do you need?"

Catherine smiled, "I need to know two things, first is their system interconnected with other factories?"

"Yes, but not from here." *He smiled back at her knowingly.*

"Can you write a subroutine, or a worm, or virus to bring them all down, every single one of them?"

"Once I get in to the actual facility, yes. It is a secure network so I have to physically be on sight and security will be extremely tight Catherine, but I would need time to write it."

"Hmmm, where is the facility you have to get into?" *Catherine patiently waited for his reply.*

Eric took a moment and then said, "It will be difficult. There are two, one is in Langley and the other is in Geneva."

Catherine patted his shoulder, "You're right Eric it won't be easy. Time's up, everyone move out." *Everybody moved swiftly at her command. Unlike many women's voices Catherine's was deeper more forceful than most. It was confident and controlled when she gave her orders, but when she spoke in private conversations it was sultrier and low, but still the voice of a woman. Her voice, like her demeanor, commanded respect and obedience.*

We reached the outside of the compound as the last of the unit was returning, and there were a series of explosions and we made our way back toward the mountains. We left by a different route than we came. The base camp had been moved and we rendezvoused with the rest of our encampment three days later.

I sat silently by the fire as Catherine approached me, "I'm sorry I could not inform you earlier." *She said as she sat down. She continued*, "We move often; when you found the camp we had to move quickly again. Satellites tend to ignore single people walking around in the country, but not in the mountains. In the country the government presumes it is simply a farmer, but only those whom the government deems to be rebels or traitors tromp about the mountains."

"Plus you would surely raise suspicion if you are being tracked and your heat signature disappeared as you entered camp." *Eric, her tech added.*

"The chopper was looking for us the day of our attack, and after tonight we will move again. After the destruction of the factory they will double their efforts to find us" *Sayid added as he sat down.*

"The time has come to decide if you want to stay for good, or go." *Sayid told me. I made no reply as Catherine informed me that I had until tomorrow night to make up my mind.*

"What about my report to President Davidson?" *I questioned* "Catherine, I told you he wants an alliance. I need to give him your answer, but you have not told me what it is yet."

"If he wants to join forces he'll have to do it our way." *Sayid stated.*

Catherine interjected, "How do you communicate with him?"

I replied, "Through the Internet. We piggy-back encoded messages through the library database and other public transmissions."

"Well I hate most technology; I'm pretty much ignorant when it comes to using it, so this is what you are going to do," *She said as she put her arm around Eric,* "you are going to teach Eric everything he needs to know." *I nodded in agreement.* "You will inform the president that we will support his resistance, but we want a meeting with the leaders of the resistance, all at once"

Then Jacob added, "Tell your president that if he betrays us or if the meeting is a trap, I will destroy them all. Not one of them will survive."

I believed Jacob could follow through on that threat too, but I responded to Catherine, "That is a dangerous meeting indeed Catherine, what if Augustus finds out? The resistance could be wiped out."

She smiled, "Then I will pray Augustus does not find out."

We listened to the BBC on a battery-operated transistor radio that night and then Eric, Sayid, and

Catherine went to her cave to converse. I continued to listen to the news. Australia had suffered for decades from holes in the ozone layer, in conjunction with pollution of their fresh water lakes as far back as in the 1980's. "Well, all the Alka-Seltzer in the world could not save their lakes now." *I said to myself. Their lakes had heated high temperatures due to the combination of increased pollution and the prolonged drought that they had been suffering. This resulted in their fresh water fish being suffocated. Regardless of how it happened, fish were found floating all over Australia on the surface of the water. Their coral reefs were also dying due to the rising temperatures as well.*

The radio journalist announced, "Pandemic is breaking out all over Western Europe today as the International Health board announces their inability to treat the Parisian Flu."

Just as Catherine returned from her meeting she sat down to listen to the rest of the news with me. "Raphael Augustus forbids cross continental travel, in his feeble attempt to isolate the spread of this fatal disease." *I informed her.*

Catherine turned the radio off, "I'm sick of all this sad news, I think the camp needs a revival." *We set off to join the soldiers sitting around the fire beneath our giant camouflage canopy. Just then Mary, Sayid's wife began to quote from the bible.*

"And Jesus answering, said to them: Take heed that no man seduce you:
For many will come in my name saying, I am Christ: and they will seduce many.
And you shall hear of wars and rumors of wars. See that ye be not troubled.

For these things must come to pass, but the end is not yet. For nation shall rise against nation and kingdom against kingdom; and there shall be pestilence, and famines, and earthquakes in places:
Now all these are the beginnings of sorrows.

Then shall they deliver you up to be afflicted, and shall put you to death: and you shall be hated by all nations for my name's sake. And then shall many be scandalized: and shall betray one another: and shall hate one another. And many false prophets shall rise, and shall seduce many.

And because iniquity hath abounded, the charity of many shall grow cold. But he that shall persevere to the end, he shall be saved."

Catherine got up quite shaken. I was going to follow her, but Sayid held my arm as he said, "Leave her be, she'll be back soon." *Her giant however followed.*

"What upset her so much?" *I inquired, as I was quite perplexed by her tears.*

Sayid told me a story and all the soldiers had sadly confirmed it to be true. "A while back, shortly after she found her brother, James neglected to heed Catherine's warnings, he believed that Christ had returned."

Sayid put his hand on his forehead rubbing it back and forth as he continued, "He came up to her one night emerging from the shadows where we slept. He excitedly told Catherine, 'Jesus has returned Cathy.' Catherine sat up startled and with a look of disbelief. He continued emphatically insisting, 'He is in the mountains just outside the city, healing thousands who were injured in the war. Take me to him Catherine. Please I can't make it there on my own.'"

Sayid found it difficult to continue as he uttered softly, "I'll never forget that night, or the ones to follow."

Sayid said this with shame and then he continued, "'No James!' Catherine replied firmly and then she softened her voice as if she were speaking to a child, 'Please trust me James. He is not the Christ. Do not be led astray.'

'Cathy, I have to go. He can heal me!' James argued, but he could see by the resolute look on her face that she would not take him. She left us then to go and pray.

James pleaded, 'Sayid you can take me, you have to. Please!'

Then my wife said with the deepest look of concern in her eyes, 'Sayid you can't go.' but I had enough of living like a rat in these mountains, so I agreed to take him." *Sayid looked so mournful as he told this tale.*

I looked with surprise at Sayid; after all he was Catherine's most devoted soldier. "I know." *Sayid continued*, "But you must understand I was not yet a believer and this way of life had made my love for my wife grow cold."

Sayid *continued the story*. "I left that night, carrying James down the mountainside toward the city. We followed the river for much of the night. I fell several times, exhausted and thinking I could carry him no further. Then I met a group of pilgrims searching for this Christ. The leader ordered a man of faith to carry James for me. After regaining my strength I followed them at a distance. By the time the sun began to rise we reached the sight of this healer. I collapsed beneath an evergreen as I witnessed this man emerge from the shadows of a cave."

Sayid stared into the firelight where I swore I detected fear in his eyes and his hands began to tremble as he recalled, "He was a very strange sight. He wore a well-tailored suit with a collarless shirt and white vest, which shimmered in the light of the rising sun. His hair was black as the night and on his eyes he wore dark black glasses. When he spoke his voice was filled with a power of a rushing wind, which was only amplified by the surrounding mountains."

Sayid held his wife's hand firmly, as if to summon courage as he continued the tale. "The man in the suit announced, 'Welcome my children, bow before me and I will fulfill your deepest desires.' One by one I saw men and women coming before him, summoned by his command and reaching toward his healing hands. Stewards of this prince of darkness ushered them forward like drones, where they all started falling on their knees, bowing before him, as they were able."

I noted a tear run down Sayid's face as he continued the tale. "He did heal the sick, the blind and the lame, but I shrank back in fear, as I saw their souls being sucked from their earthly bodies, like a dark mist and enter his mouth. Then I witnessed a red mist fill each person who genuflected before him. Those who bowed down let out and evil cry of laughter, as the red mists gained entry into their human host. I knew in that moment that demons were rejoicing at gaining corporeal form.

With each new soul I witnessed his pale skin becoming transformed into a healthy color. With each healing his brilliance and power appeared to grow. I ran away in fear, in desperation, and in despair. I delivered James to his eternal demise."

Mary gave her husband's hand a squeeze and rubbed her hand up and down his back as he continued this horrific tale. "I hid in the mountains crying and despising my own wretched and weak nature. I hid like this lost and alone for three days, and then in a dream an angel appeared to me and told me to return to Catherine. I obeyed without delay, I returned to her that very night. Still, I was soulfully sorrowful and deeply ashamed."

"I returned to Catherine on the third night and before I confessed to her my sin she said, "My brother is gone, his body is healed and a demon now resides inside him."

It was at that moment that I knew she was a warrior of Allah. I begged her forgiveness and Allah's forgiveness too. After I received it I pledged my allegiance to her forever. She told me to pledge it to the Father, the Son and the Holy Ghost, to Elohim and no one else, especially a mortal."

"I was not yet ready to pledge my life to Elohim, the one known as the Lord God, Almighty One. I did however begin to search for Him more earnestly than ever before." *Sayid concluded his story as Catherine emerged from the shadows holding the giant's hand and then she sat between us as she placed a hand on my shoulder and said,* "Peter, you are not the only one who has yet to believe, but I believe you will both come into the light."

I did not know what to make of Sayid's story, but I could not fathom such a thing occurring. I had witnessed many soldiers over the years claim to witness many strange things but my eyes, though seeing great evil done by men and women across the globe, had never witnessed the spiritual. I believed that Sayid was sincere in his experience, but insane asylums and the city streets are filled with deranged people who believe they too have witnessed such things. Regardless something in his sharing led me to distrust him less as my ingrained suspicion of him gave way to what, I did not know.

Then Catherine led us in some prayer and songs, which rang out through the darkness, as they found warmth and fellowship by the fire's light. I smiled as I watched Catherine singing joyfully beside me. Her radiance grew with each song sung. I was with them, but I did not share in their singing. Still, I took pleasure in that moment, as I listened to Catherine sing with them. She had the voice of an angel herself.

I was not one of them, but I had sensed that Sayid's attitude softened somewhat toward me since he shared his experience, or at least he no longer glared at me through the darkness. Perhaps I had misjudged him, and he had me. Years of war made us paranoid and distrustful, but hatred could not easily survive in Catherine's presence.

After everyone dispersed we were alone in her cave and I said, "Sayid is very loyal to you, as are all of your troops."

"Yes and no," *She replied and then she explained,* "Sayid is my right hand, he would lay down his life for me, and Jacob is beyond reproach, there is no one I trust more, but only my inner circle is loyal to me. The rest of the troops are loyal to Sayid. They're his recruits, including his former seal team."

"Seal team! I take it back I am not the best trained here next to Sayid.*" I was impressed.*

Catherine poured me some wine and asked very seriously, "Who are you loyal to, Peter? Are you loyal to the president, or me?"

I answered, "I'm here under his orders Catherine, and he is my commander-in- chief."

She seemed pleased that I answered honestly and then she asked firmly, "How did you come to find the camp Peter?*" Her laughter and bliss from before had disappeared and now she questioned me with intensity in her eyes that told me that she was now playing the role of commander.*

"I heard rumors in Aspen." *I replied to her inquisition.* "The whole city was talking about you. Whenever they arrest the zealots or those resisting the World Federation They're tortured and broken. The underground also shares the news along various lines of communications. I traveled alone in the wilderness for four weeks looking for you. I already told you I was under orders from the president himself to find you. After reaching the higher elevations I found myself too cold to sleep during the nights. I slept longer and longer under the warmth of the sun by day. Finally one night I saw a light like fire burning in the distance of a mountain. I followed it along the river bank, which led me to you."

"Well if you found me on foot the enemy can too. Thank you Peter, the sun will be rising soon, get some sleep. I have some work to do." *She said this gently as she patted my hand. I held it for a moment and kissed it. She grinned and said,* "I have to go." *Then she bent down and kissed my lips, and softly ordered,* "Get some sleep." *With that Catherine left me in the darkness, as the last embers of the fire in her cave faded and the first rays of sun peaked over the mountain ridge.*

I sat alone in the shadows of a rock contemplating my future. I could not foresee what my destiny was, but I was compelled to believe that the fates had placed me in Catherine's hand. I still had some suspicions of Sayid and Jacob, as they probably did of me as well, but they were beginning to diminish. I hoped Catherine would learn to trust me, but I did not trust her god. How could I trust in a god who allowed so much darkness to prevail? I suspected there was more to Catherine's story than she was telling me, but I was left alone with my suspicions in the darkness.

Chapter Ten:
A Traitor in Our Midst

The following evening Catherine ordered a complete dispersion of the camp. Catherine told me, "A large force could not manage another winter in the mountains without a substantial supply of food and water, and a sufficient amount of heat. The nights are already far too cold."

Small groups could survive, but large ones were impractical. Everyone was divided into groups of no more than seven men and women. Catherine gave her troops the order, "Head for the lowland forests and to stay out of sight. There is no more we can do together until the winter passes. Go with God." *Everyone in the group hugged, each other, save me and Jacob. We stood like sentries on either side of Catherine. After the last goodbyes we headed off in separate directions.*

Her followers never questioned her, they simply obeyed. Perhaps they were accustomed to her sudden change in directions but I was not, so I asked her, "Why did you ask me if I was going to join you if your troops were going to be separating from the camp so quickly after my arrival?"

She apologized, "I'm sorry, but the future is not always for us to see." *This did not give me any explanation at all. She simply ordered me,* "Take the rest of us to see the president of the United States."

I agreed, "Alright, but first tell me who is Jacob; what does he mean to you? I'm tired of being left in the dark." *I understood Sayid's allegiance to Catherine and I assumed Jacob was her personal bodyguard, but I needed to be sure there was nothing more. He was overwhelmingly protective of her and they spent much time alone.*

"I am her guardian..." *The large African American spoke, but he was stopped mid-sentence as I noted a look of warning from Catherine which nearly silenced him. He stood before me and I noted how he appeared to choose his words carefully. His voice was gentle and deep as he continued,* "Catherine is in my charge and it is my sole responsibility to protect her from harm."

He offered nothing more and Catherine informed me as to why she had suddenly decided to meet with the president, "Last night I had a dream of an American and Canadian flag waving in the wind, one was in your hand, the other in mine." *I thought she was crazy for allowing a dream to dictate her course of actions but I said nothing, since this enabled me to fulfill my mission for the president, while remaining at her side.*

I felt a pain in my divided heart between doing my duty and longing to remain with the woman I had so often dreamed of. I did not know if the president would want me to stay with him, or allow me to stay with Catherine acting as a liaison.

I was perplexed by her initial response to my arrival and her apparent refusal to spend time with me privately now. She never said anything about the matter she simply spent more time with Jacob in prayer and when she was at camp she was working with Eric and training physically with Sayid.

She often worked while I slept, but at least I could join her in the physical training. She was good for me. I have never been this fit. I knew she was better than I on many levels, but Sayid and Catherine made me push myself, harder and faster than I ever could if I were training alone. We sprinted up and down a mountain trail several times prior to sunset. Initially I thought my lungs would burst. The air was so thin up high, but as the months passed I also ran the mountain with ease, I even gave Catherine a run for her money.

I was elated as I inquired, "Wow, What's changed? I no longer have to struggle to keep up with you two."

Sayid smiled, "We train up high and our lungs double in size. We can take in two and some of us like

Catherine, three to four times as much oxygen as a normal human who trains at lower altitudes."

I raised an eyebrow and she laughed when I said, "I feel invincible."

Catherine put her arm around me and said, "Just wait until we go to sea-level for a mission. You will be able to run farther and faster than you can imagine. You will feel like you can run all out at your top speed forever. Then you will know what invincibility feels like."

Jacob reminded us, "Just remember, you are all mortal, no matter how you feel."

Sayid said, "Yah, yah big guy, don't worry, but Roberts, you're gonna love the feeling. It is quite a rush."

Jacob shook his head and sighed and we laughed together. I treasured these times with Catherine, even Sayid and Jacob grew on me, however I missed spending time alone with her. Every day after training we made our way toward our meeting location with the president.

I didn't know why Catherine did not spend much time alone with me, but I assumed it was because of her duties. She had to fulfill her responsibilities and protect her followers. This must have come into conflict with her desires for companionship. I suspected her faith divided us as well. I remembered Edward telling me that believers could not become unequally yoked with unbelievers. This angered me and I resented it, but I respected her faith. It gave her a strength and conviction others lacked, still I missed her free spirit and I longed for her to lay in my arms once again.

Our troop arrived in Utah and made our way carefully toward Salt Lake City where we waited to hear from the president. I took Catherine, Eric, Sayid, and Jacob out one night and we met with the president's men. Jason and Mary had to stay away in seclusion, since neither of them had any military training. We could not risk bringing them on any of our missions. The president's men brought us to a secret rendezvous. The president wanted to meet with Catherine privately, but none of us would leave her side.

We reached the meeting place that was an abandoned farm on the outskirts of town. The president announced, "Welcome Ms. Miles. It is an honor to finally meet you in person. I have heard glowing reviews of you from Captain Roberts."

Catherine took his hand and shook it, "President Davidson, you may call me Catherine."

"Alright Catherine," *He replied and continued,* "It appears that you and I are fighting on the same side. I too am a Christian and I intend to do everything in my power to fight the evil dictator that is trying to rule this world. Americans, Canadians, Chinese, French, Japanese and a select number of Russian cells have made plans for strategic attacks against our common enemy."

President Davidson was in a precarious situation. His power was limited by Augustus and his forces, but Americans still acknowledged him as their chosen leader. Augustus was a dictator who forced his influence upon the United States from afar. Few Americans supported the new order, but hunger, thirst and peace superseded the desire for freedom and independence as a nation.

Throughout the winter in the fourth year of Augustus' reign, the president was forced to become a ruler in exile, like Bourbon of France. Both the French president and our own had to remain in hiding from the world dictator. My commander and chief made his way to an undisclosed location in Canada while we continued to attack a series of targets. The resistance had little resources and I had little hope, however some distant dream of democracy compelled me to not give up.

Catherine was especially driven. She had been working with Eric for months and her plan was ready for implementation. She sent secret communiqués through me to the president, She informed him at our meeting in Utah, "I want to meet with all the of resistance leaders at once. We have a sure-fire plan to cripple our enemy."

"I think that would be too dangerous and too difficult to arrange Catherine. You don't know what you are asking." *The president replied.*

Catherine declared, "I am not asking, this is not a request. Bourbon is hiding out in the Appalachian region; you and I are already here. The leaders of the Chinese, Russian and Japanese cells can teleconference in if they can't get here, but I am confident they can arrive within three months. I will implement my plan with, or without you. I would prefer if we worked together, but I don't have time for petty politics or maneuvering. We will meet in three months' time and then we will implement the plan."

Catherine turned to leave. President Davidson did not know how to respond. He was not used to being spoken to in such a way, but Catherine did not care for diplomacy or small talk. The president pleaded, "Ms. Miles, Catherine, I will see what I can arrange, but you give me little time. Augustus controls all world travel and telecommunications."

Catherine responded with a slight edge of impatience in her tone, "You have one week to let me know if they are willing to meet and three months to have them here; it is more than enough time, Mr. President."

She began to walk away again and the president added, "I'm grateful you journeyed this far to see me, but if you are able to sacrifice a little more time I would like to talk to Captain Roberts alone."

She obviously did not fully trust the president, but she looked at me and said quietly in my ear, "Peter, do you want to stay with me, or go with him?"

"Do I have to answer that?" *She gave me a look that demanded a response so I assured her,* "I want to be with you, you should know that." *She gave me a slight grin barely detectable, but her eyes showed her pleasure in my response.*

"Then may I speak my mind with him and act as your commander in this?" *She had a coy look in her eye.*

"As you wish." *I replied and she turned to face the president.*

"President Davidson, why do you need to speak to the captain privately?"

He responded, "Oh, well I just wanted to give him further orders."

Catherine announced, "He will be coming with me. He will continue to act as a liaison between us if you wish."

President Davidson replied, "Yes, that was exactly what I was planning to inform him of."

"Good, then our meeting is finished. You may inform us later of when and where the meeting will take place." *With that she turned and left and we followed behind with Jacob and I walking on either side of her, Eric holding the door in front of her and Sayid close behind.*

I was ordered via email to stay at Catherine's side and keep the president fully informed. I was also ordered to continue to record everything in writing and keep a journal while on this assignment. I felt like I was betraying Catherine. I failed to protect Edward, probably the only real father figure she had ever known, and now I betrayed her by secretly keeping a journal and reporting to the president. My duty and circumstance always seemed to keep me from being truly honest with the woman I longed to love.

Through the course of many months we attacked a number of microchip factories on both sides of the 49th parallel. Eventually we had no more installations left to destroy; all those in our vicinity had been destroyed.

Catherine had acclaim among the resistance leaders and the president informed me that every one of them would be at the meeting. I believe they simply had to meet the legend for themselves. Within three days of our first meeting, the final details had been arranged. We were meeting at a private chalet just outside of Aspen in the late spring.

Catherine's inner circle kept up a daily training regimen. All through the winter we ran through deep snow and made our way up the mountainside. I thought training in the summer was difficult, but running in snow was extremely challenging. Few things in all my years of training were this difficult. Come spring I was the fastest, the strongest and the most fit that I had ever been in my life.

The winter passed quickly and Catherine came up to me one night and asked, "Peter I asked you this question once many months ago and I will only ask it one more time and never again. I need to know if your loyalties have changed. Where does your first loyalty lie, with the president or with me?"

"I took her in my arms and replied, "Months ago I said that I would always be a soldier first and a man second. That has changed.*" I kissed her softly and she returned that kiss passionately and then she pulled away, but I would not let her go, I pulled her closer and I added,* "You have my heart, you have my service and you have my undying loyalty." *She kissed me so passionately that I thought she would lose control. I sensed she wanted to, but she forced herself to pull away again.*

She smiled and said, "I have to be careful Peter, you are my kryptonite."

I grinned and replied, "Well, at least you did not call me Delilah."

She laughed and then said, "Seriously Peter, you are my only qualified officer who is trained in military strategy. For my plan to succeed I need you to help plan and coordinate our attack against Augustus. I'm trusting you. I need you."

I loved hearing those words, even though it was not the context I wanted to hear them in, regardless I replied, "You can trust me Catherine, I won't let you down." *Following that we went to meet with Eric and Sayid and go over the plans.*

The mountain snows had started to diminish. The meeting date had arrived and we made our way down the mountain. We were the last to reach our destination. We were watching from the forest until everyone was identified via Eric's facial recognition software. The Chinese came by helicopter and the Russians pulled up in a hummer. The Japanese walked out of the forest like us and they were in the house only for a couple of minutes before Catherine received word that the perimeter was secured.

Eric reported, "It appears that everyone has arrived and there are no other uninvited guests, only the leaders and their personal security guards."

Sayid declared, "I will keep watch; you four go ahead. I have some of our troops stationed along the mountain road. I will tell you immediately if anyone else decides to make an appearance."

Catherine smiled and we made our way around the back of the house through the forest. We all emerged from the forest together, with the exception of Sayid. Some of the leaders were gathered in the kitchen and saw us walking toward them and crossing the lawn. The president walked out to welcome us, "Catherine, I'm so glad you made it. Everyone is awaiting your arrival with great anticipation."

Catherine shook his hand, but she did not return his smile. The president led us inside and announced, "Let me introduce you to everyone."

Catherine interrupted, "There is no need, President Davidson; we all know each other. Does anyone object to having this meeting on the deck, outside?"

The Japanese rebel leader, Hideki Yamamoto replied first, "I believe that is a wise decision."

The president interjected, "Now everyone, our drinks and food are already set up. Please sit down."

Yamamoto moved toward the door and held it open for Catherine as he bowed to her. She smiled and bowed lower to him. Jacob followed her and all of the other leaders followed behind them.

Yamamoto pulled out a chair for Catherine at a round table on the deck, "Domo Arigato Mister Yamamoto."

He smiled, "Please call me Hideki, and what would you like me to address you as Ms. Miles."

"Catherine is fine." She replied.

Everybody sat except for Bourbon who brought Catherine a glass of French Merlot. He leaned over and asked, "May I give you a glass of wine Catherine? It is from my homeland in France."

Catherine took a moment to enjoy the bouquet and then she took a sip and held it in her mouth and then delicately swallowed as she said to him in French, "Merci beaucoup Monsieur le President, Merlot est mon favorite. Comment saviez-vous?"

He smiled and replied, "Your most welcome mademoiselle. I did not know it was your favorite, but you have exquisite taste, it is my favorite as well."

She smiled at him and she won him over immediately. Catherine was sitting at a table where all of the leaders were men and Catherine had them mesmerized, with the exception of President Davidson and the Chinese leaders.

Catherine ordered Eric, "Begin the sweep." *He nodded and went back into the house to scan for listening devices.*

The Russian leader said, "Catherine is an exceptional name. I see you too have the adoration of many men like your Russian namesake."

"Catherine the Great, You flatter me Yuri."

"Yuri nodded to her; I only speak the truth of what I witnessed." *He replied.*

Catherine noted, "An honest man with a brave heart, your reputation precedes you Yuri. From what I hear you have many female devotees who have risked their lives to hide you from authorities as well."

Yuri and the French president laughed out loud and then the Chinese leader spoke, "Well Catherine, your reputation is reaching historic status. You are much smaller than I expected."

"I am no smaller than your own personal bodyguards President Chang. I hear that one of them is the best martial artist in the world." *Catherine looked directly at his bodyguard. He bowed his head acknowledging the compliment; Catherine returned it ever so slightly.*

Chang responded, "Yes he is the best, we must all protect ourselves. We live in very dangerous times."

"Yes we do." *Catherine agreed and continued,* "That is why our attack must be coordinated with the utmost secrecy and precision."

Eric returned, "Catherine you were right, the chalet is bugged in both the kitchen and in the living room."

"What about out here?" *Chang inquired.*

Eric replied, "It is clean, but there is a traitor in our midst."

"That is not surprising." *Chang replied,* "These are treacherous times."

Catherine remained calm and in control as she said, "I am not surprised either, I expected this. Captain Roberts is giving everyone a secret set of instructions concerning your cells and your role in our attack. You may communicate with me through the contact information provided." *I passed out the sealed envelope with the instructions to each rebel leader as Catherine continued,* "Just let me know if you are in or you are out. Then I will know if we can proceed as planned in crippling the dictator Augustus. Please do not open them until you are safely away from this place, and please do not inform one another as to your directives."

She stood up and walked toward Eric so that none of the other leaders could see her face as she said, "Eric and I are the only two aware of the entire plan." *Then she turned toward the leaders and continued,* "Thus, even if some of you are betrayed the others will still succeed."

Hideki Yamamoto looked at Catherine with approval and they all stood up and prepared to depart. Catherine then got word from Sayid through the RF device she carried, "An army truck filled with soldiers is making its way up the mountain. Abort meeting. I repeat: Abort meeting."

Catherine responded, "What is their ETA?"
Sayid replied, "five minutes."

"Intercept and destroy" *Catherine took command,* "Gentlemen if you will follow me, we must leave immediately. My troops will succeed in eliminating the first truck, filled with soldiers coming up those mountains, but more will likely follow. You cannot return the way you came, so please follow me."

Chang said, "I can take the Russians and the Japanese I have a stealth helicopter."

Catherine looked impressed and then she requested, "I may need Yuri and his men. Would you mind taking President Bourbon and President Davidson instead."

"As you wish Catherine, but I cannot take the presidents with their entourage and Yamamoto as well, there is not enough room."

*Yamamoto said, "*We will go with Catherine and ensure you all get away safely."

Everyone nodded in agreement. Sayid reported as we made our way from the house, "Catherine our guns will not fire, we cannot detect a chip. Several men had the soldiers in their sights and no chip was detected, I repeat we are unable to fire, no chip is detected."

"ETA."

"Three minutes*" Sayid replied.*

Catherine spoke calmly, "Gentlemen our soldiers' guns are unable to fire; they only shoot if a microchip is detected. These soldiers have none. All of Augustus' forces have them, but for some reason these men do not. My men cannot intercept them. We can run for the forest, but they will track us down quickly. I believe we may have to engage them in battle here. Suggestions?"

Yuri spoke, "You need weapons? I have weapons. Come quickly!" We made our way to the back of Yuri's black hummer. He opened a case full of semi-automatic weapons."

"Beautiful" *I said as Yuri handed them out to us. He was giving one to Catherine when Sayid ran toward us from the security of the forest. Yuri aimed his gun at Sayid and was about to fire when Catherine moved with lighting fast speed and disarmed Yuri.*

Yuri looked at her with shock as she said, "He's with me."

She gave Sayid her weapon and Sayid said aloud, "One minute until they arrive."

Yamamoto said, "These men will be in body armor and they are difficult to kill, but they are poorly armored in the neck and the mouth, where the face shield ends."

Yuri added, "Very small target yes, we have faced such forces before in Russia, but these guns have excellent accuracy."

Catherine ordered, "Alright everyone take cover." *We all managed to find cover as the troop truck came around the last bend in the road.*

Catherine had climbed up to a barn loft and waited by a window with Jacob and I. Eric had a sniper's rifle and made his way to the top bedroom of the chalet. Yuri set up behind his hummer with two of his men.

I did not see where Yamamoto and his two men had gone, they moved swiftly and silently, but we were all prepared for the ambush. The truck pulled up below our position in the barn.

There were eleven of us all together and Catherine ordered the rest of her troops to hold to the forest, should more troops arrive. As the truck pulled up bellow us we could see two men in the front, the driver and one soldier riding shotgun. Catherine ordered, "Eric and Peter you two cover us. Jacob and I will take out the two in front."

Eric replied, "Roger that Catherine, I got you covered"

"I will lay down cover fire from here as well." *I said, then I kissed her and whispered,* "Be careful."

She smiled and both she and Jacob jumped out the window. Catherine jumped on to the roof of the truck and Jacob landed on top of the soldier riding in the passenger seat, as he stepped out of the vehicle. Jacob crushed the man with his weight and before the soldier could rise Jacob bent down and snapped his neck. Catherine moved like a panther and swung over the side of the truck onto the driver's side and as he was about to get out Catherine slammed the door on him and pinned him. As he reached for his handgun with his free hand, Catherine used her knife and slit his throat.

Soldiers had started to file out of the back of the vehicle two at a time; Yamamoto's men took out the first two before they hit the ground. Two more behind them started firing in the direction the shots had come from. Meanwhile the side flaps on either side of the vehicle lifted and suddenly about thirty men, all the size of Jacob were making their way off the vehicle. I took one down closest to Jacob and Eric took out one closest to Catherine. Yuri's men opened fire as well. They had excellent precision and I saw three more soldiers fall before they could even leave the back of the truck.

By now the soldiers began firing back at us in all directions. They were excellent marksmen as well. I saw Eric take out another soldier, but he took some serious enemy fire after that. He did not return fire anymore, so he had either moved or was down.

Sayid emerged from the barn below us and shot one of the soldiers at close range and then he prepared to engage another in hand-to-hand combat. Sayid was an exceptional fighter, he managed to defend himself well, but these men were bigger, stronger and faster. One of them was about to break Sayid's neck when a bullet went through the soldier's head. Sayid nodded to Yuri for saving his life then picked up a weapon and disappeared from view.

Yamamoto's men had changed position and they were now firing from a different location. I saw them each take out three different enemy soldiers. Yamamoto and his men were small, but they were very fast. I lost sight of them.

I estimated that there were eight to twelve of enemy combatants left. Catherine and Jacob were fighting two of them in hand-to-hand combat; meanwhile Sayid had begun fighting with another, using his knife. Catherine and Sayid used their knives in battle, while Jacob required no weapon to take them on. He was his own fighting force. Sayid and Catherine both managed to slice their opponent enough to disable them but for some reason they did not finish the kill. They both turned to face the same opponent when the man Sayid disabled pulled out a handgun and was going to shoot Sayid. I shot him before he could fire.

Yamamoto shot another of Augustus' men. Two had reached the house and were making their way inside, while another two provided cover keeping Yuri and his men pinned down.

I signaled to Catherine that I had to go and make my way to the house and see if Eric was okay. I started to turn away from the window when in my peripheral vision I saw that one of Augustus' men leaped from the hood of the truck and into the open window of the loft. A gunshot just flew passed his head. He then kicked me across the length of the loft before I could get a shot off. I was shocked at how hard his kick was. If I were quick enough to block it I would have broken my arms. I was thankful for our body armored suits, and a soft hay landing.

Later I had learned that one of Yamamoto's men saw the soldier jump from the truck. He sprinted across the open ground and jumped with ease onto the hood of the truck, then to the top of it and then sprang up into the barn as well. He did not make a clean jump, but his hands grabbed a hold of the sill and he pulled himself into the room. I saw him stand before the soldier with his handgun pointing at him. The giant swiftly turned with his weapon aimed at the Japanese warrior.

To my surprise the giant said in a thick Austrian accent, "Hey little man, would you like to see how good you really are."

Yamamoto's man smiled and nodded. They both put their handguns down. The Japanese man bowed and the giant nodded in return. They began to engage in hand-to-hand combat; meanwhile I pulled myself up and stepped towards the combatants, ready to help my ally only to discover it was not necessary.

The giant was fast and strong, but Yamamoto's man was faster and more agile. The Japanese martial artist avoided almost every hit and redirected the force away from him. The giant said, "You are very good, little man."

"Are you toying with me?" replied the Japanese warrior. The giant laughed as he began to circle like a boxer. They had very different fighting styles. The Japanese fighter was quick with a flurry of rapid strikes and redirections, whereas the giant waited for a swift, but deadly punch or kick. I think the Austrian was accustomed to easier opponents in the past and he seemed to relish in the opportunity to face a worthy adversary.

I could not stay; I had to check on Eric. I saw my rifle on the ground level. It had flown from my hand when I was kicked. I made my way down from the loft and picked up my weapon.

I left through the back of the barn, and as I passed by I shot one of the soldiers who was firing toward Yuri. The second soldier turned to fire at me as I sprinted by them. As he turned toward me one of the Russians killed him. I continued to run toward the house, and the Russians fell in behind me.

We got in the house and we made our way upstairs. We heard a single gunshot and then silence. When we arrived at the top of the stairs there was a soldier standing in the hall, aiming his gun into a bedroom. All of us opened fire immediately; Yuri and I dropped low, while his men stood tall and fired their weapons over us. The giant guard had so much body armor that we didn't take him down despite the amount of shots he was taking. As he turned his weapon on us however, Eric shot him in the neck from inside the room and he finally fell to his death.

I rushed to Eric's side, He had already minimized the bleeding from a gunshot wound and he said, "It is shot through and through." *Eric grimaced as he continued,* "I will be alright, but that brute shot me in the leg, before he aimed at you."

I looked down at another soldier who lay bleeding on the bedroom floor. Damn Eric was a good shot. I said, "You did good kid." *Despite his pain, Eric beamed with pride. He was small and slight and he could be no older than twenty-five, but he had faced the strongest of men and won. I tended his wound and said,* "We have to get you out of here. More will be coming."

The largest of Yuri's Russian guards said, "I will carry him."

I heard a helicopter in the distance and I ran to look out the window. I saw Jacob, Sayid and Catherine running across the yard. I looked over the horizon and I saw the helicopter coming towards them and firing its guns. They were targets in the open and the tracer bullets were homing in on their position when suddenly the Chinese chopper appeared behind it and shot it out of the sky with a missile strike.

We made our way downstairs and congregated near Yuri's truck and I heard Yuri compliment Catherine and she said, "You didn't do so bad yourself Yuri, your vehicle is a little dented, but you and your men are unscathed."

Yuri patted his vehicle and said, "Bullet proof."

I interrupted, "We have to get out of here more will be coming soon."

Sayid said, "Two more trucks are making their way up the mountains, filled with more soldiers. Shall I order our troops to use the sticky bombs?"

"Do it." *Catherine replied and Sayid relayed the order.*

I said, "Catherine we must hurry, air support will not be far behind and we don't have the necessary equipment to stop them."

"Yes we do" *Yuri opened another compartment in his Hummer and revealed two Rocket launchers. Yuri gave me and Eric a wink. The giant Russian put Eric down. He took one rocket launcher and gave Jacob the other.*

I put Eric over my shoulders in a fireman's carry, and we began to run toward the forest when we saw two explosions. Sayid announced, "Both vehicles were destroyed; our troops are retreating to the forest."

Seconds later two fighter planes raced toward us shooting their nose mounted machine guns, and Jacob and Yuri's man shot them both from the sky. Yuri yelled something in Russian at the flaming wreckage, then turned to us and said "I don't think they were expecting such a hot reception!" *Yuri chuckled at his own joke as the big men reloaded and sprinted to follow us into the forest. A chopper came up behind us as we reached the woods and Yuri's man fired his rocket launcher again and took out the chopper. He said,* "We only have one more rocket, after that we are finished."

Yamamoto said, "I will be surprised if there are more, I am sure they thought they sent more than enough men to kill us."

I added, "I agree and the closest air force base is too far away to matter, they can't get them in the air and fly here in time to find us, but we must keep moving."

Catherine knew I was right, however first she stopped by a tree and opened a bag, and shared, "I have six extra suits for you all to change into. You must put these on before we can proceed so that the satellites can't track us. You must change quickly. I'm sorry Yuri, I have nothing in extra-large for your big man."

Yuri smiled and replied, "Don't worry we are all wearing our own." *The three men opened their flak jacket and shirt and showed her.*

The Japanese had them too, "Good, is anyone's damaged? *Catherine inquired.*

Sayid lifted his good hand and Eric's was obvious, one of the Japanese had a damaged one too. "Alright Peter you help Eric get another one on, just put it over his existing one and Jacob can you please help Sayid, quickly." *She gave out the suits and just as we finished dressing the injured men, Sky arrived, jogging out of the woods.*

Catherine warned everyone "He is with me." *She ordered Sky,* "Lead us out of here." *We traveled by foot at a rapid pace. We walked for the rest of the day and throughout the night too. Catherine handed our guests night vision goggles. We only stopped for water. As darkness began to fall on the second day Sky led us into the base of a mountain cave camouflaged by some trees. The cave ran deep into an old abandoned mine shaft.*

Sky announced "We can rest here for as long as we need. It has not been used for over a hundred years. Nobody knows about it." *When we arrived Mary and Jason had already set up camp inside the mine.*

Mary ran toward Sayid and embraced him. He only embraced her with one arm, the other had been broken. "Oh Sayid, I have never seen you look so beat up? What happened?"

Jason had tears running down his face as he tended to Eric. "Catherine, what happened?"

She informed them briefly of what had occurred in the battle, while Sky took care of Eric's wounds and then he set and splinted Sayid's arm properly. He gave them both some painkillers.

Yuri spoke when Catherine had finished telling them what happened, "You all should be thankful, none of us died. The last time I faced Augustus' elite forces most of my men were killed."

Yamamoto said, "Yes these new soldiers are enhanced in size, strength and ability, much like your man Jacob, and although you are small Catherine, like yourself."

The Russian inquired, "Are you and your protector genetically enhanced, has the government tampered with your DNA?"

"No" *Catherine smiled*, "The government has not altered our DNA, we are only what God has made us."

Yuri inquired, "Hmm… Well little lady I have never seen someone as small as you fight so well. How do you explain that?"

Catherine replied, "I already have, we are simply what God made us to be."

Yamamoto said, "Well the rumors about you are true and they are not exaggerated. It is an honor to have fought with the legend."

Catherine bowed her head in appreciation and then she said, "Tell us what you know about these elite forces."

Yamamoto said, "All we have is rumors, but we have fought them before. In the past year Augusts has developed a genetically enhanced fighting force. Some say that regular soldiers are injected with advanced anabolic steroid and a special sequence of growth hormone."

Yuri cleared his throat, "It is not a rumor, Vladimir here has been administered six doses and he has grown, in strength, speed and agility. He has grown a foot taller than he was last year".

Catherine asked, "Are there any side effects?"

Catherine looked at Vladimir who in turn responded, "My natural emotions are intensified and I heal extremely fast. That soldier you did not kill Catherine is probably already up limping around and he should be fully healed by this time tomorrow."

Catherine looked at Yuri and inquired, "Do you have any more on you? How many vials do you have?"

"I have another six. I was going to administer them on myself." *Yuri replied honestly.*

"Don't, we must have two of them at least." *Catherine said with her commanding tone.*

Yuri replied, "Why, two will not help you in any significant way, it requires six doses to produce such a soldier. They are numbered in sequence and must be administered on a specific schedule, or else you can kill the recipient if you administer the dose too closely together."

Catherine explained, "I don't want to use them, I want to give them to our medic, Sky, to study and if safe replicate. Then we can match their strength and speed on a much larger scale."

Yamamoto agreed, "Yuri this is a much wiser use of it. We could build our own army all over the world. It would put an end to the slaughter our resistance cells are now facing."

"Catherine*,"* Jacob interrupted*, "It is not my place to correct you, but I feel compelled to warn you. If you do such a thing you are creating a new thing in creation. Don't play God."

Yuri said, "This new creation already exists and we are not creating, we are enhancing."

Sayid spoke up, "It is an abomination."

Jacob agreed, "It is a perversion of what the Lord has made."

I spoke up, "You cannot defeat Augustus without it. He has already altered the course and development of human evolution and if you don't use this weapon to defeat him, you may alter human history itself."

"Captain Roberts is right." *Yamamoto agreed*, "If we do not do this we will lose the war, we will lose the right to be free, and we will be forced to submit to his rule. We cannot last much longer. The resistance diminishes in strength and numbers with each passing day. We must capitalize on this opportunity."

Catherine said, "Let me analyze it and see if we can replicate the concoction, and then I will pray about it. Those of you who hear from God ask, and then we will reply to each other in three months' time, just those of us who are here tonight and share in the final decision. Agreed?

All that were present replied in unison, "Agreed"

Then Catherine added, "And please do not tell anyone of the existence of these vials, no one, not even our political allies."

Yuri went to a satchel he carried and gave Catherine the six vials. "We will not tell a soul, especially our friendly politicians, no, just us my dear Catherine. I thought there was a reason you had those politicians fly out together. Which one of them do you think is the traitor?"

"I have my suspicions, but it is not worth mentioning without proof. We do not want to destroy the resistance from within with gossip and innuendo." *Catherine answered as she took the vials from Yuri and then she continued,* "Thank you Yuri."

Yamomotto said, "Catherine you are a very wise leader."

"Thank you Hideki" *Catherine turned to Sky, and handed him the vials and he placed them in his medical bag.*

Yuri said, "I wish. I had some Russian Vodka"

Catherine laughed, "Well Yuri we do not have any vodka, but we have some excellent Irish Whisky."

Yuri smiled as he winked and said, "Ah Catherine, I think I am falling in love with you, you are a woman after my own heart."

I took my place beside her and I placed my arm around her as I said, "Back off Yuri, her heart is already spoken for."

She kissed my cheek and said, "Don't worry Peter, from what I hear, Yuri loves many women."

Yuri pretended to take offense and said jokingly, "Now Catherine, I thought we were not going to take part in gossip and innuendo." *Then he smiled proudly and confessed,* "… but I must admit it is all true. I can't help it. I love many women and they love me. It is how I was made."

Everyone laughed and Jason brought us the whiskey, serving poor Eric first, who was now sitting up by the fire with us. Eric's leg would be okay after all, the bullet did not break the bone. He then served Sayid water, who was also injured, but no one would know it aside from the splint on his arm. He was the toughest man I've met. Navy Seals really are the best, I respected this fact before, but seeing him fight those giants made me respect him even more. Catherine was given her whiskey next and then the rest of us. Once everybody was served Yuri raised his glass and toasted, "To our new alliance. May it help build a new world, and may our actions lead to freedom and victory."

We all responded in unison, "To freedom and victory."

Mary brought everyone some stew and bannock, it was delicious. Then Jason served us another round of whiskey. For the first time in many months I was optimistic that we would finally achieve that freedom and share in the victory we toasted to. I would have to confirm who the traitor was, but like Catherine I had my suspicions. We had to go forward and strive for victory even with an enemy in our midst. I dismissed such thoughts for another day.

Tonight we sat by the fire and drank, assured that we were in good company, and that at least for tonight we could enjoy a camaraderie that only soldiers know. Tonight I drank with warriors at my side, I was one of them and it had been a long time since I felt this way. It was a good night, but we were all tired and we did not stay up late.

Chapter Eleven:
Silent Serenity

Catherine let everybody know where they would be sleeping and said that we would have to meet shortly after sunrise. She bid everyone good night and then we made our way toward her tent that Mary and Jason had set up prior to our arrival.

When we were far enough from the others I said, "Catherine, you gave President Davidson a very chilly reception both times you met him. Why?"

She looked at me and I could tell she took no offence and she replied candidly, "I don't trust him; he rubs me the wrong way. He feels like a typical politician."

"Well you seemed to get along with Bourbon very well. Talk about a typical politician." *I retorted.*

"True, but he gave me a glass of Merlot." *She smiled.*

I hugged her and teased, "Is it that easy to win your favor?"

Catherine looked up at me and coyly said, "It worked for you, the first thing you did was buy me a drink, and you bought me quite a few if I recall."

"I could not help it. You lured me in, and I didn't know you drank like a sailor." *I jested.*

Catherine slapped my arm and then she said, "You cheek. Seriously though I sense Bourbon is an honest man, he is light-hearted, but I believe he would fight by our side if he had too. He is a warrior who has the disposition of a king. Like the kings of old who led their men into battle. Whereas President Davidson is not a soldier, he is nothing but a man grasping for power and who cares more about appearances than substance."

"How did you come to such a conclusion in such a brief encounter with them?" *I questioned her with only a hint of surprise in my tone and then I inquired,* "Is that why you lied to him when you said only you and Eric know the entire plan?"

"Yes, I was protecting you. I did not want him to know you were involved in the planning at all. Our meeting merely confirmed in my heart what I suspected from my research. I had Eric provide me with dossiers on each of them. I read their speeches, writings and political posts on their careers." *Catherine replied as she moved behind a screen to change and wash up and brush her teeth.*

She came out brushing her long hair and I took off my shirt and washed up and brushed my teeth and then I asked, "Is that what has been keeping you so busy lately, research and planning, or have you been avoiding spending time alone with me." *I deliberately had not put on my clean shirt as I came out to see her answer. She bit her lip and I could see she did not want to answer the question.*

She walked passed me to put her brush back in its place and as she turned I inquired as I took a step closer, "Well Catherine, are you going to answer me?"

She did not look up at me as she replied, "Of course I've been avoiding spending time alone with you."

I grabbed her shoulders gently and said, "Why?"

She looked deeply into my eyes and answered, "You know why." *Then she ran her finger across my abs and she said,* "It is because of this." *Catherine then gently rubbed her hands along my chest, shoulders and biceps as she continued,* "and because of this, and this, and this."

I smiled and then I added, "…and because of this." *I kissed her softly at first and then she responded passionately and we kissed as seconds turned to minutes and time lost all meaning.*

She pulled away, but I could tell she didn't want to, still she did and she said, "Especially because of that." *She walked toward our sleeping bags.*

"Catherine, I love you." She looked back at me, but she said nothing.

I moved closer to her and I repeated, "I love you." *Still she said nothing so I kissed her again and I could tell she loved me too, even if she couldn't say it. Kisses don't lie.*

Then she said, "Peter I can't, please, I know you don't understand, but I can't make love to you."

I conceded, "Your right, I don't understand, but I love you enough to wait. Come on let's get some sleep. You must be exhausted."

She kissed me and she said, "Okay, but put your shirt on, I'm not that strong. You have no idea how difficult this is for me."

"Yes I do." *I reminded her*, "You said... what was it? Oh yes, that I was such a sweet temptation."

She blushed but said, "Yes you are, but you promised to be good."

I laughed and I put on my shirt and we climbed into our sleeping bags that were zipped together for us. Catherine fell asleep in my arms and we did not wake up until quite late the next morning, when Jacob came in to get us.

The Russians and the Japanese all slept in too and since the mines were safe it was agreed that they would stay with us one more night to fully regain their strength and then they made their way back to their countries of origin.

Catherine thanked them both for coming and the Japanese leader was thanked in his own tongue. After they left I said, "I had no idea you could speak any other languages, French and Japanese, how many other languages do you speak?"

"None" *Then she took my hand and then she informed me,* "I only know how to speak some French because I am Canadian and as for the Japanese, you can thank my dad's old record collection for that. I use to listen to his Styx albums all the time."

I laughed and Eric said, "Styx, what's that?"
I turned to Eric and replied, "You're a genius, look it up."

Eric said, "I will."

Eric said sometime later, "Catherine that song was awful, I thought you had taste."

"Hey ease up. I was only six, and besides I didn't say it was a classic. I just said I listened to it. It was my dad's old vinyl collection." *She said as she defended herself.*

I defended her too saying, "That was not their best hour, go listen to their earlier stuff then come talk to us."

"Earlier stuff, I don't have access to an endless supply of historical records" *Eric said with a hint of shock on his face.*

I smiled as I teased, "Just another decade, it isn't ancient history."

"Are they long since dead?" *Eric sarcastically retorted.*

"Some of them." *I answered*

"Then it's ancient history." *Eric replied.*

We all laughed and went to train, except Eric who was still healing. I was surprised that Sayid came with us. Sky said, "Sayid you have to take a couple of days off at least."

Sayid said, "Why? I wasn't shot. Don't worry Sky, I won't injure it more."

We ran up and down the mountain a few times, and when we returned Jason approached us. He was tall and lean, almost lanky and he asked, "Can you all train me?"

Sayid said, "Why? You don't even like guns or any violent weapon."

Then Mary joined in, "I want to learn too"

With a stern voice Sayid questioned, "Why the change of heart you two? Neither of you have a killer's instinct. You are both emotional creatures. You can't have any kind of weapon unless you are prepared to use it to kill."

I agreed with Sayid, "It is far more dangerous to put a weapon in the hands of someone with a gentle heart. If you hesitate it will only be used against you."

Jason said, "You are all the best of the best. Sayid is a navy seal for Pete's sake. This recent battle shows that we must be prepared to fight to defend ourselves, if…if you all don't return."

Sayid and I looked at Catherine who seemed only slightly sad, like a mother who has to let her children grow up and face a dangerous world on their own for the very first time, but she knew they were right. She sighed and then said, "We can't train you two to fire guns right now, and we only have our guns that will not fire without a chip detected. The few Russian guns we have, we will need for when we go into battle and our ammunition is too limited. Shooting well takes practice, but we will show you how they work and allow you to fire the Russian guns once."

Catherine then looked to Sayid and me, "You two train them to fight with knives, after they learn basic hand-to-hand combat and Eric is well, he will train you how to fire a bow. Become excellent archers. It will help you to survive in more ways than one. When you have his approval you must go hunting with Sky, who will take you both out and teach you to shoot and gut the animals you kill. If you cannot kill a creature of the forest, you will not be able to kill a man."

Sayid was going to protest, "But Catherine I can't hit my wife, you know she will have to learn to take a hit. I…"

Catherine held up her hand and silenced Sayid as she interrupted him in mid-sentence, "Sayid, everyone has a right to defend themselves and there may come a day when she will have to. I will help train your wife and Eric will when he is well too. Roberts and you may focus on Jason, but don't hate me when I hurt her Sayid."

"Go easy on her Catherine." *Sayid pleaded.*

Mary protested, "No, don't go easy on me." *She continued and looked up at Sayid,* "Sayid, will the enemy have mercy and go easy on me?"

He said, "No they will kill you. Your best chance of survival is to run and hide. You can never stand before the men we have fought and live."

She replied with an adamant tone. "I'm not planning to go to battle Sayid. I hate war, but what if you are not here and they bring the battle to me? I don't want to shake in fear with no hope of defending myself. Besides, Catherine is a woman."

Sayid said, "Don't be ridiculous, Catherine is more like a man than a woman. She is a warrior."

"Thanks Sayid," *Catherine uttered sarcastically and then she declared,* "but I am a woman."

Catherine placed her hand gently on Mary's shoulder and cautioned, "Mary, Sayid is right in that you must be realistic. I have been prepared for this my whole life and I'm not an ordinary woman."

Catherine turned back toward us and added, "That being said, Sayid she can learn how to defend herself. She must learn." *Catherine was adamant in her last statement.*

Eric had overheard us speaking and he said, "She's right Sayid, don't worry I will help her and Jason become excellent snipers too. Catherine, we must get more weapons and ammunition."

"You're right Eric." *Catherine agreed,* "We will, but first I need you to take off the electronic inhibitors on the weapons. With these genetically enhanced soldiers, it is obvious we can no longer play it safe. Anyone who is not with us is our enemy. Mary and Jason you must embrace the reality that you must now kill, or be killed."

They nodded in agreement and she said, "Let us begin; first we must make you stronger and faster.

"What do you say guys, you up for one more sprint up the mountain?" *Catherine did not wait for a reply and she ran up with ease. Sayid and I were both tired, but we were driven by pride to compete with each other and by our male egos to impress our women, so we ran all out as well.*

Jason came up the last part of the mountain with Mary following a little more behind. We had recovered and were sitting at the top waiting for them. Jason was gasping for air, as he could barely speak he said, "My lungs are on fire."

"Don't worry it only happens for the first couple of weeks. It will get easier." *I assured him.*

"When it does," *Sayid added* "You must push yourself harder.

Jason was keeled over heaving as he gasped, "Great."

Mary made it up dragging herself along in a very slow jog, but she made it. She couldn't speak and then she keeled over and threw up. "Sorry about that." she said.

Catherine put her arm around her and said, "Don't worry; we have all been there Mary."

"Have any of you ever thrown up?" *She asked us, once she caught her breath.*

We all looked at each other and I said, "No, but we have all been training hard since childhood. Don't worry in six weeks you will be in much better shape than you are right now."

"Yah honey, you did well, and Roberts here almost lost his lunch the first time he ran with us." *Sayid joked.*

Catherine defended me and said, "If I recall Sayid, the first time you ran with me you were gasping for air like poor Jason here."

We all laughed and made our way down the mountain and Catherine said, "We will train you two as

198

VL Parker

soon as we arrive at the next camp. Pack up and we will hike at double the speed we normally do."

Catherine gave the other rebels six months to return before the attack. She knew they would require extra time to make it safely home, and Augustus would surely be doubling his efforts trying to find us.

Catherine's troops were all congregating deep in the mountains, preparing for the united attack. We made our way through the mountain ranges to another abandoned mine in the neighboring state. This mine was large and deep. Her followers had everything set up by the time we arrived.

They setup the rest of our supplies and the daily training began. Catherine had some of the veterans begin to engage the women and children in basic training. They were in boot camp eight hours a day. Even the older men and women were ordered to hike up and down the mountain at least once a day.

We had two obstacle courses laid out, one for the children and another for the adults. Catherine was building a small army. Everyone in the camp had contributed before, but now every person would be able to help in its defense should it ever be attacked or should we fail to return.

Jason and Mary were the only two who received private instruction from Catherine, Sayid, Jacob and I. Few would approach Catherine or her inner circle to speak to her candidly. I think a part of them feared us, although we did not intend it as such. Mary came to us as we were all eating lunch and she said, "I have a request to make of all of you, including you Jacob."

We all looked up and Catherine said, "What is it Mary?"

Mary bit her lip and then took a deep breath as she informed us, "Well, all of the children have been training very hard and your sub-commanders have promised the kids, well a kind of graduation ceremony. I was asked by the children when you, all of you, would be teaching them. They all have different favorites, you have become like heroes to them." *She took another breath and then requested,* "Will each of you take a class and teach them."

Sayid replied, "I have never taught children before."

Jacob said, "I have not either. I might scare them."

We all looked at Catherine, "Don't look at me; I've never even been around children before."

Sayid said, "Yes, but you are a women."

Catherine glared at Sayid and retorted, "I thought you said I was more like a man than a woman, remember?"

Sayid said sheepishly, "Still, you are a woman."

Catherine punched him in the arm and Mary said, "Look you two I have no more experience with children than you and you act like, like you are afraid of them."

We did not reply, but I think that we all blushed a little.

Eric commented, "I can't believe it. You are all afraid of little children. You have faced the most fearsome warriors on earth and fought in the most horrendous battles and you're all afraid of kids."

Eric laughed out loud and Mary gently added, "There is nothing to fear, they love you, especially you Jacob, your one of their favorites."

We had no excuse so Catherine said, "When is the ceremony?"

Mary smiled as she replied, "Tomorrow afternoon."

Catherine informed her, "We will teach them a class after their graduation ceremony."

The next day the ceremony was short and sweet. Some of the best students demonstrated what they had learned, and Catherine was asked to speak. She got up and asked Eric, Jacob, Sayid, Sky, and I to join her in the center battle ring. We did not know what she was up to but as always, we obeyed.

She smiled at the children and congratulated them for their hard work and said, "I have heard that some of you think of us as heroes. We are not. Every single one of us is simply walking in our destiny and functioning in the skills, abilities and gifts that God has given us. We are all who God has designed us to be.

God does not make mistakes. Some of us, like Jacob, are built for strength, speed, agility and with an undying sense of loyalty. He is designed by our creator to protect. Some of us are like Sky: a healer, a hunter, a cook, and one with nature and man. Some are like Sayid, built with drive, determination, insight, wisdom and a spirit of such strength and depth that few men have known. Others, like Eric are given a problem-solving capability and intelligence that is unsurpassed and reaches genius levels; he is an amazing sniper too. His rational and intelligent brain was given to him by God. He is exactly who God has designed him to be, in every respect of his being."

She smiled at Eric who smiled back and then she continued, "Captain Roberts here has been trained like Sayid and I since childhood to become an elite warrior and leader. He is gentle, honest, determined, loyal and rational. He has been given a gift of an unbiased and objective view of the world and everyone around him, which many of us need. He is the epitome of balance and self-control.

Every single one of us who stands before you is just like all of you in two ways, firstly we are all made by God and secondly we each have unique skills and abilities. Every one of us, like every one of you, has a purpose and a destiny to fulfill, but we must each choose to work hard and develop those God-given skills and abilities.

Discover what your gifts are and develop them to the best of your ability. When you walk forward in life, walk with the knowledge that even when you face an enemy in your darkest hour, you are not alone. God is with you. You are all made in his image and likeness and God does not make mistakes, so walk with humility and gratitude, but also walk with confidence and in the strength of your creator. For he is greater than any other and there is no power on heaven or on earth that is greater than our God, and you are his creation."

With that everyone clapped and Catherine said, "Alright let's get a little training in before supper." *The kids' cheer ended and they came running toward us with excitement and we began to pair off. Catherine and Jacob took one group, Sayid and I took another and Eric and Sky got another.*

I smiled as I saw Catherine training a young girl informing her how to approach defending oneself when you are surrounded.

I caught her looking and smiling at me as I taught a young boy how to target your enemy's weakest zones. "These are the kill zones, target them whether you have a weapon or not. A proper strike, even from a child's hand, can result in a kill. It requires speed and precision."

One of our young men was attacking his target with rage, Sayid stopped him and bent down, "You must never fight with rage, and vengeance belongs to God. We must never take pleasure in killing, then it becomes murder in our heart and our righteous action becomes tainted with sin. We must remain calm and clear-headed. Rage will interrupt your clarity of thought, which is one of the most important strengths in any battle. Secondly rage disrupts you breath, so if you feel yourself losing control to anger or fear, take time to breathe deeply and slowly."

"Do you take time to breath?" *He was asked.*

Sayid knelt down and answered the boy with his hand on the child's shoulder, "Yes, I always take time to pray and be still before Allah, seven times a day, but Catherine has taught me the value of breathing deeply. Catherine says, that when she sits still and breaths, she not only rejuvenates her strength and spirit, she purifies her mind and hears from the creator himself."

"Do you hear from God, Sayid?" *The boy inquired.*

"Not at these times, but he speaks to me in dreams." *Sayid replied.*

"Then why take time to breathe deeply every day?" *The boy asked*

"It enables you to breathe in battle when pain, your anger, or fear can take control of you." *I replied.* "Such a discipline should become a second nature to you, and then you will not succumb to panic."

Catherine had heard our conversation and added, "Breathing will also make you stronger than anger."

The boy said, "I don't believe it."

Everyone surrounded us and Catherine ordered, "Bring us that board."

A thick board was carried to us from the mine's entrance and Catherine ordered Sayid, "Hold the board firmly." *Then Catherine said to the boy,* "I want you to fill your thoughts and emotions with that which angers you the most. Allow your mind to be filled with rage and then punch the board and break it"

This came easy for the boy; he yelled and punched the board after calling some dark emotions to the surface. He punched the board with all that he had, with the heel of his hand. It did not break and his hand hurt him.

Sayid then said, "I want you to ignore the pain."

"Ignore the pain, it hurts! I think I broke my hand." *The boy would have cried, but he was still too angry to cry.*

Sayid told the boy, "Anger will allow you to function through the pain, but breathing deeply and filling your mind with peace will make it diminish."

Catherine said, "Close your eyes and breathe deeply and slowly" *With each breath his pain subsided and then she said,* "Take another deep breath and call to mind your most peaceful memory. Let that peace consume you. I want you to take another deep breath and when you strike the board breathe out, simultaneously allowing the energy to flow through you as you focus on a single point. When you release your final breath strike hard and fast, are you ready?"

The boy nodded so Catherine said, "Take your last deep breath and strike as you exhale. Hit the board."

The boy did as he was told and the board broke in two. The boy looked amazed and everyone clapped for him. Catherine placed one fist in the other and as the straight hand enveloped the fist she said, "Peace over power." *She bowed." The boy returned the gesture; Sayid smiled at him and nodded with approval.*

"Sky, take a look at his hand and make sure it's okay." *Catherine smiled at the boy and then we all went to supper.*

As we walked to supper I asked her, "How did you know he could break the board?"

"Master Ming used that lesson and I witnessed it work every time." *She replied.*

"Did he use it on you?" *I asked.*

Catherine replied with candor, "Yes he did, I was an angry child who had to learn the value of peace too."

I kissed her cheek and I said, "I wish I knew you then, I would have fallen in love with you at that time too."

Two little girls giggled behind us when I said this. She blushed a little and then she took my hand as we walked to the river and we washed our hands before going to sit by the fire and eat.

That night we all rested peacefully in the serenity of the mountains and Catherine and I made our way to the river. We sat and looked at the stars and the beauty of the full moon. She was so beautiful as she looked up at the stars, I watched her. I wanted to tell her I loved her again, but it was now married to the hope she would return those words. So I remained silent.

We sat like that for a long time and then I told her, "Catherine I don't want this season to end. I am so happy here with you. I don't think there has ever been a time in my life when I have felt so at peace. These moments are so fleeting."

"Me too" *She replied* "Let's just stay in this moment and forget about everything else."

I held her close and we saw a shooting star. It is silly, but I made a wish. I wished I could have Catherine completely and she could have me. I loved her and I wanted her. She was the most amazing, complicated, deep and beautiful woman I had ever known and I wanted her to be mine. Except for her bondage to her religious beliefs she was perfect. I was sure that it was religion that kept her from loving me. How can love be wrong? It was irrational. I could not help but love her as she sat in silent serenity looking at the stars above.

Chapter Twelve:
When Darkness Falls

One night we heard an announcement over the BBC radio that the rise of a great prophet had prophesied the coming of God. This god was revealed to be the miracle maker who had healed James. News of his miraculous powers swept across North America. He travelled to the Temple in Jerusalem and raised the dead. He announced that he was God at the beginning of the fifth year of Augustus' reign.

He declared he was angry at the hate and the killing and that he would establish one religion for all of mankind. Raficial Augustus was the first of the leaders to bow before him and submit to his will. Many followed. Muslims, Jews, Hindus, Buddhists, Catholics, all of the world's nations and religions embraced him as God except for a few who heeded the voice of two other prophets, who were also present in God's holy city.

Two prophets outside Jerusalem spoke against this self-proclaimed god and no one could touch them. They too were reported to have miraculous powers that few could fathom and many feared. When the police tried to arrest them, they blinded them and even burned them with nothing, but a word. The military attempted to use a flame thrower upon them; they held up their hands and the weapons immediately stopped functioning. The prophets' then said, "Burn." The soldiers burned up and turned to ashes instantaneously. The two prophets in Jerusalem killed all who attempted to arrest them by what was described on the news as, "A breath of fire."

Reports of the miracle maker himself showing up to secure the prophets' arrest and condemn them to death were later released and their bodies hung outside the walls of Jerusalem. Three days later, news spread that their death was inaccurate and that they were indeed alive. Catherine seemed sad at times and then content at others, but never once did she appear surprised. It just sent her back to a life of prayer, fasting and isolation. I hated these times when she pulled away from me.

Most of the resistance fighters in Russia, Europe and North America had been arrested. Only a few cells remained. They were tortured publicly and murdered. Still, their loyalty to their god did not waver.

I was compelled by both duty and some deep attachment to stay close by Catherine's side, but I still did not believe in her god. I began to fear that Catherine was insane. Like Edward before her, she followed her faith blindly; but she was growing more distant, disappearing for hours, and at times for days, to pray. Her heart was often heavy. I longed to reach out to her and lighten the burden she carried, but she withdrew from me even further and continued to seclude herself in prayer and solitude. She frequently immersed herself in long private conversations with Jacob.

I remember one night shortly after the arrival of the great healer in Israel; Catherine's forces had joined together in the mountains of Washington State for battle. Most of her units returned from our winter separation, except one, which we later discovered had suffered martyrdom for their cause.

It was late summer when the BBC announced one night that China had instigated a terrorist attack on France's nuclear facilities upriver from Bordeaux at Langon, on the Garonne River, in protest against their support of the French, American and Russian alliance.

Sayid commented, "I guess China is out. I suppose that Chang did not like Davidson and Bourbon very well. I wonder what happened on that helicopter after they left us. If Chang was against the alliance why didn't he attack Moscow? It does not make sense."

Eric said, "Chang must have attacked France for a deeper reason. Who knows, the Chinese are so difficult to read." *France would not have survived these attacks had not a dramatic shift in the winds occurred, causing the cloud of nuclear radiation to drift away from the heart of France and out over the Atlantic Ocean.*

I replied, "No it does not make any sense. Chang said he is with us and our attack on ARON is set. Even though we had to postpone the date, he said he is in."

Catherine then replied, "Don't worry about Chang, he is still in. everything will proceed as planned.

Catherine poured us some wine and sat down beside me. She leaned in close as I put my arm around her. Eric was sitting with Jason across from Catherine and me. They looked very good together. Eric was a lean white male, small in stature with dark brownish-black hair, and soft brown eyes. Jason was taller and also slender. He had dirty blond hair and blue eyes that lay behind rimless glasses. Jason spoke with a British accent as he said, "Catherine, Nostradamus was right. He prophesied this very thing would occur in the 1600's."

Sayid said, "Didn't he simply read a lot of bible prophesy and reword it?"

"I don't think so." *Eric stated*, "I think he dreamed his prophecies."

Catherine interjected, "It does not matter. He is long since dead. Don't trouble yourself with prophesies from this source, or any other, the only relevant question is: if you two believe prophecy is being fulfilled and the Lord came for you today would you be ready? Could you enter Heaven's Gate?"

They did not reply, but Jacob spoke, "No man is worthy to enter Heaven! It is only possible if you are covered by the blood of the Lamb. All men and women sin, it is a reality you are all forced to face. Men are weak. Your sin is not the main issue, rather it is: are you forgiven? His blood washes sin away and makes you clean. Make a choice soon for tomorrow you may die, but in Christ you shall live."

Eric had already given himself to Jesus and Jason was still on the fence. I was quite confused because I was brought up in America and the Christian right hated homosexuals. Catherine and I retired for the evening and I asked her, "Please don't go away and pray tonight. I need to talk with you. Stay with me."

She came over and sat beside me. We were in her tent all alone; it was our only place of solitude, even though Jacob was just outside. "Catherine, how could Eric become Christian when his religion says that he is dammed if he is homosexual?"

It does not say that, "Jesus told us not to judge and to love one another as he loved us."

"Catherine it says in your bible, that there will be no homosexuals in the Kingdom of God." *I retorted.*

"It says there will be no adulterers or sinners at all."

"How do you explain that?" *I asked in frustration.*

She smiled, "It is not a warning Peter, it is a promise. We are not bound by the flesh and its desires in heaven. We are the perfect reflection of the Father's love. There is no marriage in Heaven, there is no sex."

I replied sarcastically, "Sayid and every Muslim martyr will be devastated."

"Peter stop being sarcastic, open your mind." *She sighed and placed her hand on mine as she said,* "We are all sinners, every single last one of us. The scriptures say, 'All have sinned and fall short of the glory of God.' The only difference is that I am a sinner saved by grace."

"You are a sinner?" *I scoffed.* "You do everything in your power to avoid being with me. How do you sin?"

She blushed and looked down as she confessed, "Peter I battle passion, sensuality and sexual sin every single day, especially since I first danced with you. You have plagued my thoughts and dreams more times than I could count."

I was angered by her phrasing, "Plagued, nice word choice Catherine."

"I mean it; there is no escape from you, no cure. I thought of you for years when you were far from me and I battle taking you every single day. You have no idea how hard it is." *She cried.*

I had to take a deep breath to hush my tone as I said, "I have no idea how hard it is? Catherine I'm not restrained by your religious rules, regulations, and archaic morality. I would have been completely content sleeping with you the first night I met you. I have wanted you ever since. I've never slept with another woman since I met you, because I knew it was pointless. You are the only woman I want. You are the only woman I've felt so completely helpless and controlled by.

I don't have some interactive god, or some ancient deep-seated faith restraining me. The only thing holding me back from making you mine is you, my love and my respect for you.

I want you to be able to give yourself to me completely Catherine, without guilt and without remorse. I don't know how hard it is? Are you mad, do you know how good-looking and irresistible you are?"

She kissed me with a hunger and intensity I had never known and always longed for. We immersed in a sea of passion that would so easily flow into ecstasy. I could have had her and I knew she would have given herself to me. God I wanted her, but something restrained me. I pulled away and said, "I want you so badly Catherine."

Then she uttered words that made me fight the hardest battle I had ever faced, "Then take me." *she whispered.*

I lay her down and I kissed her again deeply and then I forced myself to pull back again and ask, "If we make love now, will you feel guilt and remorse? Will you have to confess and repent before your god?"

Tears rolled down her face, "Yes."

I got up and I began to leave and I said, "You say God is love, and you do not judge Eric and Jason, or Sayid and Mary because they love, and yet you consider what we could have a sin. You may want me Catherine, but you can't love me. You hold yourself to a higher account than everyone else, and if you do want me then I was wrong. You are guilty of sin, sin against your own heart. If you do love me, then by forcing us to never be able to show it free of guilt and shame, then you sin against love itself."

With that I left her crying and alone. I walked to the river and was filled with a flurry of emotions. Jacob for the first time ever left his post and joined me by the river.

He said, "Just breathe."

"You of all people should know Jacob; this is no time for joking."

"I am not. You truly are a man of God, Peter Roberts." *Jacob said with a deep voice filled with compassion as he continued,* "Catherine was completely weak and vulnerable to you tonight. She would have failed the test before her, but you passed it for her, because you love her."

"You heard every word, huh." *I asked knowing the answer already.*

Jacob was humble and he said, "Yes, and I want to thank you."

"Why?" *I inquired*

Jacob replied, "For putting Catherine first, for honoring her and honoring love. By restraining your own natural desires, you honored God tonight."

"That is totally twisted Jacob, and I don't believe in God." *I replied.*

"No, but you do not need to believe to be used as an instrument of God." *After Jacob said this he walked away and returned to his post.*

I returned sometime later and got under the covers, Catherine said, "I am so sorry Peter, please forgive me."

I held her in my arms and I said, "I'm sorry too Catherine." *We fell asleep exhausted and confused.*

Catherine pulled me aside the next day and asked me to walk with her. She led me to a secluded place near the river and said, "Peter I know you have yet to know God, but I can't help myself, I love you too. I have prayed for God to spare your life in the coming battle because I love you. Without you I am weak and with you I could easily be made weaker. I will not betray my God, but in trying not to love you, you were right, I betray my heart. Only Eric and Mary could understand such a deep struggle. Yet mine is far worse, because I have seen God and I hear his voice. The ache in my heart runs so deeply. I am yours and I am God's child. There is a painful division in my soul because of it. I can't be with you the way I want too, but I can't live without you either. I do not have all the answers, but I wanted you to know that I do love you."

We sat down by the river bank as she continued, "I'm sorry, I wish I could make you understand. One of the fundamental pillars of being a Christian is walking in self-control. It is a sign you are walking in the Spirit of God. Every Christian must submit to the Lord and lay selfishness aside. I'm selfish, I am sorely lacking in self-control and it is selfish of me to expect you to be mine when I am forbidden to give myself to you. My body is not my own, it belongs to God and I want to give myself to you. You are not a Christian and you have far more self-control than I do."

She hung her head in shame as she declared, "It is cruel of me to expect you to restrain yourself forever. I should tell you to leave, but I can't let you go either. I am so sorry." *She paused, and then she said.* "Anyway, I had to let you know, but I'm certain that you cannot understand and I fear that I may drive you farther from

God. Still, I had to let you know before this night is through, before we fight side by side in battle once again, that I love you Peter."

My heart soared, I did not understand about what battle she spoke of, but at that moment I could care less about it. I felt like I could fly and face any foe, no matter how great. Catherine loved me, I held her face in my hands and I wiped the tears from her cheek. I declared, "I love you Catherine. You have had my heart since I first met you and even if I die, I don't fear it because I have your love. I hope we both survive the battle you speak of. I've survived many before and Fate could not be so cruel as to make us find one another only to lose each other again. We will be together. We will survive. When the battle is over marry me. Marry me before your god and I will share you with him. Will he share you with me?"

"Yes, I'll marry you on two conditions. First you must believe that your vows are said before the Most High, and second, our children must be raised in his light." *she replied*

I was scared, but I replied honestly, "I will mean my vows and I consider love sacred and the most high of all, but I cannot think of it as you will as being before some interactive entity that I have never heard or seen."

She smiled and said, "That is okay, because God is love Peter. Are you willing to accept that I will I raise our children as children of the light?"

"As you wish Catherine, anything to make you mine." *I kissed her with such love and passion, that in one kiss I felt that years of lost love were poured forth in a single moment in time.*

Then Jacob reminded us of his presence. I smiled up at him and he raised an eyebrow in response. Catherine left my embrace and patted his shoulder as she went by and walked back toward the camp. I followed and said to Jacob, "Did you hear that big guy, she loves me!" *Jacob said nothing, but I didn't expect him to. He took his place at Catherine's side, and I took my place on the other as she prepared to address her assembled troops.*

Catherine embraced her brothers and sisters in Christ and announced, "Our final battle is at hand." *She told them,* "I've just sent Eric, and many of our fighters away to lead our families and friends to safety. They are fleeing from Augustus' elite soldiers who will be here soon. Eric must participate in an attack that will weaken Augustus, so let us pray they all escape. We must stay and fight and let them believe that they have discovered our camp so that we alone will face them. We have to act as if we were not expecting them. This will ensure they do not hunt down the rest of us.

God willing, our sacrifice will lead to the defeat of Augustus' forces, but Satan and his anti-Christ will not fall by our hands. *She quoted a line in Daniel saying*, "He shall be broken without human hands." Still, we have one final battle to fight, for our families and our friends."

She continued, "You all know Jesus is the Corner Stone, he is the Rock which will destroy Satan. He is coming soon, but many of you will not see him on Earth. Before sunrise we, like Christ before us, we too will be betrayed. We will enter into combat this night. We will not surrender and no white flag shall ever blow in this battle. The enemies of our God have waged war and we will die for Jesus, as he once died for us. As our blood soaks into the soil of this mountain we will find life and victory in Christ our Lord. Be courageous warriors for Christ, the King.

Do not fear Augustus' forces, the men you will do battle with. Do not stand in reverence of their power and strength and genetic superiority, for you should only fear your God. Revere him alone. For you will not escape death, so let your soul soar high and reach toward the heavens as you do battle on the earth. He is with you in battle and through your death you will find everlasting life. Jehovanissi!"

They all shouted like a roaring thunder, "Jehovanissi, Jehovanissi, Jehovanissi*!" I later learned this meant," The Lord is my banner". Sayid then fell to his knees and bared his arms and said* "I'm ready for the branding."

Catherine came over and blessed him as he was sealed by God's mark. On one arm he got a Latin phrase, meaning, 'In thy light we see' and on the other below his Navy Seal tattoo he was marked with, 'Jehovanissi'. The brand was quick and was comprised of a special stamp that shot forth black tattoo ink into the arm all at once with hundreds of tiny needles. It only took a matter of seconds, and as Sayid rose to his feet, Catherine's brother James entered the camp.

We looked up to see Catherine face her brother, cold and emotionless as James approached her and said, "Catherine, my sister, I am so glad I found you.*" He embraced her with a kiss and declared*, "Look Cathy I'm healed."

A tear of shame ran down Sayid's face as Catherine said, "My soul weeps for my brother, but you are not him."

James grinned wickedly, as an owl flew over the camp and shrieked out a haunting cry. With that omen, James replied, "Oh Cat, you chose the wrong side in this war. Come with me peacefully and your men will not have to die today."

Catherine glared as she said, "It won't be my blood that soaks the earth, snake. It will be yours."

With that said Catherine pulled out her combat knife and moved quickly to stab her brother. He leaped back just in time as enemy soldiers entered the camp.

He laughed and said, "Cat you always were fast, but you are not quick enough. Surrender now and I won't have to see them kill you."

Catherine's soldiers scrambled for their weapons and Catherine growled, "Shoot them!"

Sayid's face had been covered with shame and guilt, but this was quickly replaced with a look of resolve and vengeance.

I knew Sayid felt strongly that you should not take pleasure in killing; nonetheless he appeared to have divorced himself from such convictions as he engaged in battle. He believed that he was fighting against those that devoured the souls of men.

Sayid shot three men in rapid succession and then one of the soldiers engaged him in hand-to-hand combat.

I was forced to dive and roll, narrowly avoiding a bullet. I took cover behind a boulder and returned fire.

I could see Catherine and Jacob slaughtering several men as James watched his sister killing the enemy with a hint of pride and satisfaction.

Jacob and Catherine moved so swiftly that all who engaged them were quickly defeated.

Jacob snapped the necks of men like they were twigs, while Catherine slashed and stabbed them with her knife. We killed all of Augustus' soldiers with ease and after the fighting ceased our men converged toward Catherine's brother. One of Sayid's men said, "Well that was easy."

I replied, "Too easy."

James grinned and said to his sister, "Last chance Cat, surrender and I will spare your lives."

Catherine would never surrender and neither would we, but I knew a far greater foe was about to engage us. We had only defeated a platoon of lightly armed men, and this would not be the only forces that Augustus would send against us this day.

I looked toward Sayid and he nodded, knowing as did I that more were coming.

Sayid ordered, "Take cover, prepare for battle."

Men twice the size of those we had already engaged in battle walked up above the rise and cutoff our only means of escape.

I had no way of knowing how many we would be forced to fight, but we had limited ammunition and could not afford to engage in a prolonged fire-fight.

I yelled, "Save your ammo! Fire only when you have a sure shot."

We were positioned securely with our back against the mountains and had good cover behind large boulders.

Augustus' troops fired their weapons to no avail. They realized quickly the futility of this strategy and began to advance toward us as they laid down cover fire.

Initially they enjoyed little success as our men took precise aim from ideal positions and killed most of them as they advanced, still more kept coming.

Their armor was exceptional and only a few of us had guns. Most of the weapons were given to the troops to protect the children.

Some of the enemy got close enough to throw grenades, and one bounced close to my position. The soldier had timed it poorly however, and I picked up the grenade and threw it back at them killing several of their men. I could see their body parts flying through the air in the distance.

I knew they would not make that mistake again and I ordered, "Fan out."

The enemy forces had an unearthly strength that only a few of us had faced before.

Just as we abandoned our previous position a grenade exploded and rocks slid down the mountainside. Had we not moved, many of our men would have been crushed.

After the explosion I dove to escape the falling debris, and as I got to my feet I found myself face to face with a genetically enhanced soldier.

He looked down at me and arrogantly declared, "Surrender or die."

I didn't respond verbally. I just pulled out my revolver and shot him in the face as my reply.

I saw Sayid stab three with his knife and I killed two with mine. I was pleased to see that despite their immense size and strength they could bleed like us.

There was only about thirty of our men and about thirty or so of theirs. We were even in number, but Sayid's seal team and I were better trained than most of these brutes.

Those of our troops who had firearms were shooting Augustus's men with deadly accuracy as we engaged them in hand-to-hand combat.

Despite the heavy armor they were falling quickly and I was confident that it was only a matter of time before we would taste victory.

Then I turned to see that Sayid's body lay crumpled on the ground, blood flowing from his side. I ran over to defend him as an enemy soldier stood over him and was about to shoot him with a final coup-de-grace.

I ran and tackled the soldier to the ground. He kicked me and sent me flying backwards as he got up. I was still alive, but barely conscious.

Catherine's soldiers fought bravely and without fear, but even more soldiers, larger stronger and faster came up the mountainside. We were outmatched.

When I was kicked and thrown clear of the melee, my head hit a rock. I saw the man I had tackled aiming a gun at my head.

Catherine and Jacob were still fighting with a vengeance. No one could stop them, but then she saw me and yelled, "Enough! Snake, order them to stand down and I will go with you. You came here for me not them."

*James yelled, "*Hold your fire.*" Then he approached Catherine and replied, "*You resisted Catherine, why should I spare your men, any of them?*"*

*As James said this he looked at me and Catherine warned, "*Because if you don't spare my men, all of them I will kill you all starting with you.*"*

*James laughs, "*Cat you are so arrogant and proud, you are in no position to bargain, I could simply begin by killing you.*"*

*Catherine replied, "*You can't kill me, I already died.*"*

*James laughed, "*Did you? Did you really, well I don't believe it. Do you think yourself immortal?*"*

*Catherine smiled, but said nothing and James said, "*You think you can't die, well let's see.*" James shot Catherine with his revolver.*

All went black.

When I awoke from the darkness I could hear a voice from the distance like I was waking from a horrid dream. "Roberts! Roberts open your eyes." *It was Sayid. I opened my eyes as he knelt to bandage my head wound.*

I could tell that he lost much blood and he was probably as delirious as me, but I asked him, "What happened? Sayid tell me what happened!"

"This is what" *he replied bidding me to survey our surroundings as he told me,* "The enemy surrounded us and shed our blood. Many have passed to the other world except Catherine's immediate unit. Jacob was taken prisoner, but he was not killed. You and I were left for dead and Catherine was captured too. I witnessed Catherine's transformation."

"What do you mean transformation?" *I questioned him.*

"Did you not see? Next to you and me, she and Jacob were the only ones able to fight off these soldiers of Hell. She killed many of them; they lay dead all around you." *He replied.*

He continued to speak as I noted only the enemies' bodies lay upon the ground and only the blood of their bodies stained the Earth. I listened confused, for I thought that they were killing us en masse before I blacked out. I noticed the distant 'caws' of black crows as they circled above the battleground.

"Catherine fought with the ability of the angels. Then, as I lay bleeding beneath the shadow of an evergreen, I saw her standing on top of the hill. The morning sun was rising and it shone upon the cross sealed into her chest like a prism reflecting the sunlight. It was as if she was bathed in the light itself. I reached toward her, but I was unable to speak.

James shot her. I saw it enter her and exit her shoulder, but no blood came forth, rather a great light shone from within. I hid my face in my hands from the blinding light, as soldiers surrounded her and placed her under arrest. I heard a voice inside my head say, 'Stay still.' and I obeyed, but I opened my eyes ever so slightly. I did nothing to help her and I saw Catherine smile at me with her eyes as she was taken away."

Sayid continued "My voice failed me and I reached for my knife, but I passed out. They must have thought I was dead."

I placed my hand on his shoulder and said, 'Perhaps the Lord simply stayed your hand to save you." *I don't know why I said that. I didn't even believe in his god.*

He smiled and said, "Perhaps brother, perhaps. Now we must follow at a distance to see where they're taking Jacob and her." *We got up and we heard an Eagle cry in the distance.*

Daylight quickly waned as dark gray storm *clouds covered the sky. The darkness consumed the land like a blanket of shadow covering the whole of the earth and my heart was filled with despair. I loved Catherine, but nothing made sense anymore. This was all madness to me. I did not know what transformation Sayid alluded to, but I was glad the gunshot injury was clear through with a clean exit wound. I was so confused, but I knew I had to find a way to save Catherine.*

Sayid and I tracked the enemy at a distance for three days. We could always hear the voices of the soldiers in the distance and at night we could see their fires. Sayid and I made a shelter and slept as best we could.

Without her, my soul was like a vacant and a desolate night. She was the light of my soul that made darkness flee, and she made peace persist. Without her by my side my world was one of silent tears, alone with the broken fragments of my heart. I grieved in silence fearing that we could never be one, though a part of her remained with me always. Her love was seared like an imprint upon my heart.

On the third day we arrived at the edge of a military compound, where we saw them take Catherine and Jacob inside. I could not see how we could help her. We felt lost without her and retreated to the woods to camp. Sayid was a muffled voice in the distance as I sat lost in my own anguish, "Don't give up hope Roberts, she will survive. With God all things are possible and he works all things for good." *I did not share his outlook.*

We had lost her, we had lost the war, and we had lost the fight for our freedom. My soul wept silently in the darkness of the night. Only a lone wolf answered my cry.

The distant lamentation of the creature of the night, howling in the wilderness, shared my pain. He voiced the torment and misery I was forced to hide deep within me. It was a haunting cry that would have pierced my soul, had I felt that I had one. If I ever believed that I had a soul, that day I was sure it had died.

I heard Catherine's voice inside my head, "What do you do when darkness falls?" *She had said once,* "You reach out for the light."

How could I reach out when she was my light and she was gone? In my despondency I saw my hope of ever being with Catherine fade like a dream with the coming of morning.

Part Three:
Where Two Worlds Collide

Chapter Thirteen:
The Mark of Man

We had to accept that we could not get inside the compound for now, so we cleaned ourselves up as best we could and went into the city of Boulder the following day. We were surprised how orderly the city was. We were fighting a war for the freedom of a nation, which was living in peace, order and appeared to be under good government. The citizens were content. They did not appear on the surface to be suffering from any crime, nor did they lack adequate food, housing, or freedom of movement.

We moved about with relative ease, as long as we avoided the scanning stations and did not attempt to purchase anything, including water. The government had failed to succeed in placing a chip in most American and Canadian citizens, thanks to units like Catherine's Night Squad. The authorities did however place the chips in ID cards that were made in other countries. Without these ID cards it was very difficult to obtain goods in the large cities.

Sayid told me about a dream he had the other night; he said, "Last night an angel of the Lord told me to lead the people out of the sewers and into his forests, where they would find clean water and food, I must obey, but I will be back in time to launch our attack."

I didn't believe in his dreams, but I knew I could count on him to perform his duty. Catherine would have wanted everything to proceed as planned. We separated and he listened to his god. I set out to find a way to help Catherine. I told him, "Well good luck Sayid. I will not be going with you. I have to report to the president and see if I can help Catherine."

Sayid placed his hand on my shoulder and said, "Go with God my brother."

"Sayid," *I sighed,* "You know I don't believe in your God."

Sayid was unfazed as he assured me, "Yes brother, I am aware, but Allah spared you. Though you say you do not believe in him, it is apparent that he believes in you and he intends to use you as his instrument on earth."

I simply responded, "Yah, I have heard something like that before, good luck. I must leave you. I will send you a coded message through the usual Internet forum and update you concerning Catherine. You must enter the city on the first day of every month to retrieve the message, so be careful, don't trust any of the people you save; it is likely Augustus will have spies among them."

"Naturally I will keep them separate from the others until I forward their pictures to Eric so he can find out what he can about them." *Sayid replied.*

I shook his hand and I said with sincerity, "It has been an honor fighting with you Sayid; you are one of the best men I have ever fought with."

"Thank you." *Sayid replied,* "I appreciate that Captain Roberts. Good bye."

"Take care, Sayid."

After our brief farewell we went our separate ways, but I heard him yell over his shoulder, "Don't be offended, but I will be praying for you." *I shook my head and made my way toward the local library.*

I longed for consistency and for peace. I was torn by my desire to be with Catherine and a growing resentment for her consuming faith and her religious family. I was not one of them. I didn't belong. I was the outsider. I could not separate myself from Catherine and I could not shake the feeling in my heart that I did belong to her. I guess we all were being thrown off guard by a world gone mad. Still, I think that I managed to hide from those around me the war that raged inside of me.

It took me a couple of days to set up a meeting with the president. He arranged for me to acquire some microchip ID cards from a local agent loyal to him. I assumed my false identity and traveled by plane to Calgary, Alberta. I rented a car and drove into Banff, where I was able to meet with the president in person.

President Davidson was preparing to come out of hiding to take his rightful place as ruler of North America. He was already in contact with Augustus and peace negotiations were under way. He promised to put an end to the resistance in return for control over the entire continent. A meeting was setup between Augustus and Davidson for June sixth to fulfill America's Manifest Destiny. I felt a sense of hope again that peace would return, but I did not trust Augustus and I began to wonder if I could trust my president.

I remember Catherine warning me about him and I told her, "You can't choose your Commander-in-Chief Catherine, as a soldier you must obey his orders. I took an oath."

She said, "He is not my commander-in-chief, I rather obey my God."

The president was in the process of being returned to his seat of power, but he was still subject to the authority of Augustus and all were subject to the dictatorship of a self-proclaimed god, who now controlled the political and religious majorities on Earth.

The president assured me, "It is apparent from your reports that you admire Catherine, but I will require a full-length written and oral report of everything you witnessed and know about her."

"Why is that sir? I have reported to you faithfully all along." *My distrust of this man was growing with each statement that fell from his lips.*

The president said, "Captain Roberts, I trust I still hold your allegiance and I can trust you to do what is right for America."

"Yes Sir," *I said standing at attention without making eye contact lest he see my insincerity. I would be loyal to America, but that did not mean that I would place my faith in any man whom maneuvered his way to rule her.*

Again I felt conflicted between my duty and the woman I loved. I was informed. "Catherine has been arrested by Augustus' forces. There is nothing I can do about that son, but if you cooperate fully, I can keep Augustus from having charges laid against you." *He had sold out for power; there was little doubt in my mind. How could I help Catherine if I too was arrested? I had to be smart about the next steps I would take.*

The President said, "Roberts, I knew I could count on your support. A man with your record always does his duty" *What the president didn't yet know was that my first duty was to Catherine. I would have laid my life down to protect her without hesitation. How could I be loyal to her and obey my orders?*

I was ordered to submit my journals and give testimony against the woman I loved. "I will sir, if you can ensure that I have complete visitation and access to Catherine at all times." *I replied. I didn't lie, but he did not know that I kept two journals, one that was cold and factual that did not express my true feelings for her and one that told all.*

"I will arrange that Captain, however it places you under the eye of Augustus. He will undoubtedly know who you are. You place yourself in danger by visiting her." *The president warned.*

"I will go in there in disguise, under one of the assumed identities." *I replied.*

The president informed me. "Very well that could be easily arranged, but I will need some time to secure a proper cover for you. We will make you a military psychologist. Word is that she is considered by some to be mentally ill."

I handed over my journal, but I did not give him my private journal that contained detailed accounts of our battles together and fully shared my affection for her. I was determined that she would not face death.

I was told that the prosecution strove to find her guilty and sought the death penalty. I could not allow that, so this was why I appeared before every panel and at every hearing.

The public was demanding vengeance. They wanted her dead. It was agreed that the trial would be publicized and aired on television. It was the case of the century.

Catherine was charged with one hundred and seven murders, for crimes that were committed over a three-year period. She was charged with evading arrest and disarming a police officer, for committing a felony while in armor, and with illegal possession of a firearm. She was also charged with hate crimes against the state, and with the destruction and theft of government property. They charged her with every crime they could think of both great and small including treason and murder. They were determined to make her face justice for the crimes they said she committed.

Through it all I was steadfast and determined to be viewed by all of America as a reliable witness for the defense, but the prosecutor was sure my testimony would serve his case well, so I was called as his first witness at her final trial. I wore a dress uniform from earlier in the war, hoping to appeal to the real American sentiment, which I refused to accept was dead.

I testified before Catherine, a board of government representatives, doctors and then a panel of judges. I was called to the stand on her court date by the lead prosecutor, a short beady eyed man with pasty white skin. In a sinister voice he said. "I would like to call Captain Peter Roberts to the stand."

I was asked to state my full name and former occupation, as well as my current status. "I am Peter Joseph Roberts, a former Captain in the US Marines. I am at present serving as Chief Liaison for Military Operations for the President of North America."

After I swore to tell the truth the prosecutor stated, "Captain, we understand that you contacted and infiltrated the defendant's rebel forces, under the direct orders of the President of America. Are these statements accurate?"

I replied, "I was under orders of the president to make contact with Catherine and her supporters, but I was not ordered to infiltrate them." *Catherine shed a single tear as I began my testimony. My testimony would determine her ability to stand trial for treason and murder, or be labeled insane. My heart broke, as I spoke.*

The prosecuting attorney continued, "Is it true that during your time with the defendant, you witnessed her lead attacks against several government facilities?"

"Yes." *I sullenly confirmed.*

He handed me my journal and a stack of papers as he inquired, "Is this your journal and are these copies of your email communiqués with the president?"

I looked over the journal and read some of the emails before I answered, "Yes that is my journal and although I have not read all of them, they appear to be my email communications with the president."

The prosecutor stated smugly, "I would like to enter into evidence, these as exhibit A and B, if it pleases the court." *The clerk took the evidence to the panel of judges.*

He continued, "Let it be noted that within these journals the defendant known as Catherine Miles has been acknowledged by my witness as the one responsible for orchestrating and leading various attacks against these government facilities."

He stopped talking and he handed me a list of various factories we had destroyed and he said, "Are these the factories that are identified in your writings the same ones Catherine Miles led her cohorts to destroy?"

I replied coldly, "Yes, they are."

The prosecutor continued to pour over my journals and emails for hours. He used them and my testimony to bear witness that Catherine committed all of the crimes for which she was charged. Within this evidence were accounts of the attacks, as well as summations of her statements, concerning her crimes. The prosecution was successfully building its case against her."

Catherine's lawyer was a tall lean man with a slight Scottish accent. He stood up and declared, "I object. My client is unresponsive and unable to respond to these accusations. Furthermore Your Honors, including the emails to and from the president is unlawful, since my client has a right to face her accuser. The journals though written by the Captain became the property of the president once they were handed to him. I move that both this personal journal and the emails be removed as evidence against my client."

The judge who sat at the center of the panel replied, "Objection noted. Motion denied."

The prosecutor smiled and asked, "Captain Roberts, did you personally witness Catherine kill any government officers during your commission?"

He was making her look like a well-trained saboteur, and I was helping him destroy her. My heart was breaking. I never meant to betray her. I wanted to die, although no one else would have known for I was a master of emotional detachment, but it was killing me inside.

"No" *I replied through gritted teeth. I wanted to ring this smug little weasel's neck.*

"How many enlisted men did you see her kill?" He inquired.

I replied sarcastically, "I didn't count how many died. I did not stop to check if they were breathing when I passed by, but I did not see her personally kill anyone." *I lied.*

"Well could you say that several bodies were shot during these attacks?" *He sneered.*

"Perhaps, we often attacked on moonless nights. We all had jobs to do. I cannot say I witnessed her actually kill anyone. She engaged in battle, but whether or not she was the one who actually killed anyone, I could not testify one way or the other."

The prosecutor glared at me as he hissed," Captain, was it not your job to observe Catherine Miles; are you telling me in the many months of your observations you did not actually see her kill anyone?"

"That is exactly what I am saying." *I replied.*

He walked across the courtroom and held up my journal and said, "Did you not often write about her successful attacks in killing government soldiers and employees who worked at these facilities."

I sternly noted, "No, you inferred that from my reports, I merely mentioned what facilities were attacked and successfully destroyed."

The little man became frustrated with me and he held up his hand to me as he looked toward the panel of judges and said, "Permission to declare Peter Roberts as a hostile witness."

"Permission denied." The center judge declared.

The prosecutor said with resignation, "If it pleases the court I have no further questions for this witness at this time. I am confident after you all review the evidence before you that you will find that the defendant is indeed guilty."

Catherine's defense lawyer cross-examined me; "Captain Roberts are these copies of emails that you collected from Edward Stephens following his death?"

I looked over the emails and then I replied, "Yes they are."

"I would like to enter into evidence the emails for the court to review. I believe once you read them you will discover both Edward Stephen's concern for my client's mental state, as well as my client's diminishing mental wellness as reflected in her written communications, just before his death. Captain Roberts, can you read aloud the highlighted portion from December 12. 2022.*" Her lawyer said all of this as he handed me a particular email.*

"Dear Edward, darkness attacks me at every turn. I battle Satan himself and every person I meet I have to hold at arm's length. So few can be trusted and yet there are so many who need to be saved. I must live in the wild to prevent capture. Others have followed me into the wilderness. I do not know how I am going to feed them all, but I should not worry, God will provide. He speaks to me often, I hear his voice in my head, and The Holy Spirit counsels me, but I must make time to listen, for her voice is like a whisper on the wind. It will be a long cold winter. I rarely get to see Jesus, but sometimes he appears to me and comforts me. He will come soon. Until he does I must fight the enemy at every turn and show them no mercy. I must be on guard, for I am sure the snake will soon infiltrate my group, if he has not already. Pray for me, I need God's strength for I feel so weak and alone. My prayers are with you."

Reply: "Catherine. I have been ordered to serve in the medical field, praise be to God. I am worried about you my dear Catherine. I fear the darkness consumes your thoughts. I wish you could be at peace and smile again. I pray that you will soon discover that you have nothing to fear. Light will come, freedom will reign and the war will end. I pray that you will be surrounded by good, loyal friends whom you can trust. Be on guard; remember to take every thought captive. I pray the winter will not be harsh for you and those with you. I pray God provides and protects all of you. Remember, all life is in his hands. My prayers are with you also." *I finished reading and I looked at Catherine, she seemed unmoved by the letter. She did not look at me and she gave no reaction.*

The attorney then gently asked me, "To the best of your knowledge, did Edward have any concerns about Catherine's mental state?"

"Yes," *I replied,* "he said she suffered from dark dreams and horrid visions. He prayed for her every day. He told me that he feared that darkness would consume her mind and lead to her destruction, if she did not find the support and help that she needed."

Then he calmly asked if I had any direct knowledge of Catherine's personal history concerning any form of sexual abuse.

"Yes, I met Catherine several years ago in Ireland, where I had prevented her from being raped by a group of soldiers." *I replied with honesty.*

"Did your relationship with Pastor Edward ever reveal any post-traumatic stress disorders due to this trauma?" *He inquired.*

"Yes, he often shared his concern with me over her mental stability and her inability to trust."

The prosecutor objected stating this testimony was hearsay.

"I have submitted Edward's personal journal and writings to substantiate my claims." *The defense declared. Edward's diary and his correspondence with Catherine were entered in as evidence. The judge allowed the questions to continue.*

"Can you describe for the court any specific examples the defendant's lack of mental stability?"

I took a deep breath. I knew this would be painful for Catherine, as this would be the first time she would be confronted with the whole truth. "After Edward found Catherine, she slipped in and out of a coma for several months. Eventually she came to consciousness and then she would suffer from horrible dreams, which haunted her and she did not share her dreams and visions with him for a long time. She battled periods of detachment, or depression and withdrawal. Then she began lucid dreaming. She would argue out loud and speak to people who were not in the room. One day he passed the library and he heard her arguing with someone who was not there and then when he confronted her delusion she kicked him clear across the room." *Catherine looked so betrayed and hurt as I gave my testimony.*

One last question, "Do you believe Catherine Miles is sane?"

I bowed my head in shame, but I had to tell the truth to save her. "I think that she is delusional, as are many of her followers. They speak to a god they cannot see, they dictate their actions based upon visions and dreams. They claim to hear the voice of God himself. They say he speaks to them, but I have never seen what they see; I have never heard the voice of which they speak. So if hearing voices and dictating the path of your life based on visions and dreams are insane, then yes I would have to concede that she and her followers are mad."

"One final question captain, was Catherine Miles an American citizen at the time of these attacks?" *Her defense lawyer asked.*

"No" *I replied,* "She is Canadian by birth. We were not considered one nation at that time

The defense lawyer said, "Thank you for your time Captain. I have no more questions for this witness."

The prosecutor cross-examined me. I was asked to reveal everything I knew pertaining to her relationship with Edward Stephens. "Catherine was a close personal friend to Edward, who served under my command before he died in a gas attack four years ago." *I answered.*

"You knew the defendant prior to your military relationship?" *The prosecutor asked this as he threw a wicked glance Catherine's way.*

"Yes I became" *I took a deep breath before continuing,* "I came to know Edward when he served under me and I recently have become quite close to Catherine, however I met her briefly several years before, I already testified to this." *It broke my heart that Catherine would not even look at me. It was as if I didn't even exist.*

"Is it fair to say you have an allegiance, if not adoration for Catherine Miles?" *The prosecutor asked.*

Before I could reply, the defense lawyer stood up and said, "I object, Captain Roberts is not on trial."

The center judge spoke again, "Sustained. A valid objection. Does the prosecution have any further questions concerning the Captain's knowledge of the defendant's attacks on the government installations, her possession of military equipment and technology, and of killings that he may have personally witnessed during his assignment, aside from his relationship with Mr. Stephens?"

He asked me if I approved of the raids I participated in with her.

"Objection" *the defense yelled before I could say anything.*

The prosecutor said "Withdrawn." *Then he came back at me and asked;* "To your knowledge did Mr. Edward Stephens believe she was insane?"

"No, he was religious and believed there may have been a spiritual element involved, but he had never seen such spirits himself. They both shared the same belief structure and he often said that her visions could be real. He was torn, so I can't say for sure what he believed." *I answered truthfully.*

He walked across the courtroom saying, "So the answer is that the one person who knew her the best felt she was of sound mind?"

"I don't know." *I replied,* "All I know is that he was concerned."

Catherine looked at me with a deep sadness when she realized her trust in me was misplaced. I was trying to save her life, but she only saw my betrayal. I stared deeply into those beautiful eyes, as I said, "I am sorry Catherine." *She looked away. I knew I must be dead to her.*

After he had finished questioning me the prosecutor attempted to prove that Catherine was not insane, but rather that her history of violence and terrorism was evident from the time she was in university. The prosecutor called her old martial arts instructor, Master Kevin Ming to take the stand.

The prosecutor said, "Master Ming, will you please tell us your relationship to the defendant."

"Certainly," *He smiled and nodded as he continued,* "I am her Sensei. I trained her while she attended Trinity College."

When Catherine saw him she looked shocked, dismayed and then confused. I heard her speaking to herself, "The monk?" *I looked toward the small Asian man dressed in his long white robe.*

"Can you tell us how you would rate Catherine's abilities?" *The pasty little lawyer asked.*

Master Ming gave Catherine a fond smile as he stated, "Catherine was my finest student in Ireland. I had the pleasure of training her for a few years in America as well prior to her desire to attend school abroad."

The prosecutor walked back and forth across the courtroom as he asked, "How long was the defendant under your instruction?"

"For four years in Ireland and for almost three in America." *Master Ming replied. Then the prosecutor inquired as to what level of training she had obtained and the monk stated with a hint of pride,* "She achieved her third degree black belt."

The beady eyed little man narrowed his eyes as he asked, "Is Catherine capable of killing?"

Master Ming answered, "As humans we are all able to kill."

The prosecutor bowed and said, "Let me rephrase the question. Does Catherine Miles have the skills necessary to kill someone or several people with efficiency?"

"Yes, she has the capability and the skills necessary, but we only fight to defend ourselves." *Master Ming replied*

The prosecutor finished his questions and then the defense successfully established Catherine's character, "Master Ming can you please share with the court what you know about Catherine's character?"

"Yes*," he smiled as he recalled,* "Catherine was an impulsive angry girl when she first came to me, but she learned the value of peace. She is a gentle and free spirited individual who, although lacking discipline, was one who abhorred violence and war. She knew to only fight in self-defense.*" This was good for Catherine's case, but she still looked confused.*

The defense inquired, "Forgive me Master Ming, but how is it possible for Ms. Miles to achieve such an advanced level of proficiency in martial arts in such a short period of time? Doesn't it take a lifetime to achieve such mastery?*"*

Master Ming smiled with pride as he replied, "Yes, usually this is true, however Catherine not only attended regular classes under my instruction, but she received private instruction as well. She was very driven to excel. In the year between her high school graduation and university her father paid me to instruct her exclusively. She worked for several hours every day with me."

The prosecutor cross-examined. He asked Master Ming, "Can you tell the court whether or not Catherine, to your knowledge had any other training that would facilitate a militaristic way of life?"

"Yes." *The sensei answered,* "She had extensive weapons training with both martial arts weapons and with firearms through military summer camps."

The prosecutor argued, "Catherine Miles possessed the skill and knowledge to not only commit these crimes for which she is charged, but as shared in the captain's journal and communications with the president himself, that she chose to share this training with others, thereby promoting rebellion."

The prosecutor placed his hands on the desk directly across from Catherine and looked her in the eyes as he said, "She is not insane. She is a cold-blooded killer, a traitor and a thief. She is a leader of a rebel group and an enemy of the state. Is she deluded by believing God supports her cause? Perhaps, or maybe she used this to manipulate weak minds to commit these crimes with her. I hereby argue that after the honorable panel of judges reviews the evidence before them they will conclude that Catherine Miles is indeed guilty of all these crimes, including, murder and treason."

The defense lawyer got up and said, "If she is as dangerous as you claim, should you be risking your life by standing directly across from her?" *After this comment the courtroom erupted in laughter. I knew she could snap that little weasel's neck like a twig. She didn't. She remained motionless, but she did meet the prosecutor's gaze and he swallowed and moved farther away.*

A gavel was hit hard as the center judge demanded, "Order in the court. Does the prosecution have any other witnesses, or evidence to present."

"No your honor, I have no further witnesses nor any more evidence at this time. The prosecution rests." *The prosecutor answered.*

Catherine said nothing in her own defense. Her lawyer said she was a difficult and uncooperative client, and that he feared she lacked the competency to stand trial.

Her lawyer was a level-headed, rational person who felt with all sincerity that Catherine was indeed insane. He seemed comfortable and confident, but I could tell he had little success in obtaining any information from Catherine.

He built his case largely based on the testimony of others, primarily: Edward Stephens, doctor Ash and myself. I also was the one responsible for supplying the court with the correspondence between Catherine and Edward.

"Then the defense may call their first witness." *The judge declared.*

The defense called Dr. Ash to the stand. She convinced many of the judges that Catherine was suffering some deep-seated physiological distress due to some very traumatic experiences. This was accentuated by Catherine's near death experience, and shock due to the physical trauma to her head during the accident. She was also convinced that Catherine practiced self-mutilation due to her belief that she was the embodiment of a Christ-like messianic figure.

"Catherine" *the doctor said,* "Suffers from a persecution complex in conjunction with paranoid schizophrenia. She needs extensive psychological treatment."

"Thank you Dr. Ash. She is your witness counselor." *With that Catherine's lawyer sat down,*

The prosecutor asked, "Dr. Ash, are you a licensed psychiatrist, or a medical doctor?"

She replied, "I am a general family practitioner."

The little man said with a wicked grin upon his face and a sarcastic tone, "So based on your obvious expertise in the field of psychology and deviant behavior, on what basis, if any, do you found your assessment of the defendant? Do you have any concrete proof to support your claims that the defendant suffers from this so-called persecution complex in conjunction with schizophrenia?"

The doctor smiled back at the prosecutor and said, "Catherine has exhibited many of the signs of someone who has been sexually violated in some way, such as hurting herself. She has seared a cross into her own flesh. This requires intense heat and she would have to be extremely detached from her pain, or feel she deserves it, in order to mutilate herself like this. She could also be hurting herself physically to override the emotional pain"

The courtroom watched as a judge ordered a security guard to open Catherine's blouse to reveal her cross inlaid in her chest and the chain melted into her skin. A few on the panel gasped. Catherine gave no reaction.

The prosecution asked, "Do you have any proof that she did not suffer this by being burned in a fire? Why do you assume it is a form of self-mutilation?"

The doctor answered, "I do not know if she did this herself or had it done to her, but the skin directly under the chain and the cross are seared, there is no damage to her skin on any other areas of her body including immediately around the cross or chain itself. The rest of her flesh is unharmed.

The prosecutor dismissed the issue as cosmetic when he said, "Aside from this cross, that is apparently seared to her flesh, which may be akin to piercing, tattoos and other forms of personal expression, how do you conclude your assessment of the accused's psychological state is valid?"

The doctor replied, "Victims can also dissociate themselves by creating different personalities to cope, blocking memories, through amnesia, and abusing alcohol and drugs. They may have mood swings, depression, suicidal tendencies, or thoughts, insomnia, sleep disorders, bad dreams, flash backs, or hallucinations. They can express their pain through violent tendencies and they may also experience what is known as, out of body experiences. Catherine has exhibited all of these symptoms to varying degrees."

The prosecutor sneered, "Do you have proof of this?"

The doctor replied, "I kept careful records during her stay with my patient, Edward Stephens. I also recorded our telephone conversations which testify to such incidences."

The court listened to many of the recordings, but they had no effect on Catherine's demeanor even though they were helping ensure she would not suffer the death penalty. One of the recordings substantiated the doctor's testimony, "Hello Dr. Ash this is Edward Stephens calling; could you please come out to the house right away and bring a sleeping prescription."

The doctor responded, "Why Edward, what's wrong?"

"It is Catherine; she has not slept in four days. She eats very little and she seems more distant and withdrawn. She still can't remember anything about her past and the few times she has fallen asleep, I have had to rush in and wake her because her dreams appear to be terrifying and..."

"What is it Edward, tell me!" *The doctor insisted.*

Silence was on the line and then Edward shared, "Catherine believes she has seen the Devil."

The doctor warned, "I am on my way Edward, keep her calm, but you must consider that you may have to admit her. You may not be the one to help her."

"If she believes she saw Satan himself, then I am the perfect one to help her doctor." *Edward calmly replied.*

The doctor informed him, "I'm on my way."

"Thank you doctor, I'll see you soon." *This was all Edward replied before hanging up the phone.*

The defense entered the recorded telephone conversations into evidence along with the doctor's notes taken during her frequent visits with Catherine and then Edward while they were under her care.

"I have no further questions for this witness." *The prosecutor walked back toward his desk.*

The defense said, "I would like to recall Captain Peter Roberts to the stand."

I sat down and the officer of the court reminded me that I was still under oath. The defense attorney said, "Captain Roberts, have you ever personally witnessed any of the symptoms that Doctor Ash spoke of, aside from the depression, hallucinations and bad dreams you testified about that Edward Stephens informed you of?"

I answered without hesitation, "Yes Catherine drank a lot of alcohol. When I met her in Ireland she drank more whiskey than any of my men and she held her liquor well. She did not even slur her speech or lose her balance."

The defense inquired, "In your experience Captain, is this a common ability for an individual to drink much with little obvious effects?"

"No." *I said,* "Only a veteran drinker can accomplish such a feat."

He continued to question, "Are there any other such instances you can testify to?"

"Yes, Catherine drank a lot of alcohol while we were in the wilderness. She was seldom without either a whiskey or a Merlot in her hand." *I answered honestly.*

The defense inquired, "Did she exhibit any of the other symptoms the doctor spoke of?"

I answered plainly, "She seldom slept. She suffered from insomnia; she went for days on end without sleep. Catherine also inexplicably became sullen and detached from me for many months at a time where she became increasingly reclusive. She and I were very close and then she became quite distant. We regained our closeness and communication, although she will not even look at me now."

Her lawyer asked me, "Did she ever have violent outbursts?"

I replied "Not in my presence, with exception to when she had to fight for her own life on the beach in Ireland. She had to defend herself from multiple attackers. She successfully fended them off until I arrived to assist her."

The lawyer prodded, "Did she ever share with you any violent episodes from her past?"

"Yes, when she was younger and a date slapped her, he showed up on her doorstep the next morning and her father let the guy in despite his violent behavior toward his daughter. She went ballistic. She threw her father against the wall and the guy out the door. She told me, 'I was livid, even psychotic.' *With that the defense finished questioning me.*

"Objection, this is hearsay." *The prosecutor protested.*

"Sustained." *The judge replied.*

"Your honor, I have contacted Catherine Miles' father personally in hopes of helping my client and establish if there were any childhood incidences that demonstrate her longtime battle with mental illness." *Her lawyer spoke as he ruffled through some files before him as he continued,* "I have before me several email communiqués that demonstrate early signs of her mental issues. I have this particular incident included in these communiqués and I would like to enter them in as evidence at this time."

The court agreed and my testimony was accepted.

The defense called his final witness, "I would like to call corporal Ian Markus to the stand."

A giant soldier wearing Augustus' elite Special Forces uniform came to the stand. The defense requested, "Please state you name and rank, for the court."

The soldier said, "My name is corporal Ian Markus, I am a former member of ARON Special Forces, I am currently a corporal in the Lumen security division.

The lawyer asked, "Do you recognize the defendant?"

"Yes." *He replied.*

"Can you please share for the court, where you know the defendant from and what occurred at that time?" *Her lawyer asked.*

The soldier said, "She was present at a raid we made in Aspen, May of last year."

The defense asked, "Did you witness this woman kill anyone during that raid?"

"No" *He lied. I don't know why one of Augustus' forces would lie. I thought the government wanted her dead. What were they up to?*

The defense continued his line of questioning, "Did you engage the defendant in combat?"

The soldier answered, "Yes, we were sent to apprehend her and she resisted arrest. She disabled me and incapacitated me."

Her lawyer inquired, "Was she armed?"

"Yes, she had a knife and a handgun. She had me immobilized and she could have killed me at will, but she refrained from such action." *The soldier replied.*

"I have no further questions for this witness. Thank you corporal." *The defense had no other witnesses and the prosecution did not have any questions for the soldier.*

The prosecution and defense then gave their closing statements. The prosecutor tried to reiterate, "Catherine Miles is a well-trained militaristic individual and a leader of a rebel group, known as the Resistance. She should suffer the death penalty for her crimes. She is not mad. She is an enemy of the state.

Whether or not she viewed herself as Canadian, American, or a devout Christian, is irrelevant. To engage in any form of opposition to the World

Federation is treasonous. We are not citizens of some former country of origin; we are citizens of the New World Order and we are all subject to that government and its agencies."

The prosecutor held up a video file and said, "Earlier I had admitted into evidence video footage of Catherine Miles resisting arrest, this was taken prior to the reign of Augustus. She demonstrated her violent behaviors, establishing that she was a threat to society even then. Catherine is a lethal killer, guilty of the murders of numerous courageous men serving the World Federation."

He motioned toward the ARON officer who testified earlier as he said, "The fact that Catherine Miles may have spared the life of one of ARON'S officers is irrelevant. The greater issue is that she had the capability to not only engage in combat with the most highly trained and deadliest fighting force in the history of our planet, but she succeeded in defeating him. She is a danger to the peaceful society our illustrious leader Augustus has created."

He pointed at Catherine and continued, "Catherine Miles is guilty of the deaths, either directly or indirectly, of hundreds of loyal fighting men. She must be eliminated. She is also guilty of the destruction of several government facilities. Her involvement alone in these attacks warrants that she answers for her treason with her life. It is my opinion that the court should hold this villain to account and find her guilty as charged."

With that the prosecution finished, but he could not prove she was in her right mind, or that she herself committed the murders and theft. I knew Eric routinely cut all security feeds before every operation, so nothing was ever recorded. The prosecution had enough circumstantial evidence because of my writings and my testimony to prove that she was involved in treasonous activity, but not enough to prove she was guilty for orchestrating it.

The defense argued, "It is clear that Catherine Miles was equipped from early childhood to develop the skills necessary to mold her to become a formidable fighter. There is no doubt that she possessed the skills to not only kill another human being, but she willingly shared that knowledge of self-defense with others. Catherine may have the capability; however the prosecution has failed to prove that she actually committed the crimes she is charged with. Did she have the physical capability? Yes, but did she actually commit the crimes she is charged with?"

The defense lawyer continued, "Even if my client committed these crimes, even if she willingly destroyed government facilities and as the recorded footage submitted by the prosecution shows that she disarmed a police officer, this too is irrelevant for she is not sane."

He smiled and touched Catherine's shoulder as he said, "Furthermore, you all have seen this recording of this so-called assault on the officer and her resisting arrest. The footage reveals that Catherine ran in fear and used minimal force to avoid capture. She did not use the weapon against him. These are hardly the actions of a murderer. You also heard one of our most highly trained soldiers testify that she had the opportunity to kill him and did not."

The defense lawyer walked toward the prosecutor's desk and pointed at him as he said, "The prosecutor would have you believe Catherine is a lethal weapon and guilty of killing many men. She may be trained, however there are no witnesses to these crimes and there is no evidence that Catherine has killed anyone. On the contrary many have testified that despite her capabilities she is more likely to hurt herself than others. All charges brought against her should be dropped, for my colleague has failed to prove beyond a shadow of doubt that she herself committed them and she is not mentally responsible."

Catherine's lawyer moved back and placed a hand on Catherine's shoulder as he expressed, "It is obvious that Catherine never had the mental capacity to do any more than she was either programmed, or compelled to do. She operates from an irrational state of mind. She bases her decisions upon dreams and in response to her own fragile emotional state. Her judgment is erratic and irrational. She suffers from paranoia and she hears voices often. Her impulse control is damaged by years of failure in dealing with the reality of her painful past, which is only exacerbated by her alcohol consumption and lack of sleep. She is sick and in deep need of psychological treatment. She needs to be medically treated for her condition, not punished for it."

Her lawyer walked toward the panel of judges and pointed back toward Catherine as he said, "Look at her; it is plain to see for yourselves, that she is not in her right mind. She has not spoken once in all these months in her own defense. Please send this woman to a mental facility, where she can receive the treatment she desperately needs." *Catherine just stared into the distance, lost and detached, her eyes glazed over.*

The judges convened to deliberate the case, as well as carefully review all of the evidence set before them. We returned to court the following day to hear the verdict. The entire atmosphere was devised to intimidate and justify their decision. They sat above you in a position of power and authority, which compelled you to feel that they not only had the authority to pass judgment on you, but make you feel inferior.

They entered the courtroom with their long black robes flowing about them. They did not smile, or show any sign of sympathy. Their eyes were stern and their heads held high as they took their seats. The judges sat above all of us looking down upon the accused. The rest of us in the courtroom took out seats as well, preparing ourselves to hear the verdict.

The judge who sat at the center of the panel spoke with a deep and resounding voice, "We have carefully weighed all of the evidence set before us. We have concluded that the defendant is guilty of resisting arrest and assaulting a police officer. It is apparent that she was indeed involved in the destruction of several government facilities; however the prosecution has failed to prove that she either planned them, or encouraged anyone else to participate in said activities. Furthermore it is the opinion of this court that there is only circumstantial evidence that suggests that she was responsible for the murder of the government employees guarding the destroyed factories. It is apparent that Catherine Miles did participate in treasonous behavior by engaging in terrorist activities against the state; however we do not sentence her to death. It is the opinion of this court that Catherine Miles is not fit to stand trial for her crimes. There is sufficient evidence to prove that she is mentally ill and therefore cannot be held accountable for her crimes. This court deems that Catherine Miles is a danger to herself and may be a threat to others, therefore we sentence her to confinement at a secure mental facility namely, Colorado Mental Health Institute at Fort Logan for further evaluation."

I breathed a sigh of relief as Catherine was found insane and thankful she would not face death. She showed no emotion as they walked her from the courthouse. People spat at her and yelled all kinds of hateful slurs at her. Her only reaction was a single silent tear falling from her face. I stayed by her side and the only words she uttered as that tear fell, "So many lost souls." *She looked at Sayid who was standing in the crowd, and smiled ever so slightly as they placed her in the ambulance.*

When she arrived at the asylum she would not allow them to mark her hand. Criminals and especially dangerous offenders had to be inserted with a microchip tracking device by law, but Catherine killed three orderlies as they attempted to put one inside her.

After I was told of this, I came to the asylum to try and calm her. When I had arrived at her room I heard crashing and yelling, and I saw that four soldiers were fighting with her. She moved with lightning speed and killed all of them within seconds.

I still recall how she swiftly kicked one man in the groin and as he keeled over she snapped his neck without hesitation. The other three men encircled her; she kicked one man in the nose and it shot forth into his brain. He died instantly. Then she quickly used a knife hand to the third soldier's trachea crushing it, following that she moved toward her final assailant. Catherine picked up a long needle from a dead man's hand and moved toward the other who was backed toward the corner of the room, he tried to strike her, but she blocked him with ease and before he could strike at her again she stabbed the needle through his eye. I could not believe my eyes. A normal man had no hope of defeating her. She was too fast, too strong, and too well trained.

I ran to her and she recognized me immediately despite my disguise. I was dressed as a doctor and I asked her, "Catherine, are you okay? Why did you kill these men? Why did you kill the three orderlies before them?"

"They're trying to put the enemy's mark on me. I will not allow it." *She growled.*

"Catherine they will force you, you can't stop them. You must submit, or they will kill you." *I pleaded.*

"Let them try. If they have the power to kill me it is because it has been given to them by my Heavenly Father, but I would willingly die before I permit any such thing." *She seethed.*

I begged, "Catherine, you can't win, they will simply send more troops to subdue you. Catherine please, I can't watch you die."

She looked up at me with resolve as she said, "There are things far worse than death; you of all people should know that. Would you have me lose my soul with my freedom? No earthly power can force me to receive the Mark of the Beast."

She sent me away, and then the Special Forces unit was sent in. It was chaos. Six men with the same strength, speed, and agility as Catherine overpowered her and sedated her. I had seen them shoot her with a tranquillizer upon entering her room, but it did not take effect immediately. She did succeed in kicking one in the face and elbowing another in the head, but she could not win against such power with a sedative rushing through her bloodstream. Catherine resisted but two soldiers held her arms and two held her legs. The other two strapped her to the bed.

It took all six to subdue her and still she struggled kicked and screamed, "No, No, take your hands off me. I won't let you do this. You can't do this to me." *They shot her with a second tranquilizer and her speech faded.*

I was escorted from the area and notified, "You will have to leave now doctor. We are sorry you had to witness us using what you may deem as excessive force, but as you can see she has killed several men already. She is a very lethal woman. You may visit her tomorrow, we were forced to heavily sedate her and she will be unresponsive for several hours."

As I left the room in my doctor's disguise I looked over my shoulder and saw that they had placed the microchip in her left hand, she was sealed her with the Mark of Man.

Chapter Fourteen:
Suffering in Silence

I visited Catherine the day after she was micro-chipped. I entered the room and I fell to my knees by her bed and begged her forgiveness. She looked at me with coldness in her eyes I had never seen before. She said, "Why did you lie about Edward?"

"I told the truth Catherine; nothing I said was a lie."

"Do you think I'm insane Peter?"

I replied gently, "I think you believe fervently in your cause, I know your followers do too. I don't believe in your god and I believe when it comes to Edward, you saw what you needed to see."

Catherine did not accept this answer and I detected a painful pleading in her gaze as she ordered me to answer the question, "Answer the question Peter. Do you think I'm crazy?"

I looked away from her as I stood trying to answer it diplomatically, "I know you have gone through a lot, hell we all have. I know you believe that this near death experience was real and that God talks to you. I know watching Edward die in that gas attack must have been very traumatic, but Catherine I can't believe in a god who allows so much pain, so much suffering and injustice, and so much bloodshed."

She looked so hurt and so betrayed as she said, "Edward didn't die, he was taken to heaven and thousands of people saw it that day. I know you don't believe in a God you cannot see, but I thought you at least believed me."

"Catherine I saw Edward die with my own eyes. The horror of watching my men die in that gas attack is so vivid that I don't even have to close my eyes to see them helplessly grasping in desperation for their masks, nor can I erase their screams. They echo to this day in my mind. I saw Edward's skin eaten from his body and his flesh dissolved before his bones hit the ground."

I tried to touch her shoulder, but she turned away from me as I said, "Catherine I have been thinking about your near death experience and I believe your encounter with Satan and with God was a vivid dream you experienced when you were unconscious. Think about it Catherine, I looked like the Devil you said, when you described him you could have easily been describing me, or even yourself in a male form if you had a fair complexion. You felt guilt over us wanting each other that night all those years ago. I was your temptation and you almost gave into me. That natural desire was distorted by your religious beliefs and by those bastards who tried to violate you. That must have been very traumatic for you.

Master Ming was obviously the monk you thought you saw in Hell. I heard you say it in the courtroom and I saw how his appearance disturbed you.

The priest being raped in Hell by the demon reflects the vile sin you knew was committed against Brother John's father and you wanted justice. The red dress you wore when you say you danced with the Devil could have come from your attempt to seduce John and the guilt knowing that his heart sinned wanting you.

Catherine your whole experience was a cruel fabrication of the mind born from guilt and childhood indoctrination. You say while you were in Hell you saw, micro-organisms swimming in your blistered skin. That is impossible Catherine; you need a powerful microscope to see something so small. It was all a cruel fabrication of the mind.

I'm sorry, but I have to tell you the truth because I love you."

Catherine stared deeply into my eyes as if searching the very depths of my soul as she inquired, "Peter do you believe in good and evil?"

"Yes." *I replied,* "I have witnessed little good, but I've seen great evil permeate the heart of man."

She sighed, "If you believe in good and evil, then surely you could conceive of a God who is good and a Devil who seeks to kill and destroy anyone he can devour."

"I have never seen either God, or the Devil." *I continued,* "I believe the world is what we make it, Catherine."

"Yes it is Peter. The world was given to man, but there is undoubtedly good and evil in both the seen and unseen world, there is no doubt about that. The only question is which side are you on?" *She did not detect that her words had any effect on me, so she continued with a sense of pleading in her voice, mingled with a spirit of resolve,* "Well I did not imagine what I saw Peter. I see a realm others can't see. I witness the spiritual warfare all around me. I see both good and evil, I hear it and sense it before I need to look. It may be a matter of faith, or even madness to you, but I know it is real. I'm not mad, I'm not mad, I'm not mad." *Catherine began rocking herself to these words, however it was no longer me she talked to so, tired and depressed, I left her all alone.*

She did not say another word to me for many months; our two worlds collided, but still I vowed to visit her every day. She often sat alone in silence, however sometimes I would hear her speaking to someone as I entered the room. As soon as she detected my presence she would speak no more.

She was slipping so far away and I feared I would never reach her again. I contacted the president and he arranged a visitation from her parents. Both had been trying to see her to no avail, but now they had an opportunity. Maybe they could snap her out of her silent suffering and detachment.

Catherine's parents were with me as I escorted them inside the facility. Her mother was beautiful and composed, she looked like an older version of her daughter, however I saw that she was unnerved by the madness that surrounded her once inside. Catherine's father was silent, and resolute. He walked with determination and composure as well, until he saw Catherine.

Catherine's mother rushed to her side, kneeling and crying as she rocked her daughter in her arms. "Oh Catherine, we thought you were dead."

Catherine looked distant and disconnected, but she did reply, "I was dead."

Catherine's father said nothing; initially he just stared at his daughter with shock and disbelief. The mother continued to weep, holding her daughter close to her as Catherine pleaded, "Don't cry Mom, I can't deal with that right now. I'm not strong enough." *Those were words I never thought Catherine would say. It pained me to see her so weak, so hopeless and lost.*

Catherine's father moved toward her, "I thought you were dead Cathy, I had no idea you were alive. If I had, I would have helped you. I only found out it was you in the televised trial when your lawyer called me."

Catherine looked at her father and said, "I did die Dad, but if you want to help me, help me now! Get me out of this place! I need you to get me out of here now."

Her dad wept as tears of weakness took over this once strong man's demeanor. "I can't get you out of here Cathy, I don't have the means. Money is useless now, you know that. I have no more power, no more influence, I am nobody in this New World Order."

"Dad I've never asked for anything before, I need you to find a way. Surely you know someone who can help. You have military and business contacts from before the war. You once knew some of the most powerful people in the world. Don't they owe you? Dad, please..." *Catherine could not get up for she was strapped to a chair, but she managed to grab the corner of her father's suit jacket as she pleaded.*

He bent down pulled her to his chest and held her tight, "I'm so sorry Cathy, I can't. Everything has changed. The world doesn't operate like that anymore. I wish I could help you, but I can't. There is nothing I can do. Maybe the doctors will help you and they will set you free when you're well."

Catherine pulled back with anger in her voice she said, "Well! Well! I am well. I'm not sick, I don't need a doctor. All they do is drug me to ensure I can't fight back. The people here are the ones who are sick. They're evil and they are not interested in helping anyone, least of all me. I am not ill and they will never let me go, never! I need you desperately. For the first time in my life, I am too weak to fight. I am helpless; I'm alone and you don't even believe me. Leave, all of you leave! Mom I love you, but I can't handle seeing you, either of you, it kills me. Please go and don't ever come back again, ever."

The security came and insisted we leave. As we left I noted that a doctor administered more drugs, so that Catherine would calm down. They motioned for me to leave as they strapped Catherine to her bed. I hated seeing her like this. I felt so ashamed, angry and helpless. I was torn by my love for her and pained by her madness. I was not alone in this; her parents shared the helpless grief. It would have been better if she did die, this was not living, it was worse than prison, but like her father, I felt like there was nothing I could do.

One day I came to see her on a Saturday night. Visiting hours were over, but the president had arranged special visitation rights for me as a government appointed doctor. President Davidson never said anything, but I began to think he was torn between Catherine's madness and his belief in her cause. I suspected he was playing both sides, but he often asked how she was doing, and if she was okay. I only answered, 'She's alive.'

I was walking down the white corridors and headed down a long desolate hallway. I could no longer remember how many times I walked down this path feeling sad, helpless and guilty. Death would have been a better sentence.

I passed people in convulsions strapped to their beds, people yelling, or laughing hysterically and people like Catherine carrying on conversations with someone only they could see. Many of these people were ex-soldiers traumatized by their wartime experiences. Others just sat rocking silently back and forth, perhaps as an attempt to comfort themselves in their delusions.

I felt a sudden coldness as I came toward Catherine's room. The soldier on guard outside her room gave me a wicked smile as I approached. The lights were out; I thought that she was laying alone in the darkness. I came in and three soldiers from the specialty unit were taking their turns with her when I entered the room. I was too late to stop it and I had no power over Augustus' forces. I lunged forward to stop them, but my attempt was in vain. The strength of the soldier from the hallway was too great. He rendered me helpless with ease.

I swear, as Catherine was being raped I heard Jacob scream out in pain, yelling, "NO!" The voice was as if it was coming from some distant place and I swear to you the walls shook at his scream.

Poor Catherine, how many times she was raped I couldn't tell, whether this was the first time or not, I didn't know, but I was sure it wouldn't be the last. They left laughing and joking, and let me go. I cried holding Catherine in my arms, "I'm so sorry Catherine, I'm so sorry! What have I done to you? Forgive me! Please forgive me!" *I blamed myself for putting her in this place and for making her available for victimization.*

I remembered what she said many months ago, "Some things are worse than death Peter." *This is what she must have meant. She would rather die than be violated and it was my fault she was here.*

I cried, "Catherine, I am so sorry, please forgive me." She did not respond to me. All she had done for months now was suffer in silence. I assumed her refusal to speak to me were because she hated me. Now I knew it was because she must have been traumatized from repeatedly being raped. She was detached from herself, resigned to her fate and unwilling, or unable to fight back. She was paralyzed by fear and hopelessness. This was not the Catherine I had known.

She appeared to be so distant and alone. She had lost her will to fight because she did not resist the rapes, nor did she attempt to escape. After that ID chip was put in her hand she simply became vacant. She was a captive resigned to her powerlessness over her situation.

I'll never know how many times she was raped, but anger, revenge and pain consumed me, married with unspeakable guilt and remorse. I felt responsible for putting her in this place, where she had nowhere to hide, nowhere to escape and no one to help her. She couldn't fight, or stop the violation, paralyzed with fear. I hated myself I wanted to kill them, kill me, but all I did was cry as I held her in my arms. I felt a heavy darkness consume every part of me and its weight was more than I could bear.

I stumbled to the basement of the hospital hoping I could see Jacob and though I could not gain access to him, I saw Jacob on his knees, with tears streaming down his eyes. This giant valiant warrior was chained to the wall, he could not escape either. I don't know what they had done to break him, but I could not stop the tears from falling down my cheeks as I looked at Jacob crying. As I continued to shed tears for Catherine I walked to my car outside. I heard Jacob's moaning resonating inside of me, as he wept, "No! No! No!"

I was mad at her god; He appeared to bless her with abilities not even I could comprehend, yet where was her blessed hope now? All glory was absent from her abused and battered body. If he was real, he had abandoned her and Jacob. "Why?" *I yelled at him as I looked up to the sky. The rain poured down, beating upon the hood of my car. I slammed my fists against the roof. I kicked the door as I stood in the rain raging at her god, shaking my fists to the sky yelling,* "Why are you allowing your servant to suffer. If you are real how can you desert her? She gave up everything for you. She killed for you. She was even willing to die for you. Why? Why don't you protect her? What kind a father are you? Where are you?" *He made me no reply.*

I cannot describe the depth of my pain and I knew what I suffered was minuscule to what Catherine was subject to. Catherine and I suffered in silence, while her god of miracles was deaf to our cries for help. I crumpled to the ground helpless and alone, weeping for all that was lost, for her suffering, for our inability to change what had happened to her. I sat on the ground weeping as the rain poured down on me.

Chapter Fifteen:
Escaping What Binds Us

I was in such anguish over what I had done to Catherine; I fell to my knees in the mud and cried. I was now convinced death was preferable to her torment. I was terrified for her future, and determined to find some way to end her misery, or at least the abuse.

If her so-called almighty and all-powerful god would not save her, I would.

The next day I went to see Sayid. He had kept in touch with me, hoping we could one day see Catherine liberated. I said, "We have to free Catherine tomorrow night." *I told him that I would use my position to get him into the compound and he would help Jacob while I freed Catherine. Together we planned her escape.*

When we arrived Sayid stayed with me. Access proved relatively easy as many of the staff had become accustomed to my face. I had Sayid acting as my subordinate, dressed in a Special Forces uniform. When we arrived at her room Catherine was strapped to a chair in front of a barred window, smiling and staring at the sky.

The sky was a swirl of colors, bright orange, crimson red, pinks, and yellow, violets and white amidst a hint of blue. It covered the entire surface of the sky in a vibrant sunset. I had never witnessed such a beautiful sky before. I heard her say, "Jehovah-Shammah" *Sayid touched her shoulder and replied,* "Jehovah-Shammah"

"What the hell does that mean?" *I asked abruptly. I had no more patience for her god.*

Sayid replied, "It means, The Lord is there."

I was disgusted and I retorted, "Well I am here now, and Catherine we are going to set you free. We are going to get you out of here."

Our future was destroyed, not when she was captured, but when I decided to speak out as a witness.

I accepted that, but now I had to save her. Without Catherine fighting, her cause seemed to lose all hope and all vision. Her followers were either dead, captured, or in hiding. She was lost too. I needed to free her. Whether she was insane or not, I had to secure her liberty. I had to help her find herself again. I didn't know if that was even possible. Her god hadn't delivered her from this hell, but I would.

Then she spoke, "Get me a sharp knife."

"You can't cut the microchip out right now Catherine. As soon as the arm temperature drops they will know the chip is no longer in you and an alarm will be set off. It requires live tissue to function." *I cautioned her, as tears streamed down my face and my voice trembled, for this is the first time in many months that she spoke to me.*

Then she inquired "How many seconds do I have to place it in a live recipient?"

Sayid answered. "Seven seconds."

Catherine looked into my eyes for the first time in months. Her eyes were filled with resolve as she said to me, "I need a knife. At nine o'clock tonight I will have a live recipient to place the chip in."

I nodded, "We were thinking the same thing. Those assholes that Augustus made don't have chips in them. We can subdue them and place the chip in one of them long enough for us to escape."

Catherine inquired, "How are you going to subdue them Peter? They are too powerful for you."

I conceded that fact and then I assured her, "Yes, they are too powerful for me alone, but not for Sayid and I together. How many are there?"

"Usually one, but often there are three and some nights there are all six." *She responded with vengeance in her tone. Then she continued,* "Two of you are not enough you must be early and loosen my straps before they arrive at nine."

I asked her, "When do they sedate you?"

She replied, "They always turn out the lights at nine, for another scheduled rape session, they drug me when they arrive and while I'm strapped in my bed." *Catherine answered calmly. I did not know how she could say this with no emotion, but I was glad at least she was beginning to act like herself again. I was sure her detachment was necessary to help her cope with what they had done to her.*

I notified her, "We will free Jacob first; he can help us if there are six of them."

Catherine raised an eyebrow, "How do you plan on achieving that?"

I shared, "I've been granted access to him as your doctor. I was given permission to speak with Jacob, since you have been unresponsive for so many months."

She smiled it had been so long since I had seen that smile, but then my emotions changed to bitterness as she mused, "God is good, even my silent suffering is being used for good."

I dismissed her foolish comment and I continued, "We will set Jacob free from his chains just prior to lights out, then we will make our way back to you with an order to administer your sedative before we leave. Jacob will make his way to us when the lights go out."

I got her a serrated knife from the kitchen center when I went to get a coffee. I returned and she asked Sayid, "What about the cameras?"

Sayid replied, "We have arranged to place them on a loop. They will not record a thing."

I gave her the knife and she slipped it under her pillow. Then she pulled Sayid aside and spoke to him privately I didn't know what she said to him, but it hurt me that it was obvious she trusted him and not me. Still, I couldn't blame her, after all what had I ever done to gain her faith?

We left her with her restraints loosened lying in her bed and we made our way to meet with Jacob and inform him of the plan. Sayid and I unchained Jacob at 8:45 pm. We made our way back to Catherine with plenty of sedatives in hand. We checked in at the desk at the end of the hall, the guard asked, "Hello doctor, back again? Lights are out in ten minutes."

"Of course,*" I replied as I handed him a requisition sheet and continued,* "I was asked to administer her sedatives tonight."

The guard replied, "Wow that is a heavy dose, I heard that little bitch is hard to handle. She killed a few of our men already, hasn't she?"

"Yes." *Sayid replied and he tried to hide his glare,* "She is lethal."

The guard chuckled, "Well doctor, go ahead. I understand why they gave you protection tonight."

He waved us past and as I walked down the hall with Sayid I said, "I'm going to kill that snake before we leave." *Sayid did not respond, but from the corner of my eye I detected a slight grin cross his lips.*

We entered Catherine's room we gave her one of the syringes to use against the guard. We then waited for a minute before making our way back up the hall. Nothing is easy. I was glad we loosened Jacob's chains. I had a feeling we would need him tonight. We did not make eye contact as six genetically engineered soldiers walked passed us. They were as large as Jacob, making both Sayid and I look small in stature, and we were not little men. I took a deep breath and sighed. As we approached the front desk, I leaned in and pretended to sign some papers, and then I quickly snapped the guard's neck when his head was turned.

Sayid had already turned to run back to aid Catherine, I followed a couple seconds behind him. We sprinted up the hall and reached Catherine's room just before the last one shut the door. Sayid jumped and grabbed hold of the first soldier's neck and broke it. He fell to the floor as Sayid placed a syringe into the neck of another surprised soldier. I saw Catherine plunge her syringe in the aorta of the one who was closest to her. She pulled out her knife and slit another's throat. The three facing her were focusing all their attention on her. The soldier that Sayid had drugged slowed little, as did the one by Catherine, but they were not immobilized. Sayid was engaged in hand-to-hand combat with the one he had drugged. I moved toward him and stuck Sayid's opponent with a second syringe. He began to lose balance and Sayid crushed his trachea.

Catherine was now out of bed preparing to fight the three standing before her. Sayid and I each took one as we attacked them from behind, kicking them in the back and kidneys. They stumbled a few steps forward and then turned to face us. We kicked them and punched them several times, but they blocked us at every turn. We did not shrink back. We blocked their strikes as well, however the blows inflicted on us appeared to produce far greater damage. The muscles covering these soldiers' bodies were immense. It functioned like body armor.

I had two syringes left in my pockets. I reached for them and with one in each hand I jumped and kicked the soldier in front of me with a snap kick to the nose. It did not kill him, but it momentarily stunned him and I took the opportunity to plunge both syringes in either side of his neck. Catherine was still engaged in hand-to-hand combat with the last soldier. He managed to lift her with one hand. He was holding her by the neck and her feet were dangling above the ground.

We motioned toward them, but the soldier warned, "Move one step closer and I'll crush her neck."

We were frozen and Catherine was barely able to breath. As soon as we stopped Jacob entered the room. He walked up from behind the soldier, who did not hear or see Jacob coming, but Catherine did.

She managed to use her knife and slice his wrist forcing the soldier to release her while Jacob snapped his neck and broke it. Jacob lifted up Catherine and hugged her and said, "I'm sorry, I did not protect you. I failed you. Please forgive me."

She caressed his cheek and replied, "You just did protect me Jacob. I would no longer be alive if it was not for you." *He hugged her again and then he placed her down.*

Catherine resumed command and ordered, "Jacob lift the soldier that Peter drugged and place him in the bed." *Jacob quickly obeyed.*

Then Catherine turned to us, "Peter you and Sayid strap him in."

We did as she commanded and then we watched as Catherine cut the microchip from her hand. She sliced the guard's skin and slid it inside his forehead. Catherine ran across the hall and dove down a laundry chute. We were too large to follow. Jacob changed into one of the dead soldier's uniforms. No one would dare to question us while we walked with what appeared to be a Special Forces escort. Everyone feared Augustus' soldiers.

We made our way to the laundry room with Jacob and we met her there. After that, we completed our escape with ease, leaving through the service entrance and proceeding quickly to my car. Catherine was in the trunk and the three of us sat in the vehicle and we tried to remain calm at the checkpoint to the compound. The guard waved us through the perimeter gates without question.

We pulled over once we were well away from the facility and Catherine changed into some clothes I had brought for her. Sayid took over the driving because I think I broke my left arm blocking a hit. I watched Jacob bandage her hand in the back seat of the car.

She and Jacob were so close and I resented it in part, but she was safe and alive again. That was all that mattered. I was so relieved to see her smile again. I no longer attempted to understand her faith or her abilities. I began to suspect that Jacob was a genetically engineered soldier too, maybe Catherine was as well. I was not sure and I stopped the questions in my head. I was just glad she was free of her bonds. I felt a great weight lifted off my shoulders as we drove off. I heard the alarms in the distance, screaming their shrill cry. She escaped, she was free.

I knew I could never fail Catherine again. I would never leave her side. I forfeited my career and my duty to my country and I vowed to myself to make her mine, if she would have me. I had always belonged to her alone. I always knew it. I did not belong to her religious world, part of me was even in greater opposition to it now than ever before, and yet I could not stop loving her. I was bound to her forever.

Chapter Sixteen:
Love Heals all Wounds

We left the city and went toward the forests. We rolled the car off a cliff and set out on foot. On the third day of our journey Catherine stood naked beneath a waterfall for a long time. It broke my heart to see her bruised and scared body. She was still beautiful though, despite the abuse she had suffered. When she turned sideways I saw a slight bulge of her stomach. I cried in silence as Jacob gently turned my head away.

Sayid met us by the waterfall that evening after Catherine was done bathing and dressed again. He led us to a camp. Catherine often stopped to throw up. She drank a lot of water, but she ate nothing for days. When we finally arrived we saw that men, women and children were hiding in caves. They were afraid to come out, sneaking around in the darkness, desperately attempting to be invisible.

Sayid revealed himself as he stepped out of the shadows of the forest. Other people emerged from the black of the night like ghosts emerging from a mist. The only thing that I could see clearly was a hint of their outline and the whites of their eyes. A trumpet sounded and the clouds cleared revealing the light of a full moon, which was reflected in the water beside Catherine, where she was soaking her aching feet. The stars were gradually reflected in the water around her as well.

Jacob stood faithfully at her side. Then he suddenly smiled as he stared in silence at the reflection in the water surrounding Catherine. I never saw him smile before this moment and I did not feel comfortable enough to ask him what he was smiling about.

After a while the morning sun began to rise above the horizon. As the daylight enhanced my vision, I could see a multitude of people surrounding us. My eyes fell upon the thousands of people that Sayid had led from the sewers into the mountains. There were so many of them. Sayid yelled, "Catherine has returned, and yesterday the war began in the Heavens. Jehovah-Shammah!"

Then from all around me like a roaring thunder, the people cried, "JEHOVAH-SHAMMAH" *Even the mountains echoed their reply.*

That morning Catherine said, "You have all been hiding in the darkness for far too long. You must store firewood and organize the cave populations into smaller units. Your security does not lie in numbers it rests with the LORD. Trust in Him. Separate into family units; prepare your hearts and souls for the coming of the King. Purify yourselves make yourselves clean and holy before God, for soon the age of grace will come to an end. Prepare your heart for you must survive the winter. Stock supplies and pray vigilantly for the King returns after the war in the Heavens, which is drawing to a close. Do not fall into sin, for the hour of victory draws near and the Devil will no longer seek your lives. He is desperate to claim your soul. Do not let him in, resist sin, for his thirst shall not be quenched."

Then she said quietly to all of us who stood near to her, "Jacob and I must leave you now. I cannot stay with any of you." *She said looking at her inner circle with a gentle smile.*

Sayid initially tried to convince her to stay with him, "Catherine you are my family now, you must stay with us"

Catherine sighed, "Sayid, our final attack must proceed on schedule. I can't help you in this. You know what you all must do."

Sayid bid her, "Come with us, I understand why you can't be in the battle, but your presence alone will inspire us."

"That is not prudent Sayid, I have to go deep into hiding and no one can follow me. It is time to fast, pray and prepare for the coming of the King." *She then looked down and rubbed her belly saying*, "I can no longer risk being betrayed. I have greater responsibilities aside from my own safety now."

Sayid stated firmly, "Catherine we can protect you and the child in your womb."

She placed her hand on Sayid's hand and reiterated as she looked into my eyes, "You must seek the Lord with all your heart and soul for time is short, so seek His grace before His kingdom comes."

Then she put her arm in Jacobs saying, "My safety is in the LORD'S hands and it is Jacob's sole responsibility to bear that burden Sayid, not yours, nor yours Peter."

We were unwilling to accept her decision. She patted our hands and walked off to pray, with Jacob at her side. I was hurt by her lack of trust in us, but Sayid took no offense. A twinge of jealousy began to flow through me, and I could not mask the pain in my eyes. I was angry at her trust in her god. He hadn't protected her before, and still she put her faith in him.

That night, Sayid, Jacob, and I sat with Catherine by the fire. She spoke to us alone. "I'm with child. Augustus will not stop hunting me. He wants the child growing inside me. Satan is deluded into believing that I am his as well. I place you all in unnecessary jeopardy. I must leave to protect you and to protect the child."

"That child was placed inside your womb against your will Catherine," *I said with a fierce bitterness.* "You are not obligated to give that child life. Get rid of it!" *I ordered.* "Those were beasts that violated you, not men. They stole your body and planted their vile seed inside you. You are not obligated to give it life".

"I could not kill this child any more then I could kill myself. I do not have that right." *she replied gently. Then she placed one hand on her womb and the other on my knee as she continued,* "This child was conceived in the darkness and they were vile creatures who assaulted me, but it is the Father who gives life. It is my Father who fashioned this child, who is growing in my womb and when he is born, he will be brought forth in the light, in the love, in the joy of my LORD."

"I can't tell you what to do about that child, it is your body, but I will not stand by helpless and let you go off alone." *I stated firmly.*

She corrected me saying, "I'm never alone and Jacob will be with me also."

I continued with tenacity, "I don't know how you survived, that prison I placed you in. I don't know how you kept your sanity, while they defiled over and over again and tortured you." *I continued with tears streaming down my face*, "I don't know how you can have hope, joy and obey any god who allowed this to happen to you. I don't know where you get your strength and abilities, but please don't ask me to suffer solitary confinement and isolation, for when I am without you I am alone. I am going to stand with you and I will never leave you again. NEVER!"

Catherine wiped the tears from my eyes and gently kissed my lips, and then she replied softly, "Do you remember what Jehovah-Shamma means Peter?"

"NO." *I replied although I didn't care either.*

She said, "It means the LORD is there. His Spirit dwells in me. I hear his voice and obey. This child is from God. I know you can't accept this, for you do not know him, but I know him. He is just and out of an evil act he alone will bring forth this life, which will be a light unto the world. When Jesus comes from the sky in glory, my son will be growing, and one day he will be fighting and leading the armies of men on earth in the service of the King of Kings."

She took a deep breath and explained to all three of us, "My son was conceived from the sperm of a genetically enhanced soldier. They were ordered to impregnate me. I could not fight off the rapes, because my own abilities were weakened by the daily drug injections they gave me, so that I could be more easily subdued.

Initially they tortured me, but they did not rape me. They relished in me fighting back. It was sport for them. They wanted to test just how strong and fast I was. They laughed and spoke crudely as they attempted to dehumanize me and they threatened to rape me, but they didn't.

Then the order must have come to impregnate me, because they tried to rape me, but I killed all who tried, so they drugged me instead.

I confess I felt abandoned by God and man. I felt betrayed and when my human father failed me as he had in my youth. I felt utterly helpless and alone. I was without hope, without strength and completely unclean. I felt sick in my being and filthy.

I knew I was being raped and yet, thank God, I could not remember the violation. The drugs were so strong that it was a blur and I felt nothing and remembered nothing of the rapes, themselves. I was only lucid when they all arrived, but the drugs acted quickly.

Just when I faced my darkest hour I heard Jacob crying for me, sharing my pain. I was not alone and then an angel of the LORD appeared before me and said, 'Catherine, the living God weeps with you, but he sends a message to you from on high. He alone will answer to a violation of the flesh and he asks if you will allow him to bring light to the darkness. A creature created by man violates your flesh and from that union God will bring forth a life blessed with the physical abilities he gave you, in conjunction with the physical powers of this man-made being. You may submit to the evil that these men will do, or he will give you the power to fight off the violation despite the drugs, but in fighting these creatures you will die. Your time in this world will come to an end, and you can return home. The choice is yours."

Catherine shed a tear as she continued, "I thought of you Peter, I thought of us. I was selfish; I did not want my only sexual experience to be one of violation, theft and abuse. I wanted my body to be restored to me and given to the only man I have ever wanted. I hated that they stole that from me. I cried as I accepted this burden, for it was not my will, I wanted to kill them, kill them all. I still do, but if I gave into my hate I would lose my only hope of experiencing what love is supposed to be. It is not that this evil act was God's will Peter, but he alone is all-knowing and all-powerful. I knew that only my God could bring good out of the evil being done to me. I know him and I trust in him, so I died to the flesh that day."

I was angry as I said, "How can you trust in some all-powerful and mighty God, when he doesn't, protect you, when he doesn't save you. He simply allows you to be used and abused and then twists it for his own purposes. Catherine this is bullshit."

Catherine sighed, "Peter how can I lead Christians if my own faith in God fails when my own life falls apart?" *She continued speaking as I looked on amazed by the words she declared with confidence.* "I was violated by people belonging to Satan's rebel army. I have fought demons and fallen angels before; they have the capacity to do great evil, but my God is greater. He heals and comforts me. Their time is short, for soon his kingdom will come."

She continued as I listened with confusion and horror, "You say I suffered in silence and this is true, but I was not alone in this and I wept often. I grieved deeply; it was one of my darkest hours. I was utterly crushed. However this is not the first time I have been trapped between shadows and death. It is at these times in our life that we reach out for the Light."

She lifted the sleeve on her arm that had a tattoo that she read aloud, "This reads, In Luminetuo Videimus Lumen; it means, In Thy Light shall we see the Light." *She rolled down her sleeve and continued,* "He spoke to me in my darkest hour. He is the Light that lets me see and gives me hope. His Spirit spoke to me in the silence of my heart. In a secret place I would hear his voice.

This temporary hell on Earth is just that, temporary, but I have seen my God, I have experienced Heaven and I know what awaits us on the other side. What is the suffering I experienced compared to that of my Lord? I will never lose heart because another has violated my flesh, for they can never violate my spirit. I won't let them Peter.

If I give up hope, I give up life and love, and then they win. I won't remain a victim trapped in despair. Life on Earth is fleeting, but my reward for doing, and letting his work be done right now inside of me and through me grants me abundant joy for eternity. I'm thankful for his love. God is love Peter."

Then Jacob quoted 2 Timothy 2; 3-4, "Suffer hardship with me, as a good soldier of Christ Jesus."

I could not hide my contempt and disgust, as I retorted, "Love, this is not love. This is madness. You should not be carrying that child. Any god that would allow such a violation cannot be love. That is not love. Love protects, love defends, and love delivers. I would not allow my child to suffer in the hands of my enemy. If I had the power to stop it, I would. You would too, so how can you still trust in such a god, or maybe he is not as powerful as you believe. It is madness to believe in an all-powerful god who is love, but who does not protect his own children. It is madness to expect you to give birth to, let alone love that baby growing inside of you and be joyful about it. No, I can accept hardship and suffering, but I cannot accept this. It's your body, your choice, but don't try to convince me some all-powerful god needs you to suffer hardship with him. If he is all-powerful Catherine, then wouldn't he eliminate all evil and all suffering? None of this makes sense and I will not believe in such madness."

Catherine knelt before me, "There was an ancient battle waged long ago between good and evil and it is still fought in both the spiritual and the physical realm every day. God is all-powerful Peter, but God is bound by his own laws, his own justice, his own rules and regulations. Just as there are laws of the universe that cannot be broken, there are some that can. The Devil cheats and lies and manipulates, but his power though real and vast is still limited. We hang in the balance between these two great forces."

Catherine hung her head and sighed as she searched for words to convince me, or at least make me understand, "Once a lifetime ago you led your men in a toast for a war declared by foolish men and you all said, 'To honor and death!' Well, we are soldiers of Christ and our flesh is continually delivered to death for his sake and God's glory. He has manifested his power and strength in our flesh and because he became man, through man and Spirit we fight this war. By man and by his Spirit we will win it." *She failed to make me understand her irrational beliefs, but I said nothing in reply.*

She stood up before her men and said, "Now Sayid" *Catherine ordered,* "You must respond to your calling and complete your mission. You and Eric must implement the plan that Peter designed before my incarceration."

Everyone nodded and complied. She walked over and gently kissed my lips. Then she said, "I still love you Peter, I always have, I was just trying to protect you, and the child inside me. We will be hunted by forces far superior to genetically enhanced soldiers. Are you willing to protect me and my child, Peter?"

"I will always protect you Catherine." *I replied*

She put her hands in mine and said, "Peter the child is a part of me, it has half my DNA, don't forget that. You must be willing to protect this child too."

I said nothing, but I nodded my assent.

She looked toward Jacob who nodded and then she said, "Peter you may follow me. Your plan is detailed enough and everyone knows what they must do. The child and I will need to be hidden and protected soon, so we will leave in the morning." *I kissed her forehead in gratitude. I was torn with relief that I could go with her and with resentment that I required Jacob's approval to do so.*

Then I walked off to be alone. I was not one of them. I could not hear their god's voice. I did not even know if he had one. I sat beneath an evergreen by a river, with my face in my hands and I wept alone in my grief. Torn by my love for a woman that I feared may be mad, but so was everyone else around her. Maybe they were privy to a world and an existence of which I could not partake, maybe it was real and they were not insane, but I never heard, nor saw God, or the Devil. I did not belong to either of them, but I did belong to her. My heart was in her hands alone and I had to protect her, walk with her, and I would never leave her again.

I did have faith in love. My devotion to her was all consuming and faithful, as well as blind. I could not help but hope that our companionship would banish and heal my despair. If she could let me, I would dedicate myself to her, and if she could allow herself to commit to me, then I believed there was nothing such a love could not overcome. Love could heal and bridge our spiritual divide. Even though her faith and our desire for each other were in conflict, I believed love would triumph.

She came and sat with me by the river and we remained silent for a while as the camp prepared to disperse. She put her hand in mine. I said, "I love you Catherine, I have always loved you."

She replied, "I love you too Peter. I'm willing to spend the rest of my life with you, but circumstances have changed. To be with you, I need you to accept my child too. A child does not ask to be born. Every child deserves love and acceptance. Don't blame this child for the evil choices that others made. Can you do this Peter?"

"Yes Catherine, I hate what was done to you, but I will not blame the child for it. I blame the men who did this to you. I blame Augustus and I blame myself for putting you there in the first place, but this child, no I will never blame the child." *I replied honestly.*

She smiled and kissed my lips and asked, "Peter, can you accept my calling, my mission, the destiny that God has called me to?"

I said, "I do not share your beliefs Catherine, but I will always stand by you in your mission. We may not share the same god, but we do still share the same enemy."

She smiled and we said in unison, "Augustus."

I then asked her, "How can you love me and unite yourself to me if you believe you're saved and I'm dammed?"

"Peter, I love you, my beliefs do not require you to believe what I believe. I believe that…" *She paused and paraphrased scripture,* "One day every knee will bow and every tongue will confess he is god. Every eye will see when the King of kings returns. I'm not worried Peter. Belief will come later. It is not my job to save you, it's his. It is my pleasure to love you and accept you for who you are. The question is: can you love me enough to accept me for who I am?"

I stood up and took her in my arms, "I already have." *I kissed her gently and then I looked down at her and said,* "So you admit you think I need saving."

"We all do Peter, why do you think you're perfect?"

I laughed, "No, only for you Catherine."

She smiled her perfect smile as she said, "On that we can agree. Come. It's time we prepare to go."

I would patiently wait for the day when I could physically express my passion for her. I didn't know when that day would be, she needed time, time to heal and then there was her god and his rules. I would wait for her as long as I had to, but in my heart she was already mine. Then I walked with a smile holding her hand remembering what she said to Sayid outside the cave not so long ago.

I remembered them speaking when she said, "I'll try to remain objective, but remember when your heart was lost to your wife?"

"Yes" *Sayid replied*. "It was almost instantly."

Then she continued, "Despite yourself, she stole your heart"

Sayid agreed, "Completely."

Then she uttered the words I shall never forget, "Well, he has always had mine, since I first met him he has had that hold, but don't worry I will guard it nonetheless."

I would be patient and let her guard her heart, she needed to, but I would not guard mine. It no longer belonged to me, it was hers and I would take that leap of faith, for her. Remembering this ended my suffering in silence. As we walked back from the river I kissed her hand and she smiled up at me. I knew we would be okay, as long as we walked together. I anticipated the day when we could become one, but for now I am just happy we are together, we are revived by love's healing touch.

This is the last page I will write for many months. I have no more paper and no more ink left, but as we make our way through the mountains toward safety I feel hope. I know this is not the last chapter of our lives and I know our future will be filled with difficult battles ahead, but Catherine and I love one another and nothing and no one, can break that bond. We have already been to hell and back together in this war, but our love passed the test and we will go on.

Peter Joseph Roberts

The story continues in the second book in the series, **<u>When Angels Walk the Earth.</u>**
Soon to be released in 2013

Made in the USA
Charleston, SC
13 September 2012